Once again Sara L. Jameson has dropped the readers into a twisting, high-stakes story that will have them flipping the pages to find out what happens next.

— PATRICIA BRADLEY, WINNER OF THE
INSPIRATIONAL READERS AWARD

TROUBLED WATERS·BOOK 3

Vengeance IN VIENNA

SARA L. JAMESON

*To my dear friend, Peggy A. Bell,
who has faithfully prayed for every book I've written.*

*And to my uncle, Robert C. Goodwin,
for our mutual love of books and precious conversations.*

1

Romantic was the last thing he'd call a moonlight sail. More likely deadly.

Interpol Special Agent Jacob Coulter gripped the mainsheet, the rope almost unfamiliar in his fingers. Sweat slicked the tiller in his right hand. Sailing lessons as a ten-year-old were a gazillion years ago. Why had he given in to Riles' badgering? Haunches clenched against the seat, he loosened the mainsheet, tacked the fifteen-foot dinghy to port.

Short puffs of air rasped from his mouth.

"Relaaax." Seated on the molded fiberglass bench across from him, Riley Williams flicked wavy auburn strands from her cheek. "We're having fun, remember?"

"Who, me—tense?" So far, he'd avoided the illuminated disks jetting water in the Wörthersee. Why on God's great earth had Austrians built a fountain in the lake?

Face tilted toward the star-studded sky, she curled her legs, rested her hand on the boat's rim. The facets in her diamond engagement ring sparkled like flames beneath the full moon.

A grin worked across his face. He'd never expected the Lord to hook him up with an opera star fiancée. But not a diva-bone in her body. Apart from her Mae West life vest, Riles was an ethereal vision in white. Pompom hat, turtleneck, down puffer vest, and cords. Perfect for October.

He tacked again. Booking their first vacation had been a good idea—if they survived the obstacles in the water.

Tonight, her thousand-watt smile lit her face nonstop. "Admit it. Aren't you glad we rented the boat?" The lilt in her voice rippled like one of her opera arias.

"Uh-huh." He'd have preferred something less risky. Something that might not endanger her. Danger he couldn't prevent. Or protect her from. Not with a terrorist financier determined to kill them.

Out of habit, he patted his waterproof-covered phone in his pocket. Scanned the port and starboard shores. Moonlight glimmered on the inky water, silhouetted the treetops and houses, mostly gated estates. Best he could tell, no movement on land. If Armand's goons showed up, he and Riles would be easy pickings.

Eighteen days since their last fiasco. Austria was hundreds of miles from London, but how long could their luck hold out? Forgiveness wasn't on Armand's must-do list. Jacob flexed his neck, but the cramps in his muscles refused to budge. It was hard to forget Interpol's insistence he make their holiday his cover. Even for an hour.

The dinghy's bow sliced through the water and glided past the last house. He glanced over his shoulder. Where was that water-ski ramp?

A gust hit the sail and whisked the boat toward the port shore. He tacked again, zigzagged them away from the dense forest looming at the water's edge.

"How about a kiss, lover boy." Riles slid from the bench and scooted across the cockpit floor. Arms draped across his knees, she lifted her face toward his, lashes framing hazel eyes, a hint of lip gloss on her generous mouth. "Let's make a memory."

"Okay, doll." They could use some new memories. Good ones. If they couldn't carve time out from his life-and-death assignments, she'd never set a wedding date. He bent toward her and pressed his lips to hers. One whiff of her Chanel No. 5, and he released his hold on the tiller, fingers itching to weave through her curls.

Craaack.

The tiller shattered. Fragments scattered everywhere.

"Sniper!" Heart clobbering his chest, he shoved Riles to the floor, dove on top of her.

Wood splinters geysered, pelted the water, *thunked* inches from his legs.

Stifling a shriek, Riles flinched beneath him.

He shielded her head with one hand, clutched the mainsheet. Somehow, he had to get her out of here.

"Armand?"

"Probably hired an assassin. At this distance, must be a high-powered rifle." Shrewd. Waiting until night, unlikely to be identified.

Or caught.

Their pizza dinner churned his stomach. How long had the killer been watching them?

He swiped his palm across his face. *Thank You, God.* If he hadn't released the tiller, the bullet would've severed his hand.

Stocking cap tugged over his hair, he angled his head over the stern-side rim, squinted toward the shore. The shooter was probably wearing night-vision goggles. Jacob rolled off Riley, and she huddled in a ball, quaking against his chest.

"Do you think he left?"

"I doubt it." Armand would insist on proof of their deaths. Jacob slammed his fist on his thigh. "How many more assassination attempts before Interpol lets intel analysts carry weapons? Or make arrests?"

"Must be under quota."

The quiver in her voice tore at him. How could he protect Riles in the middle of a lake?

The dinghy wobbled like a rubber duck in a bathtub.

Adrenaline jolted through his veins. No tiller meant no rudder control. Saliva fled his mouth. To reach the dock, he'd have to row or work the sails.

In full view of the sniper.

* * *

LYING on his side in the cockpit, he snatched the mainsheet in his hand. "Call the police. One-three-three. Phone's in my pocket. You can dial and speak through the cover."

Craaack.

Another bullet *thwacked* the fiberglass hull, inches from where he'd been sitting.

Riles jammed her fist to her mouth.

Cold sweat pricked his brow. He touched the hole's frayed edges, and water burbled over his fingertips. Acid pitted his stomach. A puncture below the waterline, big as a hamburger slider. How long before the boat sank?

"That's no pop gun he's using." One direct hit and they'd bleed out in seconds. Somehow, he had to get them to safety.

Shallow breaths heaved her chest, a flurry of exhales feathered his cheeks.

If she inhaled any faster, she'd hyperventilate. "You okay?"

"Yep. Never better." Fingers trembling, she unzipped his windbreaker pocket, yanked out the cell and dialed. "This is Riley Williams. I'm calling for Interpol Special Agent Jacob Coulter. A sniper is shooting at our sailboat from the north shore of the Wörthersee." Her voice revved into overdrive. "One hit below the waterline, tiller destroyed. We're about a kilometer from the boat dock at Velden."

Good thing they were both fluent in German. There'd be no misunderstanding with the police. Wörthersee was almost eleven miles long, nearly a mile wide. Last time he'd checked, three other boats on the lake. None of them close. None a speedboat manned by an assassin.

Water gurgled into the dinghy, seeped inside his nylon slacks, sloshed around his bottom athletic shoe. Numbness crept up his ankle.

Would they capsize?

With a sniper taking potshots, no way could he bail out the inflow.

"*Danke.*" She disconnected the call. Taut lines etched her mouth. "They're on the way."

Craaack. Another bullet pierced the boat near the joint of the stern.

Gasping, Riles yanked her knees to her chest.

In seconds a chilly gusher saturated his hip. Breath lodged in his throat.

Another hit below the waterline. God had protected them so far. But one more bullet between the last two, and the police would carry them out in body bags.

Jacob eyed the starboard shore. With buoyancy vests on, they couldn't swim below the surface. Apart from his navy-blue windbreaker and pants they were a floating target in white. Hull, sails, Riles' outfit. "How are your swimming skills?"

"I do laps." Her teeth chattered. "In a heated pool."

"The brochure said this is Austria's warmest lake."

"Right. A regular hot tub."

"If we stay with the boat, it'll be easier for the police to find us."

"And the assassin." She zipped his waterproofed phone inside his pocket. "Is he toying with us or just a lousy shot?"

A chuckle strangled in his throat. "Want me to ask him?"

"Yes." Fire flashed from her eyes. "When you catch him."

The dinghy listed to port. Soon they'd be exposed in the cockpit. They'd have to shift to the starboard side to delay capsizing. Or jump overboard. Either way the killer could pick them off blindfolded.

"Riles, the boat's sinking. Take off your Mae West, the hat, and puffer. Put on my jacket so you're not such a white bull's eye."

"Aye, aye, Captain." She wiggled on the cockpit floor, squirming out of the vests, then whipped off her hat.

"Once you're overboard, hold the life preserver away from you. Keep your legs below the surface." With one hand on the mainsheet, he shrugged out of his jacket, wadded her puffer inside her hat as best he could. "I'm going to release the boom. When I say go, slip over the starboard side. Stay away from the stern. I'll draw his fire there."

"O-okay." She zipped his jacket over her turtleneck. "See ya, lover boy." She smooched the air but a muscle tic near her eye jittered an SOS. Her back to him, she crouched below the seat, fingers twisting the life-vest strap.

God, help us. They'd have mere seconds to make this work. If the boom's shift hid Riles' exit from the boat—

Heart thudding, he released the mainsail and the boom swung to port. "Go."

She scrambled on the seat and splashed overboard. In one smooth movement, the boat careened to port, and the mainsail bellyflopped on the water.

Fingertips grasping her pompom hat, he slithered into the lake. Ice water shocked his lungs. His diaphragm seized. *I can do all things—all things—through Christ—*

Every inch of his skin pebbled beneath his sodden clothes. Arm shuddering from the chilly water, he flicked her hat beyond the stern. The puffer dangled from inside the cap, bobbing like a giant jellyfish.

A gulp of air and he swam beneath the boat, life preserver undulating in his right hand. Once clear of the dinghy he lifted his head, gasping.

A few feet from the bow, Riles treaded water, her breaths short puffs. "Some choice. Freeze to death or bleed to death."

Craack. Riles' hat exploded. Bits of fabric, yarn, and down swirled in the air like a Minnesota snowstorm.

Bingo. The sniper had bought the deception. Now what?

"N-not s-sure I c-can sw-swim to sh-shore." She dogpaddled closer to him.

"Yeah." He tried for another stroke, but his arms splatted on the lake's surface. Already his biceps weighed a ton. How many yards could they swim before they'd succumb to hypothermia?

2

Police cars veered toward the lakefront promenade, sirens shrilling. *Thank You, God.* Blue rack lights strobed across the water, competing with the Velden Casino's purple-and-pink neon marquee. Jacob squinted toward the opposite shore. Would the sniper try to finish them off before the police reached them?

Or worse—wait and pick off everyone?

"Cavalry's on the way."

"R-r-right." Her face was as chalky as her sweater.

"Hang on, honey." With erratic strokes he splashed toward her, grasped her sleeve. He couldn't lose her. Until she'd waltzed into his life, he'd given up hope finding the right woman to share his life.

An engine roared, and a motorboat hurtled from the dock, sped toward their dinghy. He shot up prayers for the policemen's safety.

The craft slowed and hove to near the dinghy's bow, waves slapping their faces. Gasoline fumes from the idling engine

8

stung his nostrils and clogged his lungs. *Thank God, they'd reached them in time.* He tried to squeeze Riles' shoulder, his fingers so numb it was a clumsy pat.

A policeman in protective gear faced the north shore, legs braced in the bow, assault rifle to his shoulder. Squatting at the side of the boat, a uniformed officer hauled Riles onto the deck.

Breath whooshed from Jacob's lips. If they'd arrived fifteen minutes later ... *Thank You, God, for sparing us.*

Leaden arms slapping the surface, Jacob thrashed toward them. His fingers grazed the hull, and strong hands yanked him on board. Rivulets of water sluiced down his body, pooled on the deck. "*D-danke.*" A few more chatters and his thanks would be unintelligible.

Someone threw a cover around his shoulders. He shuffled over to Riles in the cockpit, cocooned in a blanket to her chin. He draped his blanket over hers and clasped her to his side, their bodies shuddering on the seat.

"*Bundespolizei*, Federal Police Chief Inspector Helmut Schmidt." Beneath the man's beret, gray hair flecked his temples. He wore a loaded equipment belt, a bullet-proof vest over his dark blue jacket, and matching cargo pants. Cool, assessing eyes swept over them.

"Special Agent Jacob Coulter, Brussels Interpol." Parting the blanket, he removed his Interpol ID from his zippered pants pocket. As soon as possible, he'd check on Tracy, make sure Armand hadn't tried to harm his kid sister too.

"And the purpose of your stay in Austria?" Schmidt studied the ID and returned it to Jacob.

"My fiancée and I are here for a vacation. Then I liaise with Special Agent Margot Müller of the Vienna Interpol office to locate a French terrorist financier, Armand Découvrir, who escaped arrest in London two weeks ago."

"And you suspect this man is in Austria?" Schmidt signaled the helmsman to return to the dock.

"Yes." The boat sprang to life. "We have sworn testimony pinpointing part of his operations in your country." Some of the information from Tracy.

The flare in Schmidt's nostrils was unmistakable. "What sort of operations?"

"So far, money laundering."

"Then ..." Schmidt stiffened. "You think he's operating in Velden?"

"No. I booked us at Sonnenhof Pension to relax. Until tonight, everything has been peaceful. Idyllic." They so needed this time to patch their relationship with no interference from his job.

"The moonlight sail was my idea." Riles laced her icy fingers in his. "I thought it would be romantic."

Idiot. He never should've given in to her wheedling, ignored the boat company's brochure she'd slid across the breakfast table every morning. Full-moon sails. Make a memory, she'd said. They'd made a few tonight. More like nightmares.

Interpol couldn't provide police protection, and his bank account couldn't cover the expense long-term after the London incidents. They'd agreed to pursue their normal lives.

Scoping the shoreline, Jacob pulled out his phone. How had Armand found them? "Excuse me, I need to call my sister. Armand put out a contract on her too. A thirteen-year-old kid."

Schmidt's intake of air was sharp. "Of course." He glanced around the lake.

Jacob speed-dialed Tracy's new Interpol-encrypted phone. A necessity after rescuing her from Armand's clutches in the UK. And if her BFF, Armand's daughter, tried to reach her, Interpol needed to know, ASAP.

When Tracy answered on the second ring, a few knots in his stomach loosened. *Thank God she was alive.* Taking in a rebellious teen while they were in Austria had been asking a lot of Riles' landlady, but Mrs. DeBeers had insisted. *The girl just needs a good dose of Belgian TLC*, she'd said. With their parents working as undercover missionaries in Iran, he'd agreed. Anything to help Tracy heal emotionally.

"Hey sis, how goes it?"

"Okay. I guess." Her voice huffed into the phone. "Nobody likes me at school."

"Give it time. Be your sweet self, and they'll come around." Boy, that was speaking something into being. Maybe if he kept telling her, she'd believe it. "Everything okay with Mrs. DeBeers?"

"Yes, she lets me call her Bomma."

"Grandmother, huh?" Maybe Mrs. DeBeers was right. A mother figure would bring Tracy around.

"Gotta go. We're watching a crimi."

Right. A crime show. He lived them every day. "Okay. Let me talk to Mrs. DeBeers for a minute. Love you." But Tracy had already disconnected the call. He dialed the older woman's cell. When she answered, he kept his voice low. "Don't tell Tracy, but we were attacked tonight. I'm hiring private security to keep tabs on both of you. Call me immediately if anything seems amiss."

Her quivering voice matched the tremor in her teacup when he'd dropped off Tracy. At eighty-five and reliant on a cane, she'd be no match for Armand's henchmen. He texted a Brussels security firm, set up twenty-four-hour surveillance on Mrs. DeBeers and Tracy, then turned to Schmidt. "Sorry to hold things up."

"No problem. You were wise to check on her." A smile flitted across the policeman's face. "What is your profession, Miss Williams?"

"I'm an opera singer." Stifling a sneeze, she tugged the blanket around her throat. "I debut with the Wiener Staatsoper in two weeks."

"Congratulations." Schmidt shifted toward Jacob. "About this evening ... Who do you think was shooting at you?"

"Probably one of Armand's assassins. He hired several men to kill us shortly before we left London." Jacob glanced over the lake. "They came close to succeeding." Just like tonight.

A muscle torqued Schmidt's cheek. "Hopefully they'll be unsuccessful on Austrian soil. If you'll come to the station in the morning to make a formal statement ..."

"Of course. We'll be there." The engine idled, and the helmsman docked the boat. Jacob rose and cupped Riles' elbow in his hand. Best get her to the Pension before she caught a cold, or a respiratory illness could cost her that Staatsoper debut.

"You know ..." Schmidt scratched his temple. "We're close to the Slovakian border. Découvrir could've hired a foreign assassin."

"Right." Slovakia wasn't the only nation bordering this side of Austria. The killer could easily be from Italy or Hungary. They might never find the sniper.

A fresh chill snaked down Jacob's spine. He was supposed to be the hunter here, not the hunted.

One thing was certain, Armand wouldn't give up until they were dead.

3

This was all her fault. If she hadn't insisted on the moonlight sail, they wouldn't be facing charges for a wrecked boat. Riley peeled off her wet clothes and flung them in the bathroom sink. But no way would she live holed up, waiting for Armand's next assault. Or from any other terrorists.

Hairdryer plugged in, she let the heat warm her neck and scalp as she squeezed the moisture from her wet curls. Right now, she had a career to build. A relationship with Jacob to forge. If these onslaughts continued after they married and started a family, how could they protect their children?

Ignoring the rumbling in her stomach, she toweled off. Her appetite always churned after performances and attempts on her life.

She slipped into wool slacks and a turtleneck sweater. Black clothes—perfect for her mood.

These days, bad-guy attacks were sabotaging her performance numbers.

At the soft thump on her door, the hairs on her nape

stiffened on alert. Her toes bunched into tight balls. During their three days at the Pension, they'd seen no other guests. But after tonight's sniper ... She sidled against the bedroom wall. Edged toward the doorjamb.

A faint whistle of "The Eyes of Texas are upon You" drifted into the room. "Riles, it's Jacob."

Breath eked from her mouth. Thank heavens they were Texan eyes and not the killer's. She flexed the knots from her toes. They hadn't used song signals since tracking terrorists on the riverboat cruise. Mostly old church hymns. Jacob might be a diehard country-music fan, but he loved binging on '30s and '40s films as much as she did. She unlocked the hand-carved door and let him in.

He slipped inside and shut the door, scanned the room like a soldier on point. "Nice digs, sugar cake."

"Uh-huh," she said, her lips quirking. His standard line every time he came inside. Tonight, no doubt, to put her at ease, but it wasn't working. Frau Propicka *had* given her the nicer room, with broad windows overlooking the lake. But the Austrian folk-print bedding and drapes, hand-painted furniture, and doors matched his.

"How about we make another memory?" He skimmed a hand across the small of her back and nudged her to him.

The citrusy scent of his aftershave washed over her. With every circle his fingers traced on her arm, volts of electricity ignited her core. But when he searched her lips with his, she nearly melted.

Thank You, God, for bringing Jacob into my life. And for sparing our lives tonight. She sank into the kiss, then stepped back from him. Breaths quivered in her chest. Whoa-howdy. Boundaries. She'd better set a few thou-shalt-nots here.

Lines creased his brow, the corners of his eyes. "You okay?" His voice hitched.

"Peachy." In his black cords and black crew-neck sweater

they could pass for a couple ninjas. Did male ninjas have cobalt-blue eyes and blond hair? She sat beside her desk and leaned against the chair's heart-shaped back. "We need a plan." Now that their vacation was ruined.

"I've called Margot."

Super-duper. Margot the Wonderful. His Interpol teammate from his last assignment. Staring at her lap, Riley nodded. He'd be off to Vienna, or Margot the Great would drive to Velden.

"Hey ..." He thumbed her chin up until she met his gaze. "I wanted this getaway as much as you. But if Margot takes the lead for a few days, we can cobble some special time for us."

"Uh-huh." She studied his face, the longing in his eyes. Did he really believe that—with a killer tracking them? "Maybe we should've gone to Cuero to meet my parents." Not that she'd call that a holiday. But in Texas they wouldn't be dodging potshots. Words maybe, but not bullets. "On second thought, nix that idea."

"I'm eager to meet your family, but with Armand still on the loose, I can't leave Europe."

"I know, I know." She twisted her engagement ring. One of these days they'd have to make the trip to Texas. She couldn't keep putting it off.

"Margot is requesting police protection for you."

"Thanks." Jacob needed a security detail too. "How do you think the assassin found us?"

"With me here on assignment, we couldn't use aliases. But Armand may have paid watchers at Austrian ports of entry."

She stifled a shiver. "Still, maybe we should get a couple of fake IDs and passports."

"Right. We can wear your stage wigs and travel incognito."

"You goose." She punched his arm. "Let's get something to eat. I'm starved after that swim."

He cocked a brow. "Sure you want to go out?"

"Yes." No way was she letting Armand make her shiver and shake in her hot-pink Nikes. She plucked her jacket from the wall hook, glanced around the room.

A white envelope lay on her top bed pillow. Odd. Frau Propicka always left the room immaculate. With the bathroom tucked near the hall door, she hadn't paid attention to the rest of the room.

"Wait." She strode toward the bed, jabbed her finger at the pillows. "Something's not right here."

"Here. Let me check." Jacob dashed in front of her. He opened the tweezers on his Swiss army knife, lifted the envelope, whipped the pillows and duvet off the mattress. Air whooshed from his mouth. "Good. No other surprises."

Pulse pounding, she moved to his side. "I guess you didn't leave me a love note."

But his cockeyed grin didn't hide his ashen pallor. "Sorry. Left my lockpicking kit in my room." He tweezered a picture postcard from the envelope. "Great shot of the marina, even has our boat rental place in the background." His voice was terse as he flipped over the card.

She stared at the scrawled block letters. Ice slewed through her veins.

YOU GOT AWAY THIS TIME. NEXT TIME, YOU
WON'T BE SO LUCKY.

4

Velden am Wörthersee, Day 1

Ominous warning notes. His, left beneath his pillow. Same block letters. Same threatening words. The violation—the danger—everything they'd dealt with on the riverboat cruise, washed over him in waves.

With Riles' hand secure in his, Jacob crept past the closed ground-floor doors marked "private." LED candles flickered in the wall sconces, pooling soft light on the Persian carpet runner.

During his temporary assignment to Interpol police on the riverboat cruise, he could fire a weapon and make arrests. But here, he was just a Special Agent on assignment to Austria. He knocked on the last door, Riles hovering at his side.

There had to be a way to outwit Armand. *So help me, I'll find it.*

The Pension's online pictures radiated Austrian *Gemüthlichkeit*—warm hospitality. Serenity. Safety. The perfect place for their first vacation. Starched bed linens and a pile of down pillows he could sink into. Breakfast chairs with heart-shaped seatbacks. Austrian wildflowers painted on the hand-carved doors and wardrobes. Even a dirndl-clad proprietor. Right up Riles' *the-hills-are-alive-with-the-sound-of-music* alley.

His too. Right now, Victoria, Texas, seemed a million miles away. He'd lived overseas so long, he'd need a city map to find his childhood home. He tapped on the door again. Only eleven at night, but Austrians tended to retire early and rise before the birds.

"*Ja?*" The voice floating into the hall held a sleepy note.

"We have an emergency."

Frau Propicka opened the door, tied the chenille sash around her dressing gown. No horned helmet and spear, but her statuesque height and long, gray-blonde braid could pass for a Wagnerian Valkyrie. Despite the bathrobe and boiled-wool slippers. Inside the darkened room, a duvet lay wadded at the foot of the first twin bed. A large mound burrowed beneath the other duvet.

"What sort of emergency?" She stifled a yawn.

"Sorry to disturb you, but we found life-threatening notes in our rooms." He warmed Riles' cold fist in his palm. "I've called the police."

Eyes wide, Frau Propicka's gaze ricocheted from Riles to him. "The police?" Her chest swelled. "Without notifying me first?"

"*Ja.*" He held out his Interpol ID. She squinted toward it, then stepped back. "How many other guests are here?"

"Only one. A gentleman checked in this afternoon."

"Let's wake him up," Riles said.

"Now?" Frau Propicka blinked. "At this hour? It simply isn't done. The Pension's reputation—"

"Unless someone else has access to your home, he's a prime suspect," Jacob said.

"I think it's best we wait for the police." Arms folded, she blocked her bedroom door.

"I think not." With a casual flick of his Interpol ID, he shifted his stance.

"*Sofort*, immediately." She snicked the bedroom door closed behind her.

"*Danke*." Riles in tow, he followed Frau Propicka upstairs to room four. Three guest rooms on each side lined the dimly lit hall. Thankfully, the area was unfurnished. No place for a killer to hide.

Frau Propicka rapped on the door. "Herr Huber?" When there was no answer, the proprietor banged her fist on the Edelweiss panel. "Herr Huber, open the door, please."

"Surely you must have a pass key." Riles' smile could charm paint off metal.

"*Ja, ja*." Using a key attached to a metal ball and small wooden paddle, Frau Propicka unlocked the door, flicked the light switch.

"May I?" Jacob peered over her shoulder. A carbon-copy of his room. Not even a whiff of the guy's aftershave, no sign of luggage. But Armand's goon had gotten far too close to them.

"If he's the culprit, how did he slip into our rooms?" Riles asked.

Crimson streaked the woman's face. "During the day, this key hangs on a hook behind the check-in desk. I assure you, such a thing has never happened before—"

"Of course not." And probably never would've, if he and Riles hadn't arrived.

After breakfast, they'd strolled through the village, reserved the dinghy, then hung out on the beach until four-thirty. Anyone could've entered their rooms with the passkey. The locks on their doors shot into place like the crack of a bullet. If Huber were in his room, he'd have heard them leave around five for dinner. From the pizza parlor they'd gone straight to the marina at seven.

"*Danke*." He motioned Frau Propicka downstairs. The room search he'd leave to the police. Maybe they'd find a fingerprint or two. "What time did he check in?"

"Precisely at four." The floorboards creaked as she headed toward the check-in counter.

In the guest salon, the antler chandelier glowed on the leather sofa and armchairs near the broad picture windows. The scent of sautéed garlic and oil hit his nose. "What time did you eat dinner?"

"Promptly at eight. Before that, I was in the kitchen pounding the pork cutlets for Schnitzel."

"A meat mallet's noisy as a jackhammer. You wouldn't have heard him take your key. What time did you take the passkey with you this evening?"

"*Na ja* ..." Lips pursed, she stared toward the ceiling. "Around nine-thirty. We watched a soccer match on television." Her cheeks flushed. "My husband likes the sound a bit loud."

"Sure." If Huber were the sniper, he could've returned to the Pension when the police arrived at the dock. Left the notes, then scrammed. Or if he were assigned to watch them, the sniper had phoned and told him to pen the threats.

"Did he have any luggage?" Jacob asked.

"A small valise with a shoulder strap. Sufficient for overnight."

"Did he make a reservation?" Riles asked.

Hopefully she wasn't going to try to assist his investigation. She was in enough danger.

"*Ja*. He called the day before and asked if I had a vacancy for two nights."

A chill snaked between Jacob's shoulder blades. They'd probably been under observation since they arrived in Velden. Why not forgo the handwritten warnings and risk a police search, and use the second night to finish the job? Or tonight, once they were asleep in their rooms.

"So where did he go?" Riles murmured.

Austrians weren't typically all-night partyers. "Unless Huber fled town or checked into another hotel tonight, most restaurants are closed."

"Apart from the casino," Frau Propicka said. "It closes at three."

"Right." Jacob checked his watch. Eleven-fifteen. "May I see his check-in papers?"

"*Jawohl.*" Frau Propicka rummaged through photocopied passport pictures in the desk drawer. Her face blanched. "I don't understand. His page is missing."

"Figures. Another dead end." Given her work ethic—always checking her watch, pens scooted into orderly lines on the desk —no way had she misplaced Huber's identity pictures. They were dealing with one cool-under-pressure murderer. "Was his German accent native, or Austrian, Swiss?"

"*Nein.* He sounded Slavic. Heavy, slow consonants. Throaty vowels."

"Then he may have snuck over the Slovakian border." Riles' tone flattened.

Never assume anything, his boss's mantra. And Armand wouldn't give up easily. "Could you help a forensic artist create a drawing of this man?"

"*Ja* ..." Frau Propicka shrugged. "Perhaps ... Medium height, dark hair, dark eyes. Average build. Trim. No facial hair or scars."

"Great." Riles squelched a titter. "That describes half the males in Austria."

He raked a hand through his hair. More needles in haystacks. "Any estimates on his age?"

"He is forty-seven. I know precisely from his passport."

Blue rack lights flashed outside the Pension. Moments later

Schmidt trudged up the hillside steps, rubbing his eyes. A female officer darted behind him, her braid swishing beneath her jaunty beret. In the porch light, she looked all of sixteen.

Slippers slapping the tile floor, Frau Propicka strode to the front door.

"Evening." Schmidt nodded his greeting. "Inspector Anneliese Liebermann will accompany you and Miss Williams while you're in Velden."

"Fine." Jacob flicked a tight smile. He'd have preferred someone with more police experience under her equipment belt.

Casting glances toward them, Frau Propicka rearranged her papers at the check-in counter.

"Call me Liesl." Grinning, the officer shook Jacob's hand, then Riles'. "I will not wear my uniform on protection detail."

But would she be armed? In London, the Met officers used a baton. "Thanks for your help." With Riles beside him, Jacob walked the officers upstairs, brought them up to date. He glanced back at Schmidt. "Do you have access to a police artist?"

"Unfortunately, I'd have to request someone from Wien."

"If you don't mind, I'll go through Viennese Interpol."

"Good." The policeman chuckled. "Then it comes out of your budget." While he and Liesl donned gloves, bagged the notes, dusted their rooms and Huber's for fingerprints, Jacob waited in the hall with Riles.

"Find anything?" Jacob gripped Riles' shoulder, her muscles rigid beneath his hand.

"Probably Frau Propicka's prints." Liesl whipped off her gloves. "What time shall I meet you tomorrow or will you spend the day in your rooms?"

"No. We'd planned a bike ride." She stared him down, aimed her razor-edged tone at his you-promised-me button.

He jabbed a fist in his pocket. "Brilliant. We'll be moving targets."

Eyes flashing, Riles yanked her shoulder free. "I told you in London, I'm through hiding in my bedroom."

That didn't mean he had to like her decision. He couldn't protect her on a bike ride. A sniper would have a clear shot.

At all three of them.

5

The police siren sing-songing on the road almost swallowed Armand's phone beeping in his pocket. Finally. Why hadn't the man reported in last night? Armand Découvrir pressed the cell to his ear. Hiding out in rented villas wasn't his style. Until a month ago, these estates had been his private fiefdoms, his ops centers while he moved freely in the towns and cities, overseeing the tentacles of his widespread business ventures. He'd moved wherever he pleased. Whenever he wanted.

"Yes?" Voice low, he squinted beyond the French doors. Best keep Amira out of this side of his business.

Morning sunlight shimmered on the lake. Seated at the patio table, his daughter spooned jam on a piece of her breakfast *Semmelkugel.* The crusty rolls cut the roof of his mouth. He'd have ordered French croissants, but Amira insisted they eat like Austrians. He turned away from the French doors. Placating a thirteen-year-old was as challenging as dealing with the stooges on his payroll. These days, finding quality employees was proving difficult.

"I'm waiting," he said.

"I tried but ..." The man's voice sounded muffled.

Armand squeezed the phone in his palm. "What happened?" With his top lieutenant in jail, contracting an assassin online had been a necessity. He couldn't afford to let Coulter and his nosy fiancée live.

"The police arrived at the lake before I could get off more rounds. But I sank the boat." If the man's heavy Slavic accent were any thicker, his English would be unintelligible.

Imbecile. "I didn't tell you to sink a boat." Armand suppressed the snarl in his tone. "You were hired to take them out."

"I barely escaped. But the notes I left on their beds ought to shake them up."

"I'm not paying you to shake them up. I want them dead. Understand?"

"*Ja*. But they aren't alone. There's a kid following them everywhere they go."

"A kid?" Had Jacob sent for his little sister?

"*Ja*. Some girl with long braids and wearing a dirndl."

Armand snatched the framed photo from his desk. Why had he kept it? The fewer mementos of Jacob Coulter and his sister, the better. Or Riley Williams. "Describe her."

"Pale blonde hair, flat-chested, looks about sixteen but probably older."

In the photo, Tracy's hair caressed her shoulders. Not even her school uniform hid her voluptuous figure. What thirteen-year-old sported braids these days? His blood chilled. "Probably police protection." He slapped the frame face down on his desk. "Nevertheless, the job is still on. Do whatever it takes. I want them in body bags, understand?"

The man sniffed into the phone. "What's in it for me?"

"A hundred-thousand-euro bonus if they're dead in three days."

"And if I can't complete the job by then—"

"Your bonus drops ten-thousand euros every day." Armand disconnected the call, jammed the phone in his trouser pocket. If his lieutenant weren't in prison, the assassin wouldn't get the bonus. As soon as he'd completed the job, he'd be lying in a ditch beside a deserted road.

After all, dead men can't speak.

WHILE JACOB TURNED in their rental bikes at the counter, Riley whipped off her sunhat, brushed the sweat from her brow. *Thank You, Lord.* A ride without mishap. Probably no fun for Jacob, head flicking left and right like an out-of-control searchlight. "Poor guy. It's a wonder he didn't crash into a trash barrel," she muttered to Liesl.

"*Ja*. But if you insist on going out, we must all be vigilant."

Riley ignored the reproach in Liesl's tone, flicked dirt from her slacks. "Right." But David didn't run from Goliath. Full of confidence, he hurtled toward his enemy, little stones in hand, God at his side. But David had also hidden in a cave to stay alive. She shut out the images. Nope. This was a David-faces-off-with-the-giant season.

A man in a helmet and skintight bike shorts tapped his credit card on the counter, sinewy calf muscles flexing. A biker or runner's legs. He glanced toward Jacob, cold eyes assessing.

Shivers rolled over Riley's shoulders. Were they being watched? Was he the assassin?

If so, best act innocent. She strolled the sidewalk, Liesl beside her. The scent of molting leaves and crisp lakeside air tickled her nose. Enjoy the moment because life was balking at her plan.

A few yards ahead, an unshaven man slouched on a park bench, scrabbling through a sack on his palm. Scruffy cords drooped around his legs and athletic shoes. He sank his head inside his gray hoodie, tossed a handful of nuts in his mouth. Each chew so measured his jaws seemed on a timer.

Unease pitted Riley's stomach. Definitely not a well-heeled Wörthersee resident or visitor. Had he left the notes on their pillows? She quickened her pace. "Thank God, Interpol agreed to cover the deductible on the sunken sailboat," she whispered to Liesl.

"*Ja*, that is fortunate." Smoothing the gathers in her dirndl skirt, Liesl did a slow 360 around the marina.

The vagrant had vanished. Giving the man beside him a once-over, Jacob pocketed the euros from the deposit and walked toward them.

"What's next?" Liesl's tone suggested she'd rather they hide under a rock.

Riley picked at her fingernail. She shouldn't have insisted on the bike ride. It wasn't just about refusing to cower in her room, letting Armand terrorize them. If today's jaunt had drawn out the killer, they could've ended this cat-skewers-the-mouse game. She glanced at the strain in Liesl's eyes. Face it. Her insistence had endangered a police officer. "Guess we could pick up lunch fixings and eat in our rooms."

Liesl's shoulders sagged an inch. "*Wunderbar*. Tell me what you want to eat, and I'll bring it to the Pension."

"Thanks." Then Liesl could go home while she and Jacob snuck in a few cuddles.

And planned their next strike.

Some vacation. In the Pension foyer, Riley flicked her shirt from her sweat-soaked skin while Jacob scoped the downstairs.

All she wanted was time alone with her guy. No—weeks alone with him. Time to make sure he was the right one for her, that his gotta-save-the-day protectiveness wouldn't morph into Dad's controlling nature. And push every one of her unhealed red buttons.

Tears welled in her eyes. Staring at the ceiling, she blinked them away. Once again, they were starring in a three-ring circus. Living in a fishbowl like the President and First Lady. How did they stand it?

"All clear." The relief in Jacob's voice washed over her.

"Good." Riley headed for the stairs. A quick shower, a quiet lunch, and—No. A well-dressed woman sat on the couch in the lounge, a man beside her, an Interpol jacket over his shirt, a computer bag at his feet.

Rats. Jacob's teammates had probably whizzed down the Autobahn with blue lights flashing. Riley forced a smile. Ingrate. They're here to help catch Armand. And the assassin.

"Where have you been?" The woman rose, pivoted on her heels.

Head ducked, the man kneaded his knuckles.

"Riles, this is Margot." Jacob nudged Riles inside the room. "Wasn't expecting you so early. We went for a bike ride."

"Whose idiotic idea was that?" Sparks flashed from Margot's brown eyes.

Fists on her hips, Riley marched across the rug, locked eyes with the woman's fire-breathing gaze. "Mine."

A smirk played on Margot's lips. "Figures."

The slim cut of the agent's gray suit nipped all the right places, highlighted a curve here, a curve there. Chic, classy. Definitely a go-getter. Riley extended her hand. "Nice to meet you."

"Likewise." Margot's handclasp was cool as a chilled fish. "You're every bit as gutsy as Jacob said."

And you're every bit as ritzy as he didn't tell me. "I guess he didn't mention I refuse to hide from terrorists."

"Then I should've brought some bull's-eye targets."

"Or bullet-proof vests and a weapon for Jacob."

The flint crumpled from Margot's face, and she glanced toward the windows. "*Ja ...*"

Was she being too hard on his teammate? Margot must want Armand caught as badly as she and Jacob did. Riley sank onto the easy chair beside the fireplace. The ashy smell from last night's fire enveloped her like a cozy blanket. She almost felt safe. For a nanosecond.

Jacob perched a hip on the armrest, and she squeezed his fingers. Why Interpol put their agents at risk, with no weapons, no backup, she'd never understand.

"We'd best get down to business." Margot whipped a folder from her purse.

The woman was a regular slave driver. Wasn't Jacob the team leader?

"I've prepared a list of known assassins Armand might've hired."

"Eastern Europeans?" Jacob swiped a hand over his face but worry still rimmed his eyes.

"Not all of them."

"Uh ..." Riley cleared her throat. "Frau Propicka said he spoke with a Slavic accent."

A slight flush tinged Margot's cheeks. "Nevertheless, I think we need to consider the men on this list."

"Thanks." Jacob motioned for the paper.

Margot the Guilt-Tripper. Riley leaned against him and read the names, inhaled his faded aftershave and dried sweat. "Some of these are Chechin spellings. The men would have Slavic accents." Despite Margot's annotations of last known sightings in Italy. Germany. France. Austria.

"Good point, Riles." Jacob beamed at her.

Margot's cheeks flamed.

"When I lived in Wien, it was common knowledge there were Chechin assassins in Vienna." But Austrian law forbade an arrest until someone had done something wrong.

"According to Interpol intel, they favor the apartments in the newer districts across the Danube. When you reach Vienna, why don't you check out these guys ..." He grabbed a pen from the side table and ticked off the Chechin names. "You may find they're your neighbors."

"Very well." Margot exchanged her list with Jacob's.

Outside, Liesl trudged up the steps, takeout food bags in hand. Her eagle-eyed gaze swept the yard. Riley's stomach rumbled. So much for a shower and a peaceful lunch.

Margot's body tensed. "Who's that?"

"Liesl, our police protection." Jacob darted toward the foyer.

"You're joking." Margot's brow shot northward. "She doesn't look old enough to know the deadly end of a pistol."

Hand to her lips, Riley stifled a snort. "Looks can be deceiving." After all, she'd been snookered by Armand's charm. And some of the people on the riverboat cruise. Goosebumps pimpled her arms. When would she learn to give people time to prove themselves first? Naïveté was no blessing. Ignorance could be deadly.

"While you were out playing catch-me-if-you-can, our police artist and your landlady developed a composite sketch of the missing guest." Margot flicked a hand at her cohort.

The man handed Jacob several copies from his computer case.

Peering over his shoulder, Riley gasped. "I just saw him. Near the bike rental shop, slouched on the park bench."

6

Velden am Wörthersee, Day 2

As they sat beside the fireplace, Jacob draped his arm around Riles' shoulders. Her muscles trembled beneath his palm. How long had the man been watching them? "Are you sure about the man?"

"Well ..." She squinted at the drawing.

But the guy at the bike rental counter had set off inner alarm bells, the shape of eyes, his jaw ... Nope, cop instincts never died. And in his experience, they were seldom wrong.

"Yes, I'm sure."

How could she be so certain? The biker matched the drawing too. "At the moment, we have an advantage. He doesn't know we've identified him as the assassin." Riles' perp would've stuck out on the bike path. "This killer's shrewd. Brazen." Jacob dug his fingers in her bicep, and she flinched. "Sorry, hon." If Armand's thug was still in town, he'd try again.

Frowning, Liesl studied the composite drawing. He wanted to ask if she were packing. Because if she weren't ...

"I ... I don't think I've seen him about town. To be honest, I didn't notice him on the park bench."

Riles shot him a wild-eyed can-we-count-on-her look.

"Okay." Jacob tried for a reassuring smile. "Lunch smells fabulous."

The tantalizing scent of *Backhendl*, specially seasoned roast chicken, and *Brat Kartoffeln*, roasted potatoes to the rest of the world, rose from the bulging sacks in Liesl's hands. Topped with a small paper bag bearing the Schatzi Wörthersee label. Riles would've chosen slices of rich Austrian tortes from the shop. Saliva pooled in his mouth. Enough food for two, but not the five of them.

"Jacob, may I speak with you?" Margot's glare brooked no argument.

"Sure."

She jerked her head toward the hall. "In private."

Giving Riles' shoulder a final squeeze, he stepped into the hall, Margot at his heels.

"I know you lovebirds want time together, but you have a job to do. Lives to save. If you decide to marry her, Riley must understand your job comes first."

Cheeks bitten, he flexed his fists. How was he supposed to juggle everything—wife and family first—job first. And where did God fit into all this? He'd lost enough girlfriends over this issue. "If you're suggesting I come to Vienna now, I don't think that's necessary."

Margot huffed, glanced sideways. She faced him, speculation sparking in her eyes. "Perhaps Interpol should appoint someone else to take down Armand."

Just what he needed. A colleague poised to oust him, his promise to Riles in shambles, and a killer determined to obliterate them.

"That's not your decision to make." *Thank God.* But if Margot contacted his boss in Brussels ...

"Your intel was invaluable on the London assignment, but if you have a problem with being a team player, now's the time to tell me." He softened his words with a smile.

Her flickering nostrils suggested a volcano threatening to erupt. "Of course." She motioned the Interpol artist to the door, strode toward the foyer, heels clacking on the floor. At the end of the hall, she paused and glanced at Jacob. "You're making a mistake. Armand is in Wien. Our latest intel suggests—"

"A heavier volume of bank transactions doesn't mean he made the deposits himself. Who's to say he's not holed up in one of those lakeside estates on Wörthersee, calling the shots here in Velden?"

"We'll see." Margot shut the front door behind her.

"Do you really think he could be that close to us?" Riles rubbed her arms.

"It'd be just like him. Arrogant. Certain we won't catch him. Tracy's police statement mentioned he'd rented a slew of villas in Austria."

"I doubt he'd be stupid enough to lease one he's used in the past." Riles stalked across the room, a caged lioness.

"I agree. And we can hardly go knocking on every front door."

Liesl cleared her throat. "I can ask Chief Inspector Schmidt to make discreet inquiries into the identities of renters, via the real estate agents." She handed him the lunch bags.

"*Danke.*" He set them on the round table in the corner. No doubt Frau Propicka disapproved of dining in the bedrooms. "See if you can get the renters' photo identification. Armand probably uses an array of false passports under bogus names."

"Of course." Liesl saluted him, darted toward the door. "Call me if you wish to leave the Pension this afternoon."

"I will, and thanks." Jacob pulled out a chair at the table for Riles.

"He's not going to ruin our lives. I won't have it." Riles slashed a hand in the air.

If only it were as simple as that. He scanned the curving street, whisked the drapes closed near the table. Four months ago, Noel, his best friend, had died in his arms. Murdered by a determined terrorist.

A terrorist who might've been funded by Armand.

THE MORNING BIKE ride had been exhilarating. Cuddling with Jacob this afternoon had been delicious. If only their lives were this calm all the time. Riley lowered her menu, drank in the black and red décor of the Yacht Club restaurant, the enormous water fountain shaped like a fluted vase. The lake glistened beyond the wall of windows. She shuddered, pulled her silk jacket closer. She'd had her fill of moonlight sails. "What are we celebrating?"

"Life. Us." A grimace creased Jacob's face. "Surviving the sail last night."

"Honey." She reached for his wrist across the tablecloth. "We have to move past that." Was it really that easy? Two rows from them, Liesl placed her order at her window-side table. The policewoman had insisted on eating alone. Hopefully she didn't read lips. "Let's enjoy tonight."

Orders taken, he smothered her hand in his warm palm. "I love you, Riles. Let's get married. It would make protecting you a lot easier." At his lopsided grin, warmth trickled through her.

"I know how you feel." If she married him now, she could share his responsibility for Tracy. But what about all the weeks she'd be away performing and auditioning? And instant motherhood. To a rebellious teenager in crisis. Was she ready for this? "But we have issues to work out first."

"Such as?"

The waiter set their first course of sauteed scallops and microgreens in front of them.

"My dad is overprotective. He likes to rule the roost, tell us how to think, what to wear, what to do." She stabbed a scallop. "And not to do."

"I'm not your dad."

"I know." She pushed the microgreens into a blob. "But sometimes ... when you tell me where I can and can't go, you remind me an awful lot of him."

Color crept up his cheeks. "I. Am. Not. Your father. I love you. I want to protect you. Take care of you."

Sounded like Dad to her. "Some years ago, I asked Mom if he'd always been like that. She said no. That when they dated, he was the perfect gentleman, always seated her, treated her with respect, insisted he wanted to do what she wanted to do. But Mom said Dad changed, seven years into the marriage, when Lacy and I were two. He was promoted to management and his job became a major stress with long hours and loads of production quotas to meet. He started barking orders at home." She shivered. "I'd have hated to be one of his employees."

Jacob set down his fork. "So you're worried I'll end up like him."

"You're already on the path."

"Huh? You knew what I was like when we met on the riverboat cruise." He jabbed a scallop, stuffed it in his mouth. Chewed as if it were rubber.

Oh, why couldn't he understand? She inched her fingers toward him, but he moved his hands to his lap. "Yes. Utterly charming, handsome. Confident you could save the world. Everything a woman could admire in a man. How could I not fall in love with you?" Blinking back tears, she looked away from the woundedness in his eyes.

"But with such a stressful job, life-and-death decisions facing you nearly every day—" Why had she chosen tonight to bring the elephant into the room, their one date night? They were supposed to be making happy memories.

Velden am Wörthersee, Day 2

Acool blast of night air hit Riley as she and Jacob stepped outside the restaurant, arms barely brushing. Ahead of them, Liesl stalked the sidewalk, head jerking left, right, body poised like a sprinter.

The chocolate torte she should've skipped roiled in her stomach. She'd tried to steer their conversations into less tempestuous waters, but Jacob's reticence was so unlike the man she knew. If they couldn't air their concerns before marriage, how would their disagreements affect them after they said I do? The last thing she wanted was a strife-ridden marriage. They were Christians. It shouldn't be like this.

Across the street, the Casino Velden's pink and purple lights splashed the sidewalk with garish hues. Outside the etched glass doors, a darkhaired man ran a hand over his brush cut, adjusted the bow tie on his tux.

"Jacob." She tugged his sleeve. If the vagrant had shaven ... Or could it be— "Is that the man who stood beside you at the bike shop?"

"What?" He squinted toward the casino entrance. "Yeah ... could be him."

The doorman parted the glass doors, and the man strode inside with the panache of Donald J. Trump.

"Quick, let's change into our evening clothes, see what he's up to."

"All I brought were business suits."

She tweaked his lapel. "I thought James Bond never traveled without a tuxedo."

"Yeah, well, I'm not the type."

Liesl sidled next to them. "What's the problem?"

"Riles saw one of the men who resembles the police drawing enter the casino."

"I can't enter without the Chief Inspector's permission. The casino has its own security personnel, and they'd recognize me. I'm known in town." Liesl cleared her throat. "Usually, at six in the evening, the casino dress code becomes smart casual. Tonight is a gala. Formal wear is required."

Jacob groaned. "You're kidding."

"Well, I can go in." Riley thrust her hands on her hips. "Lucky for us an opera singer is never without an evening gown."

"Not without me," Jacob said.

"Try and stop me." Great. She'd picked another argument.

"Oh, no, you don't." He grabbed her arm. "You're not going in there without me."

"Don't be a ninny. This is our chance to get a lead on Armand."

"That guy's probably gambling his down payment on killing us."

"We'll never know unless we follow him."

"Not happening. We report this to Chief Inspector Schmidt." Jacob dialed the policeman.

Peering over his arm, Riley punched the speaker button on

his cell. Ten rings later, a voice message kicked in, 'call the station for immediate help.' "He must be taking a night off."

"Can't blame him, after the ruckus we've stirred up the past twenty-four hours." Jacob pocketed his cell. "Any idea where he is, Liesl?"

"He's out of town. A family birthday."

"That settles it. I'm changing clothes." Riley headed for the car, Jacob and Liesl dogging her steps.

"Riles, you're not going inside."

"Oh, yes, I am. One of us needs to tail him. You can sit on the park bench and wait for him to leave. Then Liesl can nab him."

Jacob yanked her to him. "You're. Not. Going after him."

"I am, and you can't stop me. Like you said, we have the advantage. He doesn't know we're on to him."

"That guy wouldn't hesitate to take you out right there in the casino." His voice rose. "It wouldn't take much, a knife between your ribs, a bullet in your brain, hands around your throat in the rest room."

"I agree," Liesl said.

"Calm down. You're overreacting." Riley hoped. God had protected her before, hadn't He?

An elderly couple in Loden coats and feathered hats strolled toward them, faces wreathed with disapproval.

"Quiet, you two." Riley flicked a loose curl behind her ear. "You're drawing attention."

"I should be the one going in there." Jacob's words strangled in his throat. "What do you know about gambling?"

"Zip. *Nada*. Never gambled in my life, and I have no desire to start. But sometimes agents do things they're uncomfortable with. Right?"

"Hey—stop right there. You're not an agent."

"Face it, lover boy." She jabbed him in the chest. "At the moment, I'm the best option you have."

SUIT JACKET BUTTONED over his shirt and wool undershirt, Jacob hunched on the bench across the street from the casino. Beside him, Liesl tugged her sweater to her chest. A line of chauffeured cars eased to the entrance and disgorged men and women in full evening dress. "Thanks for manning the fort while we changed clothes."

"That's my job. Fortunately for us, the suspected assassin is still in there."

Fortunate? With Riles in there? Jacob checked his watch again. How long was she planning to stay? He tugged at his tie. Crossed and uncrossed his legs. "She shouldn't be in there without a body mic, some way to communicate with her."

"Such needs are rare in our town." A breeze fluttered Liesl's skirt. "Is Frau Riley always so impetuous?"

"She has a tendency to follow trouble, or it gloms onto her." He'd left the Dallas PD because of broken relationships with a woman he'd hoped would marry him. If he could've invested the proper time in their relationship. *I'm marrying you, not your job*, she'd said. *I can't live with the fear every time you step out of the patrol car, you might be murdered.*

Jacob shoved his fists in his pockets. Being a protector coursed through his DNA. He couldn't change that. But Interpol was draining his personal life like the police department. And proving far deadlier.

Now his fiancée's life was in danger.

Elbows dug into his thighs, he cradled his face in his hands. Had Riles refused to set a wedding date for the same reason as his ex-girlfriend? Or did she think she had to take down every enemy before they could marry? Was that why she'd insisted on lassoing the lion in the casino? Or was it really all about her dad?

"Look." Liesl gripped his arm. "Trouble just walked in the door."

"No way." He jerked upright. Pink lights gleamed on the man's gelled hair as he strolled through the casino foyer.

"It was the other suspect, the one on the park bench."

"Are there two assassins?" Heart clobbering his chest, Jacob dashed across the street, burst through the casino doors. How could he have let Riles go in there without him?

The black-suited attendant blocked the doorway. "I'm sorry sir, formal dress is required tonight."

"Interpol." Jacob pulled his ID from his breast pocket. "I'm sure you can make an exception."

"I'm sorry. No admittance without a tuxedo."

"I'm not here to gamble. I'm on a case. And you're harboring an assassin."

Liesl darted to Jacob's side. "You must honor the rules."

"Is he with you?" the doorman asked.

"*Ja.*"

"Do you have a search or arrest warrant?"

Her cheeks flushed beneath the purple neon light. "*Nein.*"

"Then I'm sorry. The dress code is strictly enforced. You know the rules."

"*Ja, ja.*" Liesl touched Jacob's arm. "Come along."

"Not yet." He wrenched free, jabbed a finger at the doorman. "If anything happens to my fiancée, I'll have you arrested for obstructing justice."

The suspect stepped back into view. He swept his gaze toward Jacob, a gold tooth glinting in his smile, then tweaked his bow tie and headed for the gaming salon.

Jacob bit back a groan.

No doubt, Riles was in the same room.

8

All she had to do was find the man in the police drawing, see if he spoke with anyone, then hightail it out of Dodge. She strolled into the first room, shallow breaths fluttering the black jet paillettes on her evening gown. Sweat glued her beaded clutch to her palm. What if Jacob was right and the assassin tried to harm her?

No, think positive. She could do this. She was David confronting Goliath.

Pink and purple neon lights clashed with the carpet a shade away from bordello red. Multi-colored circles embedded the flooring, subliminal suggestions of enormous coins. Icicle lights dangled from the tray ceiling.

Ka-chings and pings chirped from the crowded slot machines. People hunkered on tall stools, faces fixated on the computerized screens. Fort Knox seemed the popular choice, a game advertised on the sandwich boards in the doorway.

Definitely not James Bond's game of chance.

42

A black-suited casino attendant in a white shirt and crimson tie walked over to her. "May I help you, madame?"

"I'm not sure." She glanced around the room. Had their target come in here?

"You must register at the Kassa and purchase a card or chips."

"*Danke.*" If only she could do this without having to gamble. "If you don't mind, I'd like to see what you have first." What had she been thinking, setting foot in a casino? If her grandmother knew, she'd roll over in her East-Texas grave.

"*Bitte.*" He gestured her inside the room.

Pretending to scan the games, she strolled along the slot machines, studying every male customer. No sign of Flattop.

"Find anything that interests you?" the room attendant asked.

"*Nein.*"

"May I suggest a game of blackjack, roulette, or poker." The man gestured toward the adjoining room.

Definitely not. "*Danke.*"

The man waiting at the Kassa turned. He swept his gaze over her.

Feet riveted to the carpet, she mangled the fifty-euro banknote and her passport in her hand. No. It couldn't be. The vagrant from the park bench, all spiffed up. Should she leave now? But Jacob was across the street, just a yell away.

The man stepped aside, motioned her to the teller.

Would he stab her in the back, shoot her here? Oh, why hadn't she listened to Jacob? "*Danke.*" Pulse throbbing her throat like a jackhammer, she stepped to the Kassa, ears straining. On this carpet, she'd never hear the assassin's steps.

"Card or chips, madame?"

A placard in the window listed the fifty-euro minimum purchase, the choice of chip denominations. Ten euros. Twenty.

A hundred. Five hundred. Color coded so everyone would know how much she was betting. If the killer wasn't playing the slot machines ... "Uh ... chips, I guess." She pushed the crumpled banknote and her passport beneath the glass opening.

The teller slid five chips toward her, his downturned lips practically saying, why bother?

"Gambling's not really my thing." Why did she feel the need to explain?

"Don't let the manager hear you." He gave her a phony smile, motioned the next person forward.

Chips scooped into her palm, she stepped aside. Glanced around the foyer. The vagrant was gone. A sigh escaped her lips. *Thank You, God.* With shaking fingers, she dropped her chips and passport inside her purse and headed for the gaming room. Why hadn't she made Jacob read her the rules for casino games? Anything past gin rummy and Old Maid was out of her league.

Beige leather banquettes rimmed the walls. Yellow neon lights bathed the room in a soft glow. At least the decor wasn't as sleezy as the slot machine room.

Men in tuxes and bejeweled women in designer evening gowns milled shoulder to shoulder around blackjack and roulette tables. Muted conversations hummed through the electrified atmosphere. At the poker tables, players huddled over their cards as if they all held a royal flush.

At the first roulette table, the black-vested croupier spun the dial. The marble clattered and bounced around the disk. "Number seventeen." He raked his cane across the green felt table and pushed the piles of chips in front of Flattop. "*Mein Herr.*"

Breath caught in Riley's chest. She'd found the biker. Now what?

Gaze riveted toward the table, the assassin smirked.

The elegantly gowned woman beside him pouted. "*Ach,*

perhaps I should put my chips on your numbers." She patted her upswept dyed-blonde hair with a beringed hand that could disable a tendon. A silk wrap accentuated her diamond and emerald necklace, the matching teardrop earrings.

"Beginner's luck." Flattop scooped the chips close to him. He glanced up, raked his eyes over Riley, and she froze.

"I doubt that." The woman beside him turned to Riley. "Countess von Felsenstein." She gave Riley a once-over. Put the woman's svelte figure inside a sandwich board and she'd still look glamorous. "And who might you be, my dear?"

"Riley Williams." Idiot. Why hadn't she given a phony name?

"You're American." A twiglike setting of emeralds and diamonds encased the countess's wrist.

"Yes." If the woman lost her savings at the roulette table, she could always pawn her jewels.

"What brings a lone American woman to the gaming tables of Velden am Wörthersee?"

"Oh ... just thought I'd try my luck." She hadn't a clue how to play any of these games. She waved toward the blackjack table nearby, slicked sweaty fingers across her hip. *Oh, Grandma, forgive me.*

"Come join us." The woman moved aside, making room for Riley next to Flattop. "But if you intend to play, you'll need to purchase some chips." She nodded toward the Kassa outside, the young man in the glass-walled booth.

"*Danke.* I have some." Her fingers iced on her purse. What should she do? Leave? Nope. David would load a stone in his slingshot. She had the advantage. He didn't know Jacob suspected the guy was the assassin.

The players scooted piles of chips onto the numbers. Wow. She wouldn't last long at Flattop's table. Or any other game.

What if she hit a run of beginner's luck? Her heels rooted to the carpet. Wait. Isn't that what gamblers thought—just one more game—then my luck will change and I'll walk out of here rich? She stifled a shudder. How easily this could become a habit, an obsession, hooked for life. Unless God intervened and set her free.

"Excuse me." She eased between the countess and Flattop. How did Christian undercover agents do this—engage in activities they abhorred or were downright criminal?

"Place your bets, *meine Damen und Herren*."

The countess nudged Riley's arm. "Take my advice, put your chips wherever he does." She flicked her thumb at Flattop. "He's the man in the know."

"Really." Riley fingered her chip.

Flattop pushed twenty chips on number twenty-one. Each worth five-hundred euros.

The countess plunked fifty chips on Flattop's number, each one-hundred euros. "Go on, dear." She motioned Riley to place her bet.

Cringing inside, she slid her lone chip on number twenty-one.

The croupier spun the dial and the marble rat-a-tatted around the roulette wheel. Two bounces and it plunked on number thirty. Groans rolled around the table. The dealer raked the chips from the numbers and pulled them to him. An older couple left the table, and the vagrant eased into their place.

Perspiration beaded her forehead. Now what? Riley lifted her gaze from the green baize. The other players plunked their chips onto the numbers.

Flattop and the vagrant stared at her as if she were their next meal.

The killer's note on her pillow swam before her eyes.

THE NEXT TIME YOU WON'T BE SO LUCKY.

Bile rose in her throat. His 4711 cologne and the countess's floral perfume overpowered her own Chanel No. 5. What had she hoped to accomplish by coming here? Once again, she'd leapt into action with no plan. Not even a backup Plan B. Or C. She braced a hand on the edge of the table, her smile tight as rigor mortis. "Know anymore winning numbers?" she asked Flattop.

Head tilted to one side, he hefted his expensively tuxed shoulders, spread his palms as innocently as St. Francis of Assisi.

Great. If he wouldn't speak, she couldn't assess his accent. She took another ten-euro chip from her purse and set the disc on number three. Stacks of bets surrounded her lonely piece of plastic like a fortress.

"All bets placed." The croupier spun the dial. The marble bounced and lodged on number twenty-one. Groans rose around the table. The croupier cleared the chips from the baize to the growing heap in front of him. "House wins."

At least Flattop had lost.

"Madame." A gold tooth glinted from the vagrant's oily smile. "Allow me to advise you." His Slavic accent swallowed his vowels and consonants like a meat grinder.

"How kind." Which man was Armand's assassin? She couldn't keep calling this one the vagrant. His tux reeked of megabucks. Probably a disguise this morning.

Dark eyes glittering, he circled the table, walked toward her.

Her heart leapt into her throat. Now what?

Hysterical laughter choked her. Maybe she should ask for a selfie with these guys. Maybe she ought to leave before—

"Pardon me." The man with the gold tooth motioned the countess aside and squeezed in beside Riley. "Your luck is about to change."

9

Eyes riveted on his gold tooth, Riley gulped. "You don't say."

Focus. Focus. Get the information and scram. Both men were about five foot ten. Dark haired. Brown eyes. One was clearly of Slavic background. Both had purchased thousands of euros' worth of chips. Which one worked for Armand?

Gold Tooth brushed against her, plunked a stack of chips on the edge of the baize.

Stinging tentacles zinged through her arm, burned her skin. She whipped away from him, collided with Flattop. "Pardon." She scrabbled her fingers over the site on the back of her arm. Blood stained her forefinger. What had he injected her with?

Shudders raced through her heart. She pressed her fingers to her sternum but the galloping in her chest raged on. Had he poisoned her? How long did she have? The circle pattern in the carpet spun like an out-of-control merry-go-round. "I—I—" Sweat dribbling down her forehead, she gripped the gaming table.

"Is something wrong, Madame?" Gold Tooth reached for her elbow.

"Get away from me."

The countess whacked his chest. "Move. Can't you see she needs help?"

"Pardon." He stepped back and the countess slid into his place.

"Let me help you, my dear. Shall I call an ambulance?"

"No, no … I … ladies' room." Could she walk that far?

One arm snugged around Riley's waist, the countess steered her toward the rest room. "Are you all right, my dear?"

"No, I—"

A female casino employee darted toward them. "Do you need assistance?" She grasped Riley's arm and hustled her toward the ladies' room.

The quivering in Riley's thighs jittered into her calf muscles. *Dear God, help.* Jacob, oh, Jacob. If only she'd listened to him. Her ankles twisted in her high heels. How much longer could she hold on?

"Breath—I—need—" Dots swirled before her eyes. A vise gripped her chest. Choked off her air.

The woman shoved open the door, dragged her to a padded chair. Riley's chin sank toward her chest. The countess's face spun like a kaleidoscope as she yanked a syringe from her purse.

"No—no. What are you doing?" Voice rising to a shriek, Riley gripped the countess's wrist.

Face hard, the woman swatted Riley's hand away, jabbed the needle into Riley's thigh.

Stings at the injection site rippled through Riley's leg. *Oh, God, help.* Was the woman trying to kill her? The tightness in her throat melted and air eked into her lungs. *Thank. You. God.* "Thank you. If you hadn't—"

"I'm never without one." The countess brushed a moist curl from Riley's forehead.

"If you're allergic, why didn't you have your own epi pen?"

"I don't have allergies. That man shot something in my arm." Riley swiveled on the chair, twisted her shoulder to check the wound.

The countess fingered the angry swelling on Riley's skin. "This is a matter for the authorities." She whisked her phone from her purse. "I'll call for an ambulance."

"*Nein*. I'll be fine." She could hardly tell the countess the police and Interpol were already outside the building. "Really." She forced a smile.

"Why would he do this to you?"

"I don't even know him." She couldn't exactly say she hadn't seen him before.

"Imagine that. I come to the casino for a good time, and I end up saving a life." The woman slipped a gold compact from her evening bag, dabbed a tissue to the glistening beads above her lip. "It's an omen."

"I hope not." Any more omens like that and she might not live to sing her Viennese debut.

The woman swept over to the sinks, wet a paper towel, and dabbed it on Riley's forehead, her cheeks. "You're so pale."

"I'm fine, *danke*."

"You don't dress as if you're destitute." The countess freshened her lipstick. "Let me guess. You're a corporate CEO determined to break out of her smalltown mold. Trying her luck for the first time at the roulette wheel."

Riley chuckled. "No, an opera singer."

"How exciting. I love the opera. Where have you sung?"

"Belgium, Germany, Romania, and other countries. In two weeks, I debut at the Wiener Staatsoper. As the Queen of the Night."

"Ah, Mozart, my favorite. I'll be there. I have season tickets."

"Thank you. It's always nice to see a familiar face in the audience." Riley shuddered. A friendly face.

Once again, God had spared her life. Jacob would kill her if he knew the vagrant had attacked her. But how could she not tell him? He'd warned her the killer wasn't afraid to get up front and far too personal. Shivers trickled along her spine. Bullets weren't the only weapons in his arsenal.

"Where are you staying in Wien?" Compact in hand, the countess fingered her updo.

"I rented a small apartment." Riley stood, willed strength back into her legs. Jacob would be furious if he knew she was playing twenty questions with a stranger.

"Then you must come see me." The countess linked arms with Riley. "Perhaps we could meet for a coffee and torte. After all, I rescued you. You're my responsibility."

"That's so kind of you but my rehearsal schedule—"

"Nonsense. I insist." The woman took her business card from her purse and pressed it on Riley's palm. "Don't lose this."

"Thank you." Who knows? She might need a friend in Vienna. Especially if Flattop and Gold Tooth showed up.

ACROSS THE STREET from Jacob's café table, the casino's pink and purple neon lights glowed like Pinocchio's visit to Pleasure Island. The black-suited employee swung back the glass door. Riles wobbled outside the foyer, fingers scrabbling over her bare arms.

Something must've happened. Jacob tossed twenty euros on the table, bolted toward the casino, Liesl at his heels. Idiot. He should've locked Riles in her bedroom.

"Are you sure you're all right, madame?" The employee darted for her elbow.

"Just peachy, thanks."

But her face was chalk white. Had she been attacked in the casino? Why, why, why hadn't he stopped her going in there? "You're shaking." Shucking off his suit jacket, Jacob wrapped it around her shoulders, matched his steps to her tottering walk across the street to his café table. His dirty dishes were perched on the waiter's white-coated arm.

"*Ein grosser Brauner, bitte.*" A large coffee with milk should help. He seated her, pulled his chair beside her. "What happened in there?"

Teeth chattering, she filled him in while Liesl jotted notes on a tiny spiral pad. "If the countess hadn't recognized what was happening, and had an epi pen, the casino employees would've rolled me out in a body bag. End of career." Sniffling, she rested a hand on his knee. "End of life with you, before it even begins."

"Thank God for the countess." Jacob tugged her to him. "Oh, Riles, I shouldn't have let you—"

"Stop right there." She patted his lips, her touch icy. "I chose to go and there was no way you were going to prevent it. I'm an adult, and I make my own decisions."

Facing the casino, Liesl strolled the sidewalk as people left the building.

"The countess wants to get together in Vienna. She thinks I'm traveling alone."

"Well done, Riles." What kind of man was he? His job was to cherish her. Protect her. Instead, she'd drawn the assassin into the open. And nearly died for her efforts. "I should've been there."

"I knew it." She slapped a hand on the table. "You're a control freak. Just like Dad."

"I've never met your father, but I'm no control—"

"Yes, you are."

"Is this what our marriage will look like—me having to ask permission to go somewhere, do things?"

"Following a killer into a casino, knowing he has your name on a bullet hardly qualifies as controlling you. I love you. I want you to be safe. I could hardly stand it, waiting outside tonight, not knowing if you were okay, or if—" He choked back a sob. Noel's death was still so fresh. He couldn't lose Riles too.

"That makes two of us." She sniffed, stroked his arm. "But the vagrant, Gold Tooth, overplayed his hand. Now we know which guy is Armand's assassin."

"And he got away."

"He'll try again."

"Yeah, great. Now we need a food taster. Bullet-proof vests, a couple gas masks." Or go home. He glanced at Riles. If she didn't have opera engagements, he'd ship her back to Texas until Armand was caught.

"Riles, I don't think you should be alone tonight. How about I sleep on the settee?" If they were under surveillance, changing hotels in the village would be useless.

"That hardwood thing?" She rubbed her arms. "That sounds uncomfortable."

"That's the point. I'm more likely to hear someone approach the room."

10

Jacob's phone vibrated against his thigh. He slipped from Riles' couch and took the call in her bathroom. "Nice to hear from you, Father." Acid roiled his stomach. Just after midnight, Austrian time, but two-thirtyish in Tehran, Iran. An odd time difference but it wouldn't matter, their chats never ended well. And he'd never received a middle-of-the-night call. Had something happened to them? "Hello, are you there?"

"Yes." Father's voice roared, Moses dealing with the Golden Calf.

"Did you receive my letter?" He was never sure the censors forwarded them to his parents. Mother and Father weren't the Great Communicators. And in a closed country, coding news was essential. Iranian officials may have redacted words like *withdrawn from boarding school.*

"Yes." Father's tone bit Jacob's ear. "Your authority is limited to medical power of attorney. How could you make such a decision without consulting us first?" Thunder rumbled through his words.

Seated on the edge of the bathtub, Jacob scrubbed a hand over his jaw. If he said too much, his parents might be thrown out of the country as undesirables. "Just this once, won't you please trust my judgment?"

A snort hit his ear. "With your track record?"

Jacob ignored the veiled reference to letting his parents assume he was an accountant, not an Interpol agent. "Tracy's doing well at her new school in Brussels."

"That's not what she says." Liar, liar, Father's tone stung.

The tub's chill seeped through Jacob's slacks. Father had contacted Tracy? Or had she called their parents? "These things take time. She'll grow to love it there." He hoped.

"You had no right to move her. Her grandparents are furious you didn't contact them first. After all, they're paying her tuition."

"Were." He'd paid for her semester in Brussels. And they were his grandparents too. He'd left them out of the loop to protect Tracy's reputation.

"Son, your mother and I have decided to revoke your power-of-attorney privilege."

The words rocketed through him. "And who are you going to find who actually cares what happens to Tracy?"

"Don't sass me."

"Father, be reasonable. You have no one in Europe who can look after her. I did what I thought best—"

"Changing her school, her country in the middle of a semester?" Father's voice exploded into the phone. "Usurping a legal right you don't possess?"

That's it. He'd let them deal with the fallout. "Tracy was in danger. There was a ring of criminals operating in the school. She was involved. I pulled her out to protect her."

The silence at the other end lasted so long, Jacob said, "Father, are you there?"

"Yes." Father choked out the word. Were those sobs in the background? Maybe Mother was listening in at their end.

The line went dead.

Jacob sagged against the bathroom door. He ought to be glad he was free of the responsibility. But he'd accepted the job and copping out was not his MO.

THE PHONE on his nightstand shrilled again. Armand struggled awake, fumbled for the cell. The clock read one a.m. "Do you have any idea what time it is?"

"The woman was at the casino tonight."

Armand sat up in bed. "She didn't strike me as the gambling type."

"She isn't. She hadn't a clue how to bet."

"Was she alone?" Tautness crept into Armand's voice.

"Yes. The man sat with another woman outside the casino restaurant, the one who rode with them this morning." The computerized chimes of a winning slot machine pealed through the connection. "Fortunately, her boyfriend wore a business suit. Tuxes only tonight."

"So they wouldn't let him in." Armand threw back the duvet. Riley was on to his man. Why hadn't the policewoman arrested him? He walked to the windows, the cold tile chilling the soles of his feet. If the police brought in his assassin for questioning, the man would tell them everything. After all, he was a temporary hire. Not a trusted lieutenant.

"The price has gone up."

"What were you doing, gambling?" Armand shoved back the drape. Moonlight flooded the patio below. Maybe he ought to hire someone to eliminate this guy before he ruined the plan.

"I think a million euros ought to cover the risk."

Armand choked. "You mean your losses tonight." He whipped open the nightstand drawer. Grabbed his pistol. "Do the job and then we'll talk."

Maybe.

STEAM BLED BENEATH RILES' bathroom door as water cascaded from the faucet. Sunlight filtered between the closed drapes. Jacob stifled a yawn. Was she always such an early riser? A nice hot shower sounded like a piece of heaven, after he snatched a nap. A text pinged his cell. Liesl.

> I stayed after the casino closed at three a.m. The two men never exited the front doors. None of the employees saw them leave the premises.

Jacob fired off a quick text.

> Odd. What's your take on that?

> Inside help? Maybe they slipped out dressed as cooks. Or hid inside garbage barrels. Who knows? Without a search warrant …

> Thanks for trying. Get some rest. I'll try to keep Riles inside today.

> One more thing. The real estate check yielded several names of interest. The corporations listed seem to be bogus.

He sat upright, texted her back.

> Yeah?

Three dots bounced on the screen.

A lakeside villa less than a half mile from
the casino was rented by Fräulein Marta
Werner. The Chief Inspector has set up
surveillance on the property.

Great. What about the other one?

More bouncing dots.

It's rented by a Grigori Malkovich but he's
due to vacate in two days. The villa is
located closer to Klagenfurt.

Klagenfurt, the major Austrian city at the other end of the lake. He texted back.

Still, it might be worth checking out.

These could be their first serious leads to Armand. Would he really risk staying so close to them? But Armand's trail of crumbs, his audacity in London ... Yes. The guy would do precisely that. Jacob sent another text.

Have a gut feeling one of these rentals
belongs to Armand.

On it. Call me if you want to go out.

Will do. Get some sleep.

He couldn't jeopardize Liesl's life. Exhaustion made agents more vulnerable to attack. The bathwater stopped running. Riles' hummed roulades and high notes pierced the silence. If he didn't get some sleep ... He curled his legs to his chest on her settee. The barely cushioned seat dug into his ribs. Would she sneak out if he napped?

His phone shrilled, Tracy's ringtone. He'd meant to call her yesterday. With Armand on the loose, keeping tabs on her was paramount. But with last night's crises ... Once again, he'd failed Tracy. "Hey, sis. How goes it?"

"Not that you're interested, but I can't sleep. Mrs. DeBeers snores like a cyclone."

"I'll ship you some earplugs. What size?"

"Oh, puh-leeze. Spare me the jokes."

"How about a couple extra pillows. You can squash them around your ears."

"Will you cut it out? I can't stand this. School is horrible. These kids are such babies."

Because they hadn't shopped in luxury stores, dined in every European capital? He bit his tongue. Nope. Not going there. "Mrs. DeBeers likes you."

"I want friends my own age."

A throbbing pain pulsed behind his eyes. If he didn't get some sleep— "That's understandable."

"Right. Like you really care. My brother the cheapskate."

"Huh? Where's that coming from? I'm giving you twenty-five euros a month."

"I can't even go to a movie and have coffee with a friend on that."

Had he set her allowance too low? After her extravagant shopping trips with Amira, spending Armand's money, no thirteen-year-old would be satisfied with less. But she'd vowed to change, right?

"I want to get a job."

"You're underage."

"I'm showing initiative. Isn't that what you wanted?"

"Yes, but—"

"You can't have it both ways, bro. Either you double my allowance or—"

"We'll talk about it when I get home."

Tracy snorted into the phone. "Right. When will that be? Six months from now?"

He cringed. "I'll be there as soon as I can." The line went

dead. Is this what parenting would be like? Maybe they'd been dropped into the worst of it. Surely the early years were a joy. Baby's first smile. Baby's first word, *da-da*. First steps. Toddling to him, arms outstretched.

The bathroom door creaked, and he shoved his phone in his pocket. Steam followed Riles into the bedroom, a towel turbaned around her hair, her cheeks so flushed and dewy he longed to caress the moisture from them.

"What's up?" She whipped off the towel, and her auburn curls tumbled about her turquoise sweater.

"Tracy. The kid hates school." He filled Riles in. "I don't know if I can do this, juggle my career and be there for her."

"She's had a tough time, no parents around. But she's guilt-tripping you. Holding you responsible for situations you didn't cause and couldn't fix."

He raked his hands through his hair. But he was fixer, a protector. Isn't that what men did?

"I wish we hadn't left her in Belgium." She flicked something from her beige slacks. "Forget that. She's safer there than with us." She sat beside him on the settee, slipped her arm around his shoulder. "How about a reward system for good grades, unimpeachable behavior, and help with household chores, rather than simply upping her allowance."

"Great idea." He smooched her cheek, nuzzled his nose against her rosemary-scented hair. "You'll make a wonderful mother."

Her chest hiked, and her hand fell from his shoulder.

A pit hollowed his stomach. Didn't she want children?

11

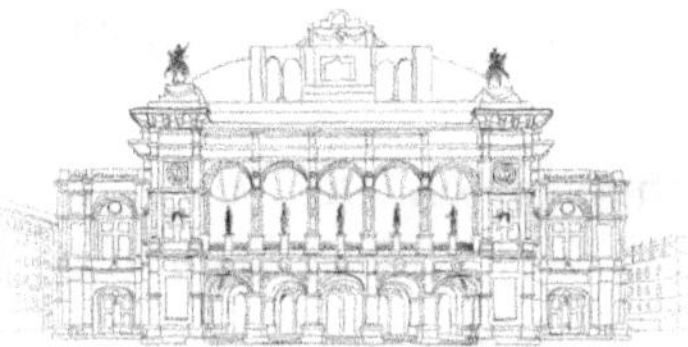

Velden am Wörthersee, Day 3

Armand sat across from Amira at the glass-topped table on the balcony. The morning breeze whipped her long black hair from her shoulders like a medieval vixen. Since he'd pulled her from boarding school, she'd become the teenager parents dreaded. Sullen. Rebellious. Wearing as much makeup as his mistress.

A sigh seeped from his mouth. At least he'd managed to protect his daughter's purity.

Beneath her false eyelashes, she shot him eye daggers, jaws snapping over a section of grapefruit as if it were a defenseless minnow.

If only Jacob hadn't forced his hand, ruined his daughter's life, destroyed lucrative business interests. The enterprises Jacob knew about. Stifling a smile, Armand splayed his fingers on his thighs. Breathe, breathe. Calm. Peace. He'd outsmart little boy Jacob.

"Why can't I go anywhere, do something fun?" Amira tossed

her spoon on the plate, jammed her fists in the bend of her arms. "I can't even go to school."

"I didn't think you liked boarding school. Now you have an award-winning tutor who's highly recommended."

She snorted. "Fräulein Werner? She's no fun. We can't go to a library or a museum. And only one shopping trip." Amira shifted in her chair, slid him a sly glance. "Funny how she disappears after supper. Must be those great recommendations, *oui*?"

A muscle twitched his cheek. How much of his private life was she aware of? "Why don't you see how Tracy's doing?"

Amira's jaw slacked. "But you told me I must never contact her. Ever."

"Perhaps I was a bit harsh." Right now, he needed her to do his dirty work for him. Lure Tracy out of her protective lair. "You miss her, don't you?"

"Terribly. We had such fun together." Amira's eyes narrowed. "Are you sure it's all right to contact her?"

"What do you mean?"

"Well ..." She chewed her lip until it reddened. "Your work ..."

Chills ripped through him. "My work?" What did she know about it? He'd been so careful, met with associates long after she'd gone to bed, or was at boarding school.

The false eyelashes dipped, curtained her eyes, her shrug far too casual. "Nothing."

Sweat slicked his palms. Had his own daughter betrayed him? He'd trusted her. But Tracy had proven a liability. A deadly one.

Shifting on his seat, he crossed his legs. Uncrossed them. Crossed them again. What had Amira overheard, did she know about the murders? Had she shared whatever she'd surmised with Tracy?

For a moment, Amira's eyes met his. Amidst her defiant gaze, pulsed a flicker of dread.

Bon. A *soupçon* of fear meant respect. All was not lost. She'd still inherit every bit of his empire. He swallowed over the lump in his throat. How could he make her understand they were hiding not only for his safety, but to protect her way of life?

She squared her shoulders, eyes brimming with vitriol. "Well?"

Fingers drumming the table, he weighed his options. No doubt his DNA thrummed in her blood. But thirteen-year-olds could be vindictive. Conniving. Could he count on Amira to make the call?

Even family members needed time to prove themselves, their loyalty. At all costs.

"Find out how she's doing. Where you could meet. I don't think one text will hurt."

───────

Seated on the settee in Riles' bedroom, Jacob wrapped his arm around her shoulders, his heart still reeling from her words. He'd never considered she might not want to start a family. "Hon, about kids—" His phone shrilled. "Morning, Margot." He put the call on speaker.

"Can you identify Amira Découvrir?"

His fingers glued to the phone. Would Armand harm his own daughter? "You mean her corpse?"

"Her face. She's very much alive."

"I—I don't know. We never met her." He exchanged glances with Riles. Her shrug wasn't reassuring. "The picture Riley saw on Armand's desk in London was taken several years ago. You know how much kids change."

"I'm sending some photos over the encrypted line. They're a bit grainy but it's the best we could do. Our men were surveilling someone else, and she strolled across the photographer's path."

"Great. We could use a break in this case." The line pinged and he uploaded the pictures. Riley dug her chin into his shoulder, squinted toward the screen. Nestling his cheek against her temple, he caught a whiff of her perfume.

He enlarged the screen image of a young woman, made up like a high-class call girl. False eyelashes, crimson lipstick, stiletto-heeled boots and a too-short skirt, a double *C* logo on her Chanel shoulder bag. "I don't know ... she's only thirteen."

A fortyish woman with long blonde hair walked beside her. Shopping bags from Fendi, Gucci, and Chopard, the exclusive Swiss jeweler, flanked her stylish pantsuit. The girl's prancing step suggested the woman was a servant, not the shopper. "What do you think. Amira?"

"Hard to say." Riley leaned closer to his cell. "That's the Kärtnerstrasse, the main shopping district in Wien. I recognize the shops, the buildings. She's in Vienna. Have Tracy send you a copy of Amira's picture."

Margot was right. Riles would make a great agent. If someone could rein in her wild streak. Did he want his wife in this business? He texted Tracy and asked for a copy of the girls' photo taken at school.

Three dots bounced on his screen.

Why?

"Because I said so," he muttered, fingers poised over the keyboard. How much should he tell her?

Riley thinks she may have seen her.

Despite his rocky relationship with his sister, she'd warmed up to Riles.

Ask Riley where she saw Amira.

Emojis of praying hands flashed across the screen.

"Are you kidding?" He typed a response.

Nope. Send me the picture. Don't want to raise false hopes. Trust me. He hovered his forefinger over the send button. Should he erase the last bit? In Tracy's eyes, he was a failure as a brother, a father figure, a provider.

A ping sounded and the download appeared on his screen. *Thank You, God.* He flipped between Tracy's picture and Margot's surveillance photos.

Riley dug her nails into his arm. "That could be Amira."

A low whistle escaped his teeth. "How could Armand be so stupid?"

"Assuming he knows about my debut, he may have let her out of the house before we arrived. For some people, shopping is addictive."

"Yeah." And if Amira's like Tracy, the girl hounded Armand until he gave in. "According to Tracy's police statement, Amira's tastes and purchases were beyond astronomical. She'd head for the most exclusive shops."

"Can't blame her. She's lived the rich-and-famous lifestyle, having her unlimited expense account pulled is a tough adjustment."

Jacob groaned. "Tell me about it. Probably feels like retirees scraping by on Social Security checks."

"Or a singer launching a career." Riles stroked the day-old stubble on his cheek. "You think Armand is with her?"

"Could be. Or he sent her with a bodyguard. If he's not staying nearby, they're probably less than a two-hour drive from Vienna." Or living half a mile down the road from them. "He could be testing the waters, letting her out. If his goons didn't spot the surveillance team, we may be in luck." He googled Vienna's outlying towns and calculated the driving time. "Armand could be anywhere."

"If he's still using his former MO, then he has hot cash to offload, right?"

"Yes." He pocketed his phone. "Now all we need is a plan."

"Piece of *Milchrahmstrüdel*. He'll send Amira out again. We stake out the first district and follow her home."

"No way. Her bodyguards probably have our pictures. Interpol needs surveillance cars in every parking garage, ready to tail them. We leave this to the professionals."

"Are you kidding? With their dismal track record?" She yanked her suitcase from the clothes cupboard.

"What are you doing?"

"Packing. If Armand's in Vienna, I'd like my debut at the opera to be trouble free. For once." She whipped her clothes from their hangers, tossed the garments in the bag.

"What about our vacation? Margot can handle this." They needed this time apart from his job or their relationship—

"If we stay here, I'm not sure we'll live to finish it." She shoved the top of the suitcase into place, forced the zipper closed.

"But the Chief Inspector's found several rental properties that could be harboring Armand."

"Where?"

He told her what Liesl had said.

"That close?"

He didn't know whether to laugh or cry. She'd nearly died last night, now Joan of Arc was back on her steed, ready to tangle with the enemy.

"But first, we're going to pay Armand a visit."

"How?"

"We scope out those two properties ourselves." She wheeled her suitcase to the door. "C'mon, lover boy. Get your duds together. And those rental addresses. We're going scouting."

12

"How did I let you talk me into this?" To say nothing of the fancy-dance spiel he'd given the reluctant boat rental clerk. If he wrecked this craft, insurance wouldn't pay a second time. Jacob tacked to the right, and the sailboat veered toward the lakeside villa. The morning breeze wasn't helping.

The house was smaller than what he'd pictured Armand renting. Autumnal-hued flowers dotted the meticulously groomed grounds. A balcony stretched across the back with steps descending the hillside to a gated dock. Judging from the windows, the house had three floors. Smaller windows on the top floor probably indicated servants' quarters. Servants he'd love to question.

Binoculars raised to her eyes, Riles arched higher in the seat. She'd changed into black slacks and a matching turtleneck that made her red life vest stand out like an emergency beacon. The boat bobbed in the wind-driven swells. "Keep her steady."

"I'm trying." He stifled the growl in his voice. This was

insane. If Armand was in the house, he could be watching them. Calling for his assassin to finish the job. Now.

"We're going to flush the bird out of his gilded cage."

"We might flush out more than that."

"Don't be such a ninny. It's time we put him on the run."

"He's already on the run. Cornered animals make fierce foes."

"Yeah, well he hasn't tangled with Coulter and Williams." She stood, feet apart, binoculars glued toward the house.

"Yes, he has. Now sit before you fall into the lake."

Another swell hit the boat, and she tumbled to the bottom. She edged back on the seat.

"I thought I saw movement at one of the second-floor French doors on the balcony."

He jabbed a fist on the tiller. "If only we had a search warrant."

"Let's row to the shore." Riley pointed toward the gated landing in front of the villa.

"No. You could get us arrested. Or killed."

"We're advancing against the enemy."

"Riles—"

The French doors on the ground floor burst open. A woman in a billowing dress and athletic shoes galumphed toward them, strands of dishwater-blonde hair escaping her bun. Chief Inspector Schmidt overtook her and strode to the landing gate. Wringing the apron around her ample waist, the woman sidled next to him.

"Halt." Schmidt planted his fists on his equipment belt. "This is private property."

Idiot. He should never have given in to Riles. They needed every law enforcement officer on their side. "I was having trouble steering the boat. No harm intended, officer."

"*Danke*, Frau Becker. You can go now," Schmidt said.

"Hmm …" She pursed and rolled her lips, eyed Riles and him, the boat.

"I'll handle this." Schmidt's tone was testy. "You've done your duty, alerting the police."

Odd. He hadn't tried to dock the boat and enter the yard. If she'd called the police, had Armand put her up to it? Jacob scanned the windows. No shadows lurking behind the curtains.

"*Bitte, gehen Sie.*" Schmidt motioned the woman away. When she headed for the house, he glared at them, his voice low. "What do you think you're doing here?"

"Out for a sail." Riles grinned. "Lovely weather, don't you think?"

"Any sign of her employer or anyone else?" Jacob asked.

"*Nein.* And no one has left the property since we staked out the place."

"At least you got inside the house without a search warrant." Riles flashed another grin. "You can have a peek before she walks you out the door. Make excuses to check the locks in case we return. Look for suspicious items. Signs of a teenager."

"Riles—" If only he had jurisdiction here. But he was powerless. Jacob's legs itched to dash into the house and conduct his own search for Armand. The man was in there. Somewhere. "Please request a search warrant."

The policeman thrust his thumbs inside his equipment belt. "On what grounds?"

"Chief Inspector, you know as well as we do, Armand is very likely renting this house." Riles hefted her chin in the air.

"Is Miss Williams always this obstinate?" Schmidt's eyes narrowed. "Interfering in police business?"

"Frequently."

"My condolences." Schmidt's jaw muscle twitched. "It must be difficult for you to do your job."

She wilted toward the bench, curls falling toward the flush in her cheeks.

Oh, Riles. With everything in him, Jacob longed to pull her to his side. "In her defense, many of her zany schemes have uncovered criminals. My colleagues are so impressed they want to hire her."

Schmidt's jaw slacked. "Really."

"Yes. Interpol has recruited her in Brussels, London, and Wien."

"Actually—" Riles perked up on the seat. "We're leaving for Wien as soon as we turn in the boat. We've checked out of the Pension."

"*Gott sei dank.*" The Chief Inspector's shoulders sagged. "Good idea. *Gute Reise.* And don't even think about casing the other property or my men will arrest you for obstructing police ops."

13

Velden am Wörthersee, Day 3

Fingers gripping his pistol, Armand dropped his bedroom drape back in place. He'd had Jacob and Riley in his sights. If that blasted policeman hadn't been standing there, those two troublemakers would be dead.

He'd been certain they'd dock the boat and find a way to enter the house. What choice had he had, other than telling Frau Becker to summon the police. The police who were sitting in a patrol car outside the fence to his property. A hoarse chuckle burbled in his throat. He'd bet Jacob hadn't expected him to call in law enforcement to check out trespassing boaters.

Thankfully, Fräulein Werner had been overseeing Amira's math test, out of sight, behind the closed study door. Armand slid the gun inside his bedside table drawer, stalked the length of the room. Caged. Caged in his own home.

If only he'd sent Amira and her tutor to Rome. Or Paris. Anywhere but here. Jacob might convince the police to request a search warrant. Or he'd try to return after dark. After all, they had a few scores to settle.

A light tap rapped on his bedroom door. "*Monsieur*."

"*Oui*?" He opened the door a crack.

In the dimly lit hall, Frau Becker shifted from one foot to the other, kneaded her hands. "Why are the police still parked outside the estate?"

"For our protection."

Her eyes widened. "But why do we need—"

"There are those who wish to harm me and my daughter. But you're perfectly safe, of course." Would the officers confront her when she left to grocery shop? What would she tell them? A pity the estate owner had insisted he retain Frau Becker on staff during the rental. "You've nothing to fear."

"That's comforting." She backed away from the door, gaze darting left, right. "Supper is ready."

"*Danke*. We'll take it in my study."

"Very good, sir." Frau Becker plodded down the hall at twice her usual clip.

They'd have to keep the lights off after dusk, make the house seem uninhabited, apart from Frau Becker's third-floor light. No point advertising how many bedrooms were in use.

Then he'd wait, gun in hand, for Jacob to return and break into the house.

His death would be ruled self-defense.

Armand locked the bedroom door, then checked the chambers in his pistol.

Loaded.

Ready to fire.

THE AFTERNOON SUN nearly blinded Jacob as he whizzed along the A2 Autobahn for Wien. Hopefully, the vignette, the toll sticker he'd purchased for two months, would outlast this assignment. He needed to wrap up this case, get home to

Brussels, and see to Tracy. He dialed Margot. "We found Armand's rental villa. Can you get a search warrant?"

"I can try. Did you see him there?"

"No. But the place of business on the rental agreement is bogus. And someone called in the police when we sailed toward the dock. Definitely over-reacting." He filled her in on the police surveillance.

"I don't know … Those aren't compelling reasons. I doubt they'll issue a warrant."

"Just try, will you? I'm certain Armand was there today. If we don't move fast, he'll escape." He disconnected the call, eased the accelerator back to the speed limit, 130kph, eighty-one miles per hour, while the forested hills passed in a blur. He checked the rearview mirror again.

Each time he slowed, the black Skoda had hung back, then passed to the car behind them when he sped up. Notifying von Bingen would have to wait. "We had Armand. I can feel it in my bones."

"Getting ourselves arrested wouldn't have helped." Riles massaged his arm, barely penetrating his rigid muscles. "If he's in the house, he can't leave. And neither can Amira."

"Not unless that boathouse has a skiff. Armand's probably a master rower."

"I doubt Amira would agree to leave her purchases behind. And he'd have to row the three of them somewhere. Unless he plans to leave the tutor there as a decoy."

"Wouldn't surprise me if he did." How long had the car been following them? Armand's assassin was likely only a phone call away. "I have half a mind to drive back to Velden and do a little breaking and entering."

"No!" Riles slapped the windowsill. "That's exactly what Armand expects you to do. He'll be waiting for you, armed. He probably watched us from a window this morning. He knows you're on to him."

"Once Schmidt pulls off his watchers, Armand will bolt." Jacob slowed, strained for a glimpse of the Skoda's driver, but he seemed hunched behind the steering wheel.

"You have the airports and train stations under surveillance, he can't go far."

"What's to stop him hopping in his car and driving to Italy? Or the Czech Republic? A nice, long road trip and he can re-enter Austria from anywhere."

"But his business interests are in Wien—"

"We don't know that for certain." Jacob put on his blinker to exit the Autobahn. The Skoda did likewise. Now what? He couldn't lead the driver to Riles' apartment.

"Apart from money laundering in every Austrian casino, Wien is the most logical place to generate substantial income."

He gripped the steering wheel, ignored the cramps in his fingers. "Wien, Wien, city of dreams. For centuries she's been a city of intrigue and spies and underhanded deals. Little's changed." Right now, it was his city of nightmares. Hunting for threaded needles in muddy haystacks that might lead back to Armand. If he could find the evidence before Armand's assassin put them in their graves.

"The city of every classical musician's dreams. Home to Mozart, Schubert, Beethoven, Brahms. Mahler. To name only a few composers." She sighed. "Living here was so romantic."

The Skoda shot into the passing lane, zipped behind Jacob's bumper.

"You didn't tell anyone where you'd be staying, did you?"

"No. But if you spend the night on my couch, you won't drive back to Velden tonight."

"Fat chance of that. We have company."

"What?" Riles whipped her head over her shoulder. "How long has he been there?"

"Probably since we left Velden. I was preoccupied with our

failed surveillance. I don't think I started watching for a tail before we hit the Autobahn."

She rummaged in her purse, turned, and snapped a picture of the Skoda. "Gotcha." She peered at the screen, then held it up for him.

"Uh-huh." Interpol probably couldn't enhance the grainy texture enough to identify the man with certainty.

Grunting, she wedged between the seats, grappled for the binocular case in the back. Lenses pressed to her eyes, she said, "Hard to tell, but the driver looks like the other man from the casino."

Sweat slicked Jacob's palms. The assassin.

"Oh, no, he's rolling down his window."

The driver's hand moved between the windshield and the side mirror.

"Jacob, he has a gun!"

14

En Route to Wien (Vienna), Day 3

Riley drilled her nails through the armrest, shoved her shoes through the floormat. *If the shooter doesn't kill us, Jacob's driving will.*

Jacob swerved into the passing lane, tires screeching. The car shimmied like a fish out of water. He glanced in the mirror, and his face paled. "Duck!" He shoved her head toward her knees.

A crack sounded and the rearview window shattered. Bits of glass peppered her head. She bit back a shriek. "Are you all right?"

"Fine." His voice was terse. "Stay down. I'm going to try evasive driving."

"What do you call this?" Her voice shrilled up an octave.

Without warning, the car lurched left. Right. Horns blared. She braced a hand on the dashboard.

"Dear God, help us. If You don't intervene, Armand will win this round." Tears clogged her voice. She hugged her knees.

With everything in her, she wanted them to live. Build a life together. And take down Armand.

Somehow, she had to get a grip. "Where are the police when you need them?" She risked a glance at Jacob.

"You'd think someone would call this in, and they'd pull us over." His eyes widened. "Stay down." He crouched over the steering wheel, jerked it to the left.

Another shot pinged off the roof.

The car sashayed in semicircles. Her head reeled with each spin. How much more of this could they take? No, no. She should thank God for His goodness. They were still alive. The assassin hadn't hit them. "Maybe we should've stayed in Velden." She tried for a chuckle.

"Now you tell me." His lopsided grin melted through a layer of her tremors. "I could make a U-turn."

"Don't you dare."

Instead, he floored the accelerator, cut in front of the semi beside her. He swung the car one more lane to the right, barely decelerating, and took the off-ramp at a dangerous clip.

She bit back another shriek. Thank heavens he wasn't a professional race car driver. Their relationship would never survive.

"You can sit up. The truck blocked his exit."

"*Thank You, God.*" She inched upright, fire shooting up her neck muscles. Tomorrow she'd book a full-body massage, or her voice would be in shambles. "Do you need directions to my apartment?"

"Nope. We're going to a safe house. I don't want him finding your place or mine." He pulled out his cell, punched the speaker icon. "Margot? We were followed from Velden." He filled her in on the chase. "Does Interpol have any safe houses?"

"Let me check. Where are you now?" The *tip-tap* on a keyboard filtered through the phone.

"Tell her we're coming in via Schönbrunn Palace," Riley whispered.

"Got that." Margot sighed. "Sorry, we haven't any available."

"Can you recommend a car repair shop? We have major bullet hole damage."

"I'll text you some names. Where will you stay tonight?"

"Somewhere a shot-out rear window doesn't raise eyebrows." Jacob eased to a stop at the red light.

"Are you coming into the office?" Margot sounded as if she'd moved away from her phone.

"Tomorrow. I'm not leaving Riles alone. Any chance for that search warrant?"

"No word yet."

"Thanks. Talk to you in the morning." He turned onto Hietzinger Allee and entered the parking garage for the Parkhotel Schönbrunn, a four-star hotel that overlooked the magnificent Baroque palace.

The attendant stared toward the blown-out rear window. "Are you checking in, sir?"

"We're looking forward to our stay in Wien."

Riley bit back a smile. Not a lie.

The man handed Jacob a ticket and waved him into the garage.

"Isn't this too close to the Autobahn?" she whispered as he cruised the parking spaces.

"It is. I want the assassin to think this is where we're staying."

"Nice. The Hietzing U-Bahn station is a block from here."

"You know this part of Vienna?"

"Yes. My first apartment was in this district. Loads of old money here, very genteel people. Charming old houses and tree-lined streets. Despite the hour's commute, it was so restful when I let myself into the backyard garden."

"Sounds nice." He pulled into a vacant slot on the second floor.

Damp air seeped through the broken window and into her bones. She rubbed her arms, flipped up her shirt collar. Humid, chilly air wasn't good for her throat.

The garage reeked of gasoline fumes and hot rubber tires. Body stiff from their wild ride, she waited beside him while he removed their suitcases from the trunk.

He did a web search for hotels. "Question is, where won't he think to look for us?"

Velden am Wörthersee

ARMAND STABBED the dying log in the grate, and sparks sputtered into the air. With the velvet drapes pulled, no light should be visible from outside. He poured himself a second glass of wine and sank into the easy chair beside the mantle. There must be a way to leave the villa and move Amira and Fräulein Werner elsewhere. Far enough so they could live the good life and disburse more of his income free from police scrutiny.

If he left, officers might question Frau Becker, show her a picture of him. No doubt Jacob had informed them he suspected Interpol's most wanted man was holed up in the villa. He'd have to leave Austria. Run his business affairs from another country. Worst of all, he'd have to live without *her*. She'd become far too indispensable to his operations.

In the firelight, the glass of claret gleamed like blood. Soon his cash inflow would attract unwanted attention from the banks' authorities. He snatched the wineglass and drained it. Leaving a paper trail for Jacob to find could be disastrous.

His grip tightened on the glass. Venice, Italy, was only 165 miles from Velden. If he let Fräulein Werner drive off the property with Amira in the trunk, would the police find an excuse to stop his car? Since he'd rented the house in her name, she had every right to be seen on the property or in town.

Sweat beaded his brow. The car registration was in one of his aliases. Would his daughter agree to such a precarious ride? If Jacob had convinced the local police to put out alerts on him, Amira's passport would set off alarms.

His phone vibrated in his trousers pocket. He braced himself for the sniper's report. "*Oui?*"

"I found their car." He filled Armand in on the chase, the gunfire. "Pretty foolish to stay so near the Autobahn exit."

Armand snorted. "You're a bigger fool than I thought. It's a red herring."

"If you assume that, all the more reason to check the hotel registrations in the area."

"I'm not paying you to waste my time." Heat surged through Armand's chest.

"There's the matter of a bonus."

"A *bonus*? You haven't completed a single assignment."

"Taking out the other man from the casino."

He'd done what? There'd been nothing on the news about a murder. "A job you weren't authorized to do." Spittle flew from Armand's mouth. A pity he hadn't recorded the call. He wasn't going down for a kill he hadn't sanctioned. "Do. Your. Job." He disconnected the call and the cell vibrated again.

About time she checked in with him. Phone to his ear, he settled deep in the chair's cushions, voice purring like a kitten. "*Liebling—*"

"We have trouble in paradise."

"What kind of trouble?" He sighed into the phone. What else could go wrong?

"Some of the girls refuse to cooperate."

"Tell the men to use force."

"Do you really want damaged goods?"

"This sort of merchandise needs to learn who's boss." Hand shaking, he poured another glass of wine. The crimson liquid splashed on the side table.

"I've never seen you so testy, *Liebling*. Think about it, clients are picky. You don't want to hurt the business."

"I *have* thought about it! I'm a prisoner in my own home." His voice echoed off the walls.

"Better there, than in jail."

Her soothing tone did nothing to calm his nerves. He guzzled the third glass of wine. What he needed was a trustworthy lieutenant. A man who got results. Not another imbecilic sharpshooter who couldn't seem to nail two people with a bullet.

"Do you still have company?"

Good. He could trust her to code her words. "Yes. Frau Becker said they insist the intruder might return."

"That must be costing the city a small fortune." She sighed. "Let me know what you want done."

She was right. He'd have to resolve the problem with the merch. It wouldn't be right to ask her to intervene. Time for a radical move.

15

Yesterday had been one gun battle too many for her. If they couldn't catch the assassin, then it was time to take down the moneybags. Armand.

He'd be expecting Jacob to show up, but she'd be the surprise he hadn't counted on.

Riley stifled a yawn. Fortunately, Gussi had still been awake and willing to loan her car for the trip. Smart move, keeping up with her Austrian friends.

At this hour of the night, the drive from Wien to Velden had taken her less than two hours. What Jacob didn't know wouldn't hurt him, right? After suggesting he sleep on her couch, she'd had to fancy-dance her way out of that idea. Convince him she had to have her beauty rest.

Outside Armand's villa, Riley crawled along the grassy knoll between the trees. Frost seeped through her black jeans and sweater, moistening her skin. Why had she promised to meet Jacob for breakfast at nine? By the time she reached their hotel, dawn would be over the horizon.

If she made it out of here alive.

Another yawn crept up her throat. Her watch dial read almost four in the morning. What if she were too late? Overhead, an owl hooted. Prickles spidered over her skin.

One foot planted on the first rung of the fence, she hauled herself over the iron railing and thudded to the soft soil in Armand's yard. She crouched to the ground, listening. Waiting. Gentle waves lapped the shore. Ahead of her, darkness shrouded the house. Clouds slid over the faint moonlight she'd used to navigate the woods bordering Armand's property. No slivers of light from the windows on this side of the villa.

Had Armand managed to escape? Had she wasted her time sneaking out here?

Belly to the ground, she slithered to the side of the house, away from the police car parked on the road. She inhaled the heavy scent of moist dirt.

Now what? She hadn't thought this plan through. What had she hoped to gain by trespassing? Jacob was the one with lockpicking skills. A pity she hadn't brought his kit.

A few yards ahead, a bolt shot back. Halfway down the wall, a door squeaked open.

Heart pounding, she scrabbled backward, flattened her body against the wet grass. Had she been spotted? Why, oh, why, had she come here alone?

No. Think like David, bold, courageous, total faith in God to deliver him.

Rubber-soled shoes darted along the concrete sidewalk to the boathouse. When the steps had passed her, she glanced up. Armand and Amira. Dressed in black, a duffle in each hand. Riley fisted a tuft of grass. They were escaping, and there was nothing she could do about it. Her car was a mile away.

If she informed the police, they'd arrest her for trespassing. She'd do jail time in Austria. Lose her opera contract. Her career would be ruined. Jacob would kill her.

The boathouse door creaked open. Shoulders hunched, Amira waited on the dock while Armand rowed the boat toward her, oars sloshing the water. The boat thumped against the dock, and Amira scrambled aboard.

With smooth strokes, Armand maneuvered the dinghy toward Klagenfurt, the other end of the Wörthersee. The clouds shifted, and moonlight glimmered on their faces. Armand's terse. A wet sheen on Amira's cheeks. Her stifled sobs carried across the water.

The boat cleared the property. Riles pulled out her cell, dialed the police, keeping her voice low. "A man wanted by Interpol for money laundering is headed toward Klagenfurt in a dinghy."

"How do you know this?" the answering officer asked.

"Because my fiancé is a special agent with Interpol."

"Uh-huh."

"No, really." She gave him their names and phone numbers. "Look, could you hurry it up? They're getting away."

A motor putt-putted on the lake.

"Wait. Not a dinghy. He's in a motorboat. The man's name is Armand Découvrir." She hung up, dashed toward the fence, clambered over the iron bars, and stumbled through the woods toward her car. Klagenfurt was only a half hour if she took the A2 and B83. But how long by motorboat? Armand probably had a vehicle waiting to whisk them over the border. She'd never find him.

Twigs crackled under her shoes as she tromped through the brush, dialing Jacob.

"What's up, Riles?" His yawn slid into the phone.

She blew out her breath. No sidestepping a reprimand. "Armand and Amira are headed for Klagenfurt."

"How would you know?" Sharpness sliced through his grogginess.

"He did it just like you predicted. Took off in a rowboat then turned on the motor." Words tumbling from her mouth, she reached the road, dashed for her friend's car.

"You didn't answer my question."

"Well, obviously I drove down to Velden. Helps to have old friends in a city."

"Riles, you could've been killed." His voice reverberated in her ear.

"But I wasn't and now we have proof Armand rented the house. I notified the Klagenfurt police but I'm certain they'd like a confirmation from Interpol."

"Yes. Hang up and head back to Wien. Now."

"There you go again, telling me what to do."

He groaned. "Don't you get it? I love you, Riles."

"I know. I love you too. But I'm not spending the rest of my life with a carbon copy of my father. We'll discuss this later." She disconnected the call and headed for Klagenfurt.

Wien

WHY DID she have to be so stubborn? He was just trying to protect her. Protect her from herself and her harebrained schemes. Jacob scrambled into slacks and a shirt. He'd like to be here when Riles arrived. But he needed to liaise with the Klagenfurt police in case they nabbed Armand when he came ashore.

Sockless feet thrust into his loafers, he grabbed his keys and wallet, took the elevator to the hotel lobby. At the reception desk, the bleary-eyed clerk straightened his rumpled red vest over his shirt and hotel-crested tie.

If only their rental car wasn't miles from here. "Can you order me a taxi to Klagenfurt?"

The man's jaw dropped. "That's three-and-a-half hours from here. Almost three-hundred twenty-five kilometers."

"I know." But who knew how long it would take Margot to dress and get here?

"Very well." He dialed for a taxi. "He'll be here shortly."

"*Danke.*" Jacob trotted outside, climbed in the taxi. He flashed his Interpol ID at the driver. "Get me to the Klagenfurt marina as fast as you can."

"*Jawohl,*" the driver said in Afghani-accented German. The Mercedes shot down the street.

Jacob dialed Margot. Three rings and she accepted the call.

"Don't tell me you caught Armand."

"Close." He filled her in.

"Riley was on the scene?" Margot's voice rose an octave.

"*Ja,*" he said through gritted teeth. Somehow, he and Riles had to come to an agreement on her non-interference in Interpol business.

"Shall I pick you up?"

"*Danke,* but I'm en route to Klagenfurt. My taxi driver has the gas pedal nailed to the carpet. Meet you there."

Drawing deep breaths, he settled in the back seat, but his heart still galloped like a pack of wild Texas horses. If they managed to arrest Armand, he and Riles could resume their vacation. If she hadn't decided to break off their engagement.

Then he could focus on taking down Armand's illegal ops. Riles would finish her opera performances, and they'd return home to Belgium and build a life together.

But would she still have him? Sweat slicked his palms. She'd threatened as much on the phone.

16

Klagenfurt, Austria, Day 4

A breeze whipped Riley's curls across her cheeks. Tucked between motorboats and paddle craft, the dinghy bobbed against the mooring pole at the boat rental dock. Her heart sank. No sign of Armand and Amira.

Had the police barely missed them? She spun toward the lakeside promenade, the *Strandbad* to her left—the swimming area with diving docks facing the Wörthersee. They could've walked to a hotel, a colleague's house. Once again, they'd be hidden in plain sight. She turned to the policeman. "Have you been here long?"

He eyed her as if she were the criminal. "Have you seen this boat before?" He shone a flashlight on the dock.

At five in the morning, it was hard to tell. "Could be. It was dark, almost moonless when Armand and Amira rowed out on the lake."

The officer's posture shot ramrod stiff. "You know them personally?"

She squelched a groan. "Armand, yes. It's a long story."

One she'd rather not share. Being snookered by suave, Hollywood-handsome Armand still made her cringe. "His daughter was best friends with my fiancé's kid sister at boarding school."

Eyes narrowed to gun slits, he fingered the handcuffs on his equipment belt. "You say he's into money laundering."

Did he think she was a disgruntled girlfriend?

Riley stepped back, planted a fist on her hip. "If you speak with Interpol Agent Jacob Coulter, he'll give you all the details about Découvrir and his illegal activities. Some of which were committed on Austrian soil." No way was she mentioning Inspector Schmidt in Velden. He'd have them arrest her. "Although Jacob's probably already spoken with your superiors, let me reach him for you." Flashing the officer a smile, she dialed Jacob.

"Where are you, Riles?"

"A policeman wants to speak with you." Stifling a chuckle, she passed him her phone. One chewing out avoided.

The officer nodded and grunted. Jacob must be giving him an earful. Kneeling on the wooden dock beside the dinghy, she motioned for him to shine his light at a tiny clump under one of the seats. She leaned inside, scooped a ring into her hand, opened her palm toward the policeman and gasped. A diamond-encrusted emerald on a gold band. A setting much too large for a teenaged girl.

"Yes. I believe this is Armand's boat. His thirteen-year-old daughter is one of his chief launderers. She has a penchant for exquisite jewelry. Must've fallen out of her duffle bag."

"How long have you known Special Agent Coulter?" He returned her phone.

"Long enough to help him solve several major cases involving terrorists." Hadn't Jacob exonerated her with the Klagenfurt police? "I wouldn't be surprised if Armand headed for Italy. Do you have a roadblock set up?"

His sniff said it all. "That is police business. Not a concern for a private citizen."

At least he didn't say *foreigner*. Or a woman. She swallowed a sigh. If Jacob were here, he'd light a fire under this guy. "It'd be a real coup for the Austrian police if they caught Découvrir." She spread her hands heavenward. "I can see the headlines now—Austrian *Bundespolizei* capture notorious terrorist financier."

"You will come to the police station until Agent Coulter arrives. We will ride in my car."

Great. Once Jacob walked in the door, she'd have to face the Grand Inquisition from both men.

Four *Grosser Brauners* later, Riley pushed aside the coffee cup. Swiped the curls from her temple, squirmed on the hard police chair. Finally. The policeman had collected her personal dossier back to her days in diapers. If her career reached international status, he could write her biography. She popped a throat lozenge in her mouth. Who wouldn't be hoarse after answering questions for three hours?

Three hours they could've been out searching for Armand and Amira. It was great the officer had located their boat, but did Armand have someone on the force in his pocket?

Jacob crossed the police station foyer.

Steeling herself for his lecture, she gave him a feeble wave.

Instead, he swept her to her feet and hugged her. "You okay, hon?"

Wow. PDA in a police station. She found a smile for him. "Just peachy. Can you convince them I'm not Armand's mistress?"

"I don't know. Might be pretty tough. What man wouldn't fall for such a beautiful woman?" He tweaked her nose.

"Aww, you say the sweetest things. But he's serious about this."

The officer eyed them like a vulture hovering over carrion.

Jacob released her and handed the man his Interpol ID. "Thank you for your swift response to my fiancée's information on Découvrir. Great work locating his boat."

The officer's nod was curt. "Fräulein Williams seems to know a great deal about your investigations."

"*Ja,* true. But without her assistance, Interpol would've missed key arrests of dangerous terrorists."

"*Ach so.*" A hint of grudging respect tinged the policeman's tone.

She stifled a grin. How about that—Jacob was defending her. Again. Why had she expected the worst from him? She slouched in the chair. The ride to Wien would give him plenty of time to ream her out for reckless behavior. He'd probably insist on driving Gussi's car too.

The station door whipped open. Margot breezed in, sporting a navy-blue power suit, matching heels, and flawless makeup. Did she go to bed dressed for emergencies? Riley plucked a twig from her hair. And here she was in her Ninja clothes, hair probably disheveled, and clomping around in mud-clotted sneakers.

Standing beside Jacob, Margot offered her Interpol ID to the officer, gave her a frosty once-over. "Have you spoken with von Bingen?"

Jacob's shoulder blades shot back. "No."

"She wants a report from you ASAP."

"Naturally."

How dare Margot undermine him in front of the police? Riley fisted her hands on the desk. Von Bingen hadn't circumvented him before. Who set that in motion? All he needed was a turf war, a cute little usurper to the throne. Little Miss Marker didn't know the meaning of team player.

"Officer," Jacob said, "let's organize a neighborhood search, check hotel records, and holiday house rentals. All border crossings should be monitored. This man is extremely dangerous."

"Sadly, we lack the manpower to provide this."

"Margot, you requisitioned Interpol police to assist before you left Wien?"

A flush crept up her face.

Head ducked, Riley hid a giggle behind her hand. Bravo, handsome hero. No doubt Margot could be a fierce enemy, but Jacob was still team leader. Unless she'd done more than alert von Bingen to developments.

Jacob pulled pictures of Armand and Amira from his computer bag. "Could you have copies of these made, please? My team and I will start canvassing local hotels and rental agents."

The officer returned with a stack of the photos.

"*Danke*. Come on Riles, we have work to do." He handed her a portion of the pages, gave another set to Margot. "Since rental agencies don't open until nine, we'll focus on hotels and restaurants for now. Don't skip any establishment, no matter how humble. Expect Armand to do the unexpected." Jacob drilled Margot's eyes until she blinked. "Text me the streets you've done. I'll do likewise."

"Of course." Margot headed out the door.

"She ought to have fun walking the streets in those heels." Riley looped her hand around Jacob's arm as they stepped onto the sidewalk. "Let's split up. The officer made me leave Gussi's car at the boat dock. I'll text you every fifteen minutes with my location."

"Nope. Armand may have goons in this town."

She dropped her hand from his arm. "There you go again, controlling my every move. Just like Dad." She gazed at the bakery across the street. "Honestly Jacob, I don't know if I can live like that."

"I'm trying to protect you." His words guttered in his throat.

"I appreciate that. But if he's still in town, we need to scour the city as fast as possible."

A muscle twitched in his jaw. "I don't want you doing this alone." His phone buzzed. "It's von Bingen."

Now was her chance. She waved, turned to go. "Don't worry. I'll let you know where I am. Checking hotels ought to be safe enough."

Right. Armand never moved without armed backup.

17

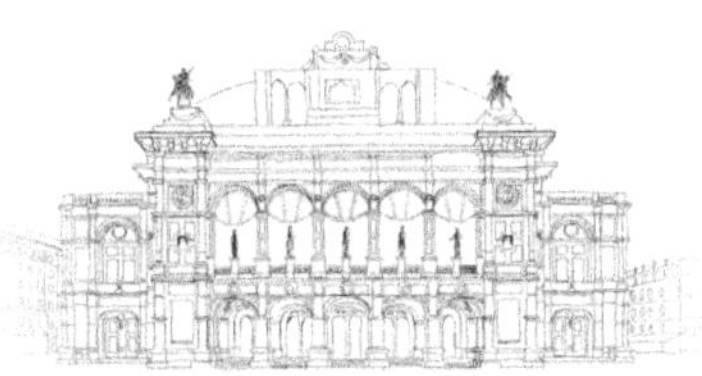

Klagenfurt, Austria, Day 4

"Coulter, I'm having doubts about your leadership capabilities." Von Bingen's words cratered Jacob's gut. He tucked inside a deserted doorway on the street, images of his boss at her desk swirling before his eyes. The work surface bare, other than a complaint filed against him, gray sharkskin suit matched to her upswept hair. In his three months working for von Bingen, Cruella de Ville was saintlier than Mother Theresa.

"Your colleague suggested you're more focused on your vacation than locating Découvrir."

The veins in his neck throbbed. How dare Margot imply that. "I disagree. We've drawn out two assassins, found a possible connection with the local casino in Velden, and early this morning Armand was observed fleeing his rental home in Velden with his daughter. We tracked them to Klagenfurt."

When von Bingen said nothing, he continued. "All of which I might add, was accomplished while my Interpol partner was in Wien." Doing heaven knows what.

"Then who is 'we'?"

Oops. "My fiancée and I."

"You've involved Miss Williams in Interpol business. Again?"

Nope. But he couldn't keep her out of it. "Not intentionally. She seems to attract the terrorists."

"You're not suggesting she be put on payroll, are you?"

"Definitely not. But she flushed out the assassins in the casino and surveilled Armand's villa this morning as he left the grounds."

"A pity she can't head this team." Acid singed von Bingen's tone.

He couldn't argue with that. He owed every success as a field agent to Riles. "May I respectfully remind the chief, the Bureau insisted we use our vacation as cover for this assignment."

"Very well. Carry on. For now." The warning in her voice hit him like a bucket of ice water. "But you've lost your colleague's trust, and that's death to true teamwork. Another report from her and you're out."

* * *

IF ARMAND HAD CHECKED into a hotel, where would he have gone? Riley scrolled through the online list of Klagenfurt hotels and Pensions. She paused on the picture of Palais Porcia. An updated Baroque building in Old Town Klagenfurt. Bedrooms in traditional Baroque or Biedermeier style. Classic Armand.

Inside the hotel lobby, the wallpapers and furnishings catapulted her back two centuries in time. The multi-colored rugs and green velvet Baroque chairs were a bit much. Given Armand's London office, the décor would appeal to him. She approached the reception desk.

"May I help you?" The middle-aged woman folded her hands on the inlaid wood, skimmed Riley's clothing.

If only she could've cleaned up first. "I'm assisting Interpol and the local police on a case." She flashed the Interpol ID card Jacob had given her after their first job together and laid the photographs on the counter. "Have you seen these people?"

The woman's eyelids twitched.

Riley's pulse leapt. A typical sign of recognition. Had she found Armand?

"Anyone could make such a card." The clerk nodded toward Riley's pictureless ID.

"True. Would you like Interpol's phone number?"

The woman stared at her so long, Riley dialed Jacob's Interpol number on her cell, held the screen toward the woman to read the caller ID. Jacob Coulter, Special Agent.

Brow cocked, the clerk almost snickered. "Madame, that does not prove he works for Interpol."

"We just left the Klagenfurt police. Special Agent Coulter can be here in minutes."

"Why do you want to know about these people?" The clerk busied herself straightening pens in a cupholder.

"Interpol wants to question them."

"About what?"

"I'm not at liberty to say." The call switched to Jacob's voicemail. Rats. Riley held up a finger. "Special Agent Coulter, a desk clerk wishes to verify my identity. Please call the Palais Porcia as soon as possible." Leaving him the hotel's phone number, Riley squelched the shrill edge creeping into her voice. Armand was here. She could feel it in her bones. And if Jacob didn't hurry over, they'd lose him again. Probably thanks to the desk clerk Armand had over-tipped.

A smirk flitted across the woman's lips.

"Obstructing justice is a criminal offense in Austria." At least she hoped it was.

"I must ask you to leave the hotel. Now."

Chin hefted, Riley glared at the clerk. "I'll let Special Agent Coulter know how uncooperative you've been."

"If there is a Special Agent, I'm sure he's aware of hotels' confidentiality policies."

INSIDE THE BOUTIQUE a few doors down from the hotel, Riley thumbed through pantsuits on the rack. The floppy-brimmed sun hat should hide her hair nicely. She grabbed a cream-colored top to go with the beige jacket and slacks, and a pair of espadrilles. Subtle, European classy. Near the Kassa, she grabbed an oversized pair of sunglasses and paid for her outfit. With luck, she'd pass for a hotel guest.

Not that she had a plan, but she had to fool Dragon Lady at the reception desk and roam the halls, check the restaurant. Offering silent thanks to the saleswoman who'd allowed her to leave the shop in her new clothes, she drew her deepest pre-aria breath and entered the Palais Porcia, striding with the ease of a self-assured diva.

The desk clerk glanced up. *"Guten Morgen, gnädige Frau."*

"Morgen." Riley flicked a wave in her direction, headed for the elevators. Now what? Would Armand request a penthouse room or stay on a floor low enough to flee with ease? And how could she flush him out?

JACOB WAITED outside the black-framed glass doors, the shaped shrubs in pots. The home rental agency should open at nine. White walls and the chic exterior spoke mega euros. So did the listing pictures displayed inside on neatly spaced racks on the wall. If he weren't here on government business, he'd bypass this agency. His paygrade would never cover the rent on their places.

But many of the properties would appeal to Armand's lavish tastes. Jacob squinted at the postings on the far wall. Possibly even the castles. And most definitely the mountaintop retreats.

Why wouldn't a successful terrorist financier keep several options in his pocket? Lease a Klagenfurt home to seal business deals and hide his activities from his daughter.

The lock clicked, and a woman in a blue suit and white blouse beckoned him inside. "*Guten Morgen.* Anything interest you?" She brushed back a long lock of chestnut hair.

"*Ja.*" Jacob sat in front of the agent's desk, pulled out his Interpol ID and Armand's picture. "Have you seen this man before, perhaps rented him a villa?"

She gnawed her lip, glanced toward another agent's desk. "I don't understand."

"It's vital we find him as soon as possible. He's a dangerous terrorist financier, responsible for deaths in Austria."

"Why do you think he's in Klagenfurt?" Avoiding his gaze, she shifted a folder on her desk.

"He was seen traveling here last night."

Breath whooshed between her rigid smile. "But as you can see, you're our first client this morning."

"It's quite possible he rented a villa online, perhaps months ago. He's known to rent estates all over Austria."

A tic pulsed the corner of her eye.

What was it with these people? They were as protective of privacy as a Swiss banker. "Among numerous other crimes, he's responsible for murders all over Europe."

"I—I wish I could help you but ..."

"Very well." He rose, laid Armand's photo on the desk. "We can continue this discussion at the police station."

The color leached from her face.

"They found his boat early this morning. We know he's here." He gave her a minute to consider. "Obstructing justice won't reflect well on the company's reputation, nor will renting to criminals. If that were to leak to the press." He took one of her business cards from the holder on her desk, and her eyes widened.

"Shall we go now?"

"Where?" Her voice cracked.

"To the police station." Some choice. Call a taxi or text Margot to pick them up.

"*Nein, bitte.*" She gripped the edge of the desk. "I have a little girl, she's only three. I could lose my job—"

Bingo. The bluff had worked. He sat again.

She whisked her laptop from its case, fingers racing over the keyboard. Shoulders hunched, she glanced toward the other desks in the office, then swiveled the screen toward him.

The mountaintop house in the picture overlooked the Wörthersee's turquoise water, densely forested hills in the background. No all-glass structure, wooing nature indoors. Long walls and shuttered windows blocked any attempts to see inside the structure. He jotted the address in his phone, noted the rental agent. The broker/owner. Why had she given him the information? Wouldn't her boss fire her if he found out?

"What makes you certain the man in the picture rented this place?" He kept his voice low.

"Herr Fournier came to the office. He's rented from our firm on many occasions."

"Always from the broker?"

"*Ja.* He handles the—how shall I say—elite clientele."

"*Danke.* You've been most helpful."

"You won't say anything ..." She nodded toward the center desk. "Or mention my name?"

"I'll do my best to protect your anonymity." He texted

Margot to pick him up outside. *"Auf Wiedersehen."* His cell buzzed as he headed out the door. Riles.

"Jacob, did you get my message? I've found Armand."

"Where?"

"He's holed up at the hotel Palais Porcia near the Lindwurmbrunnen, the dragon fountain."

"How do you know?" He waited for Margot by the curb. Riles filled him in.

"Hon, that's no proof."

"That's not what my gut tells me."

Woman's intuition. Great. Why hadn't men received a couple of those genes? "I'm headed for a villa he rented under the name of Fournier. The rental agent recognized Armand's photo. Says he does business there a lot."

"No, you're wrong. He's at the hotel."

He gripped his forehead. "For once, please let Interpol do its job, okay? I want you to camp out in a café near the hotel and wait for me to pick you up."

"Right now, before you head to the house?"

"No. Have a coffee or two. I'll swing by after I case out the villa."

"By then he could be over the border."

"So let's stop wasting time. I want your word of honor you will stay out of the hotel."

"Girl Scout's honor."

"I didn't know you'd been in the Scouts."

The line disconnected in his ear. He shoved his phone in his pocket, dashed for Margot's Mercedes. Maybe he should've insisted on picking Riles up now. Would she be safer with him?

18

Klagenfurt, Austria, Day 4

The hotel phone buzzed again. Grunting, Armand shifted beneath the duvet. He'd asked not to be disturbed. Surely the hundred-euro tip he'd slipped the desk clerk had been generous enough. He floundered a hand toward the device. "*Ja?*"

"Forgive me for disturbing you, Herr Breitbach, but a woman came to the desk, claiming to work for Interpol. She had pictures of you and your daughter." Her voice dropped to a whisper. "She wanted to know if I'd ever seen you."

Adrenaline surged through his chest. Word on the street was Austrian Interpol had launched a search for him. "How odd. I don't know any woman employed by Interpol."

"Confidentially, her ID seemed phony. No picture on it. She called a Special Agent named Jacob Coulter, but his voice mail activated."

A vein throbbed at his temple. Riley Williams. How had she found him? He threw back the covers, shoved his feet into the hotel's slippers. If she were in town, then Jacob was probably here too. If he caught her, he'd strangle her himself.

"I'm a wealthy man. You know how it is, people always want a piece of you."

"I sent her away." The woman sniffed into the phone. "I assure you, she never heard from me you're our guest. We value our clients' privacy."

"I appreciate your tact." He yanked a pair of slacks from his duffle. At four-thirty this morning, the lobby had been deserted when they'd arrived. She was the only one who could identify him. "The hotel is fortunate to have such loyal employees." Oil oozed from his voice. How much would it cost him to buy her silence? He paced the end of the gilt bedframes. "When does your shift end?"

"At noon, *mein Herr*."

Less than three hours. Fräulein Werner wasn't due to arrive with their suitcases and a car until mid-afternoon. "Your kindness will be generously rewarded."

"That's most thoughtful of you, *mein Herr*." Her voice almost tittered.

"Not at all." He disconnected the call, flopped on the crimson velvet couch. The crystal chandelier and red-striped wallpaper closed in on him. Riley and Jacob had been nothing but trouble since the day his girlfriend had introduced them.

From her bed, Amira groaned, shifted beneath the duvet. Or was she faking sleep? He dug his fingers into the side of his head. These days, whom could he trust? He'd traded one prison for another. The last month at the villa, he'd been able to move about the property. Here, he dared not set foot out of the room. If Riley had tracked him here, Interpol or a police officer might pose as a bellhop, a room service waiter.

He flicked on the shower, stepped inside the marble enclosure. In London, Riley had proven a tenacious enemy. Impossible to kill. But toying with Jacob ... Armand scrubbed his scalp until the skin was raw. He'd outsmarted them then. He could do it again.

He had to.

Or his empire would crumble. And there'd be nothing for Amira to inherit.

Toweled off, he slipped into the hotel robe and padded into the bedroom.

Amira sat up in bed, eyes narrowed at him. "Cat prowling too close to the mouse?"

"Watch your tongue, young lady." He replayed the conversation in his mind. How much had she overheard?

"How much longer do you think you can outsmart them?"

He whirled toward her. Hands crossed on top of her head, she smirked, eyes soulless as a sphinx.

After all he'd done for her, how could she be so cold, so calculating? Why couldn't she be like sweet, adoring Tracy?

But then, to run his ops, Amira would have to be ruthless.

<hr />

Letting Jacob assume she'd been in the Scouts wasn't really a lie, was it? She and Lacy hadn't made it past Brownies. But no way would she sit in a café and drink more *Grosser Brauners*. Her stomach would rebel. Then she'd be no match for chasing down Armand.

Finished casing the hotel's second floor, Riley took the elevator to the top floor. The hall furnishings were even more luxurious than below, much more Armand's style. She'd left the restrained lines of Biedermeier for gilded curlicue Baroque. These days, none of it was cheap in antique shops.

Her feet sank into the plush rugs topping the carpeting. Soon the housekeeping staff would be out with their carts, and her presence would arouse suspicion. She strolled along the closed doors, ear cocked toward the wall. Water surged through the pipes outside the last room. If Armand were still asleep, she'd never find him.

Cell out, she clicked on the compass. Given a choice of rooms, which direction would he prefer—toward the lake or the *Innere Stadt*, the historic downtown? She headed for the opposite side of the hall, started with the room nearest the elevator. A quick escape might be useful.

Faint voices drifted toward her. She hurried to the door, laid her cheek against the wood.

"I told you to get dressed now!"

"No. I won't leave. You keep me a prisoner at home, force me to come here in the middle of the night. I'm not leaving again. I want breakfast."

Riles' breath caught. Armand—the voice was unmistakable. Arguing with Amira. She yanked out her cell, dialed Jacob.

"If you won't order room service, then I'm going downstairs."

"You do that, and you'll be picked up by the police." The snarl in his voice carried through the wood.

"I don't believe you. You used to be so—so powerful. Nothing rattled you. Look at you. Running like a coward."

A whack sounded from the room. Amira screeched. "How dare you hit me?"

If Armand was losing it, he was more dangerous than a wounded lion. The animal would do anything to regain its lost pride and power.

Oh, why didn't Jacob answer? His cell kicked into voice mail. Why couldn't he answer when she needed him? Hand to her mouth, she whispered into the phone. "Jacob, Armand is in room five fifteen at the Palais Porcia Hotel. He's arguing with Amira. Get over here right away—"

The adjoining door swept open, and she lurched away from Armand's room, phone gripped in her hand.

Every inch of the man's girth filled the doorway. The hall

chandelier glinted on his silver hair, his three-piece suit. He took three steps toward her. No doubt she looked guiltier than a backslidden sinner.

"*Morgen*, I-I—" What could she say? She was eavesdropping on a wanted man? "A thirteen-year-old child is being abused in that room."

"May I see your identification card?"

She drew herself taller. "And who may I ask, are you?"

"Herr Dr. Helmut Krank, chief magistrate of the Vienna Criminal Court."

"Well, I can assure you I'm not the criminal here." She pointed at Armand's door. "But the man inside is wanted by Interpol." She held up her phone. "In fact, I was notifying Special Agent Coulter when you opened the door."

The elevator clanked open, and a maid shoved a housekeeping cart over the threshold.

"Maid." The judge motioned her over. "Notify the front desk and hotel security this woman is trespassing."

With a nod, the maid placed a call on her cell, gaze riveted on them.

Riley swiped her fingers across her forehead. What had she gotten herself into? If she went quietly, maybe Armand wouldn't know she was out here.

The elevator pinged and Dragon Lady strode toward them. She squinted at Riley. "Take off your hat, please."

Moving in slow motion, Riley pulled it off, and her hair tumbled around her shoulders.

"This woman is an imposter. She claimed to work for Interpol. She showed me a man's picture, asked me if he's a hotel guest."

"And I was right. Armand Découvrir is in that room." She spun toward the judge. "He's a dangerous terrorist financier, as Agent Coulter will confirm." She told him about the attempts on their lives in London. "Agent Coulter is my fiancé."

How could the judge keep his face so impassive? She'd hate to meet him in a courtroom.

Armand's room was silent as a tomb. Was there a fire escape outside his window? "Make her open the door." By now, he could be blocks away.

"Herr Doktor, that man is Herr Breitbach." The desk clerk spread her hands like a plaster saint. "This woman is mistaken."

"No, I'm not." Riley's voice rose. "Open the door, and I'll prove—"

The door swung open.

Clothed in the hotel bathrobe, hair sodden, Armand stepped into the hall. He grabbed Riley's arm and snugged her to his chest. "There you are, *Schatzi*. I've been so worried. The psychiatrist said you'd have days like this, but I never dreamed—"

"No! Don't. He's lying." She struggled against Armand, espadrille stomping his foot.

With an ironclad grip on her arm, he dragged her toward his door. "You must forgive her. Sometimes she's delusional, but quite harmless, I assure you."

"He's a murderer." Riley dug her shoes into the carpet. "Call Interpol." She yelled Jacob's number as Armand strongarmed her inside his room.

One hand smashing her lips to her teeth, he shut the door. The locks clicked.

The pulse in her throat jittered like a machine gun. Spots swam before her eyes. *Dear God, help.* If the clerk and the judge refused to call Jacob, she'd never leave the room alive.

19

Klagenfurt, Austria, Day 4

Hidden behind an outcropping of boulders on the west side of Armand's rental property, Jacob returned Margot's binoculars to their case. "No sign of life. Not even a stray cat."

She grunted, brushed mud from her heels and skirt. "Let's knock on the door. We've checked the place from every possible angle." She scrambled to her feet and stomped around the grassy knoll leading to the front porch.

"Hey, wait. It could be dangerous." He shot after her. Doubly so since they were unarmed.

Margot pounded the door like a battering ram. Outfitted like a CEO when they were in the field seemed to bring out the worst in her. Still, she'd raced to Klagenfurt in the wee hours before dawn.

"We need a search warrant. Armand's hardly likely to answer the door," he said.

"Such things take time." Margot headed toward the car. "By

now, he's probably halfway to Italy. Fancy a trip? We can show his picture to the border police."

"First we pick up Riles."

Margot whirled toward him. "That's more important than apprehending a criminal?"

If he'd had his own vehicle, he could send Margot border hopping while he checked on Riles. He slammed the car door, fastened his seatbelt.

Gear thrown into reverse, Margot executed a screeching U-turn and headed toward the road to Italy.

Bracing himself in the seat, he texted Riles.

Where are you?

When there was no answer, he checked his voicemail. His heart leapt into overdrive. "Turn around. Riles found Armand. He's at the hotel."

"Are you sure?"

"Absolutely. He's in room five fifteen." And if she knew that for certain, she'd either broken into it or confronted him. Either way, his gut screamed she was in danger.

Mortal danger.

God, help! Riley struggled against Armand's grip, kicked his ankles. Surely he was bluffing. If he killed her here, every police officer in Austria would be after him. "*Hilfe, hilfe!*"

Hand clamped over her mouth, Armand whispered in her ear. "Shut up or I'll shoot you now." A gun dug into her ribs. "Silencers are wonderfully effective."

Her heart battered her ribs. *God, help me.* She had to calm down. Convince Armand she wouldn't bolt.

He shoved her deeper into the room. Blood red everywhere,

drapes, couch, wallpaper. Amira cowered on the bed, clutching the yellow duvet to her chin, her eyes saucers.

Would he murder her in front of his own daughter?

Riley faked a calm breath, exhaled slowly over his hand. Forced her shoulders to droop. But he rammed the gun barrel between her ribs, mashed her lips to her teeth. The metallic taste of blood oozed on her tongue. Why had she thought she could outwit him, the master deceiver?

He pushed her onto the couch. Jabbed the gun against her forehead.

This was it. He was going to kill her here. Breaths heaved her chest. Our Father, who art in Heaven, hallowed be Thy name, hallowed be Thy name, hallowed be—*Oh, God, spare me.* If not—she hefted her chin, stared at his glacial-blue eyes.

"No, Papa, you can't be serious." Amira leapt from the bed, white nightgown straining at her legs as she dashed to his side. "Don't do this. Not here."

"Shut up." He cocked the pistol.

Riley gulped.

"What's happened to you?" Amira's voice rose to a shriek. "I don't know you anymore." She tugged his arm, but he brushed her aside. "Think. If-if you kill her here, you'll ruin everything."

How had the world become so depraved? Even his daughter thought murder was okay. Just don't get caught. She was in worse moral shape than Tracy.

The barrel trembled against Riley's forehead. He blinked. Squeezed his eyes shut.

The cold metal dug deeper between her brows. Riley stifled a gasp. Fire seared every nerve ending in her nose. "You know, Armand ..." Somehow, she kept her voice soothing. "Amira's right. As long as I'm alive, you have an insurance policy out of here."

"That won't be necessary." He locked an arm around his

daughter's throat, yanked her to his side. "This one will do nicely."

Fingers clawing at his wrist, the child riveted stricken eyes on Riley. "Papa, please ..." Her whimpers sliced through the electricity charging the air.

Heat seared Riley's chest. How could he be so cruel, and to his own flesh and blood? "You. Beast." She spat the words. "Go ahead. Shoot. You'll never make it out of the hotel."

He threw back his head and laughed. "What a spitfire." He released Amira, stepped closer to the couch. "I'm going to enjoy watching you die."

"I can't stand this." Amira whipped her clothes from the foot of the bed, grabbed her shoes and duffle bag, locked herself in the bathroom.

How did the girl have such presence of mind in a crisis? Seconds later, the bathroom door banged open, and Amira dashed out into the hall.

If only she'd alert a maid. The housekeeper would call the police. The last ounce of adrenaline sieved from Riley's body. What did it matter? She'd be dead before the girl reached the elevator. "You'll have trouble explaining this one."

"I don't think so. My insane former girlfriend drew the gun on me. When I tried to take it from her, the gun fired accidentally." At the soullessness in his eyes, shudders rippled through her spine.

Why hadn't she seen that before? Or had his London defeats rattled him. She feigned a chortle. "The police and Interpol already know that's a lie." Where was the maid, hotel security? "Nope, you need me now. Alive." She drew a breath, brushed away his wrist. Hands braced on the cushion, she wobbled to her feet. If she could just convince him—

A flash of white robe and something slammed the back of her neck. She tumbled to the carpet, whacked her forehead on the coffee table. Groans cascaded from her mouth. Throbbing,

throbbing, throbbing ... Bile spurted into her throat. What ... how ... Another blow whacked the top of her skull. Spots whirled in her eyes. Fire blazed across her scalp. From her temple, red trickled between her lashes, blurred her vision. *Oh, Jesus, I'm Yours.* A black curtain dropped through her head. Blessed ... peace ...

FROM MARGOT'S CAR, Jacob rang Riles' cell for the umpteenth time. Still no answer. He should've listened to her intuition. Or made her come with him. "Can't you drive any faster?"

Margot pulled out a blue light, slapped it on the roof of the car, floored the gas pedal.

Sweat glued his armpits. He drummed his fists on his knees, flexed his knotted calves. Surely she hadn't knocked on Armand's door. Yeah, right. This was the woman who'd brazenly entered terrorists' bedrooms and barely escaped alive.

Oh, Riles, don't have done anything stupid. He shot up prayers for her safety. What if this time he arrived too late?

Colorful Baroque buildings and onion-domed steeples walled them in. Margot blasted her horn at the snarled traffic clogging the narrow streets. His feet itched to dash from the car. "What's the matter with these drivers? Can't they see your flashing light?"

"Where can they go?"

The minutes stretched until he wanted to scream. The traffic inched forward. Finally, several cars peeled to the left and right, and Margot shot her Mercedes through the gap.

Breath whooshed from his mouth. *Thank You, God.* Brakes screeching, she stopped in front of the Palais Porcia Hotel. Seatbelt unlatched, Jacob scrambled from the car and jogged inside. The desk clerk stared at him, jaw agape.

"Interpol. Urgent business." He flashed his Interpol ID at

her, sprinted toward the elevator. He'd notified the police en route. No sign of them outside. If Armand were still here, only armed officers could arrest him.

The elevator crept upward. His fists worked at his side. Why hadn't he taken the stairs?

The doors glided open, and he bolted for room 515. Where were the police? Was there another emergency elsewhere, or did Armand have key officers on his payroll? He banged on the door, jiggled the handle. Locked. "Riles, Riles. Can you hear me?" He leaned his ear to the wood.

Idiot. He should've gotten a passkey from the desk clerk. But all he could think about was Riles. He glanced around the hall for a housekeeper.

At the other end of the corridor, a woman in a black uniform and white apron came out of a room, arms laden with wadded bedding.

"*Bitte*, let me in room five fifteen." He dashed toward her, ID in hand. "Interpol. It's an emergency."

The maid hesitated.

"Come on, woman. The police should be here any minute. If you refuse, I'll have you arrested for obstructing justice." Another bluff, but maybe she didn't know Interpol analysts were impotent.

She lumbered down the hall, key card in hand. He wanted to snatch it from her, do the job himself.

With agonizing slowness, she swung the door back. Scanning the room for signs of Armand, Jacob dashed inside. Riles lay sprawled near the couch, her head against the coffee table. Blood stained her forehead, her throat, her jacket.

"Dear God, no." Kneeling beside her, he searched for a wrist pulse. Beating. But erratic. He dialed for an ambulance. "Riles, Riles, can you hear me? I'm here honey." Late. Once again. Choking back a sob, he cradled her limp body in his arms.

The maid hovered inside the doorway, apron twisted in her fingers.

"Did you see a man and a teenaged girl leave this room?"

"A girl hurried to the elevator from here. She was carrying a duffle bag."

"What time was that?"

The woman shrugged. "*Na ja* ... Perhaps twenty minutes ago?"

"And the man?"

"I was busy cleaning another room, but ..." She glanced at her watch. "Maybe fifteen minutes ago. Not long after the girl left."

"Did you hear the elevator ping?"

"*Nein*. He took the stairs. He also had a duffle bag."

Jacob groaned. Fifteen minutes ago? Armand could've been in the building when Margot pulled up. He dialed his partner, filled her in.

"I'll check inside the hotel and canvas the street." A car door slammed. "Are the police with you?"

"Not a whiff of them." And man, how he needed them. Now.

A soft rap on the door. The desk clerk peered inside the room, wringing her hands. "Is she all right? I had no idea— Herr Breitbach said—and she seemed to be an imposter. The judge thought so too."

"All right?" Jacob dabbed the blood flowing from Riley's head wound. Had she lost too much blood? Ear close to her mouth, her faint breaths brushed his cheek. Shallow. *Dear God, please let her live. Let her be all right. I can't bear to lose her too.*

20

Klagenfurt, Austria, Day 4

Hands fisted in his pockets, Jacob paced the emergency room hall. Not even his Interpol ID gained him admittance to the triage cubicle. *'Sorry, you're not a legal family member.'* If they were already married, he could be at her side, hold her hand, hear the doctor's orders.

The usual hospital smells of urine, floor disinfectant, and fear shrouded him. Two hours since the medical team had examined Riles. What was taking them so long? Was she still unconscious? What if she'd suffered a brain injury, an aneurysm, a blood clot. No, don't go there. Keep the faith, keep the faith.

The phone in his pocket vibrated against his thigh. Tracy.

If only it were Margot with a lead on Armand. Thank God, his sister was checking in with him. "Hey, what's up, kiddo?"

"I want my allowance raised. Now."

He rubbed the throb in his temple. "Why the urgency?"

"Because you owe me."

"Owe you—for what? Are you doing my dishes, cleaning my apartment, doing the laundry?"

"Nooo." She huffed into his ear. "I need spending money."

"For what?"

"Things."

"If I'm paying for these things, I'm entitled to know what I'm financing."

Thuds and stomps penetrated his ear. Fire breathed into the microphone. "Is that your final answer?"

"For the moment."

"Oh, you—beast. Don't say I didn't warn you."

His feet glued to the floor. "Warn me about what?"

"Good luck trying to find out." She disconnected.

Did all parents go through this, or was he doing something wrong? Maybe he could arrange a four-year assignment overseas, be totally out of the parenting picture when he and Riles had teenagers of their own.

If she survived the head injury.

"Herr Coulter?" A voice drifted over the intercom.

He darted to the reception desk, flashed his ID. "I'm Special Agent Coulter."

Flashing a sympathetic smile, the nurse said, "*Herr Doktor* wanted you to know he suspects a brain bleed. He's ordered a CT scan immediately."

After two hours of waiting? "*Danke.*" Jacob plopped onto a chair near the wall and prayed harder than he'd ever prayed before. *Dear Lord, please intervene. You're the same today, yesterday, and forever. You haven't stopped performing miracles.*

The phone buzzed again. How long had it gone off? Interpol HQ in Brussels flashed on the screen. Had Margot contacted von Bingen behind his back again? With Riles in danger, he'd forgotten to update his boss. He braced himself for von Bingen's latest diatribe. "Special Agent Coulter speaking."

"Hartmann in Communications. You asked to be notified if your sister received a call from Amira Découvrir."

Jacob jerked upright on the seat, snatched a pen and a magazine from the side table. "Yes. Fill me in, please."

"I'll do one better. We were able to record the conversation."

The recording played, and his fingers tightened on the pen.

"Amira!" Tracy squealed into the phone.

"*Shh*. Keep your voice down. I'm not supposed to call but I had to. Papa—" Sobs shook Amira's voice. "Papa ..." Crackling sounds as if she were shielding the phone. Her whisper shrank so low Jacob strained to hear her. "Papa tried to kill me."

"He what? When? How?" An emotional kaleidoscope spilled from Tracy's voice—disbelief, anger, panic.

Fire blazed through him. The guy would kill his own daughter? Wake up, Tracy. Armand wasn't the loving papa he'd pretended to be.

He scribbled notes on the inside page of the magazine.

"This morning. In the hotel."

"Why would he do that?"

Silence filled his ear. Amira must've been present when Armand snatched Riles.

"He-he was angry with me."

"But why? He adores you."

Good girl, Tracy. Keep picking at this. Jacob nearly crushed the pen in his fingers.

"I-I can't say. But I ran away."

"Where are you now?"

This time the silence lasted so long he wanted to yell, *where are you? Tell us, tell us.*

"I'd better not say."

Right. He threw the magazine on the table. Plead the fifth. Not that they did that in Europe.

"Can I see you?" The wistfulness in Tracy's voice ripped at him.

No, no. no. Tracy, stay away. Amira's bad news. Don't you remember?

"Are you going back to him?"

At the conspiratorial tone in Tracy's voice, chills slithered through him. Surely all she'd endured in London with the police interrogation had made some impression on her, hadn't it?

"I-I don't know."

"But how will you live? Do you have any money?"

"Some. I guess I could pawn a few things."

Jacob shifted on the chair. Demanding an increase in her allowance could've been Tracy's attempt to help her friend. If so, why had she called his refusal a warning?

"Does Papa Armand know where you are?"

"I hope not." Tremors skittered through Amira's tone.

"I might be able to help you out soon. It wouldn't be a lot of money but ..."

Was Tracy still expecting that raise, or did she have some other scheme? The warning, the warning ... what did she mean?

"I need a place to stay where he can't find me."

"Gosh, I don't know anybody. Wait. Can you get to Brussels?"

"Sure. I think ..."

"Great. Let me know when you arrive. I'll hide you in Jacob's apartment. He's in—away right now."

Bingo. If Amira took the train, she could be in Brussels tomorrow. He'd have an Interpol reception party waiting for her. Kudos to Tracy for not revealing his whereabouts. Maybe all wasn't lost with this kid.

"Talk to you soon."

At the excitement in his sister's voice, he sank in his chair. He wanted her to have friends, but with kids he'd be proud to parent.

Hartmann came back on the line.

"Any way to trace the call?"

"The call was made from the train station at Velden am Wörthersee."

"Then Amira's on the run. By now, she could be on a train to Wien." From there, she could take the overnight train to Brussels. He tore his scribbled notes from the magazine and pocketed them. Placed a call to Margot.

"How is Riley?"

Wow. A touch of concern in his partner's veins. "No word yet. I'm waiting for the results of a CT scan." He filled her in on the Amira-Tracy phone call.

"This could be our break. Maybe you should fly to Brussels."

He slapped his forehead. So much for the kindness. "Not until I know Riles is out of danger and Armand isn't hanging around to finish the job." He struggled to keep his voice even. "The situation is under control."

"Really? Sometimes we must make unpleasant decisions." Her cool tone washed over him like a bucket of ice cubes. "Especially in leadership."

Working for von Bingen was bad enough. And now his partner seemed cut from the same bolt of burlap. After their shared London assignment, Margot had seemed the perfect teammate. Intelligent. A creative thinker. Dedicated. "That is my decision to make. If Amira is foolish enough to show up in Brussels, or my apartment, she'll find a well-armed reception committee. Any luck tracing Armand's movements?"

"One of the chefs recognized Armand's picture. Apparently, he left the hotel via the kitchen. I canvassed the shops and restaurants in the area and alerted the taxi drivers to call in if they'd driven him."

"Great. Keep on it." He disconnected the call. They'd let Armand slip through their fingers—again.

He placed a brief call to von Bingen and brought her up to date.

"Are you sure you can handle this, with your fiancée in the hospital? Perhaps I should have Margot take over—"

"No. It's not a problem. My dealings with Armand far outweigh her experience." Had von Bingen forgotten London?

Her sigh reached into the phone. "All right. For now. Keep me posted." She disconnected.

A doctor in full scrubs and blue booties padded across the room to Jacob's side. "Miss Williams has not regained consciousness."

"And the CT scan?"

"No brain bleed, but the lack of consciousness concerns me. Head injuries can become life-threatening without warning."

Icicles slew through Jacob's veins. Like Natasha Richardson's skiing accident, her sudden death days later. No, don't go there. He needed to believe God would heal Riles, speak life-affirming words over her.

"I'm admitting her to the ICU. I wish I could be more encouraging."

Jacob nodded, tongue glued to the roof of his mouth.

21

Klagenfurt, Austria, Day 5

Jacob walked another lap around the ICU waiting room. He'd had no choice where the ambulance took Riles. He'd have to trust she was in good hands. Phone in hand, he ignored the families crowding the couches and chairs, murmuring amongst themselves. Despite the air conditioning, the air reeked of overactive armpits and sour breath. These people had been here far longer than he had.

Cell to his ear, he stepped to the doorway while Interpol pulled up the reports. "You're sure Amira wasn't on the train?" But if she'd flown from Vienna to Brussels ... "Did you monitor the airport?"

"Yes. She didn't travel to Brussels via plane or train. Would she be stupid enough to hitchhike?" the Interpol policeman asked.

"Yeah." Jacob sighed. "Not much we can do about it if she did. And Armand might have his goons hunting her down. I'll bet she could unravel far more of his ops than Tracy did." He asked the question he'd been dreading. "Did my sister go to my apartment?"

"We have a team posted there around the clock. She hasn't shown up."

"That's one good piece of news. Please keep me informed." He pocketed the cell and sank onto an empty chair.

If only Tracy weren't so susceptible to Amira's suggestions. Maybe he should increase her allowance. He *thunked* the back of his head against the wall. What was he thinking? No matter how much more her gave her, it could never compare to Armand's handouts. He yanked a tattered magazine from the side table, flipped through it. No, Tracy had to learn self-discipline and right values.

Bribing her wouldn't solve anything. Character had to be built. Not bought.

He tossed the magazine aside, drummed his fists on his knees. But Amira's disappearance was concerning. No doubt she was resourceful. In full makeup she could pass for seventeen, but she was still a minor.

And probably more than willing to fulfill some man's wildest dreams.

Venice, Italy

CELL AGAINST HIS EAR, Armand glanced out the balcony window overlooking the Grand Canal. Venice wasn't his city of choice, but he'd been fortunate to make it out of Austria. Three-and-a-half hours beneath a blanket on the back seat floor of Fräulein Werner's rented Peugeot had left his spine bruised and sore. There'd have been no room for Amira. "It's good of you to call."

"How are you, *Liebling*?"

Did he detect a note of frost in her tone? He sank on the brocade bedspread. Everything had happened so fast, leaving Velden. "I've missed you, our nights together."

"As have I." Her voice quivered.

Was it passion or something else? She'd do well to fear. Disloyalty was punishable by death. But right now, he needed her. If she refused to move his funds through the channels, his money laundering ops would stagnate. Not to mention a few other businesses. His duffle bag could hold only so many millions of euros.

"Aren't you missing something of great value?"

"No."

"Shame on you, Armand. How could you treat your daughter like that?" The chiding in her tone amused him.

But how did she know? "I suppose she called you."

"Something like that."

Had Amira gone to her apartment? Very resourceful. His daughter was more like him than she cared to admit. "Do you know where she is?" He had to find her, make amends. A million euros spending money ought to appease her.

"If I did, I wouldn't tell you."

"So you *do* know."

"I know how you treat disgruntled employees. *Liebling*, if you ever hit your daughter again, you will regret it."

"Are you threatening me?"

"*Aber nein*. But if you try to murder your daughter, you'll never see her again. She'll run so far you'll never find her."

Had he really meant to kill Amira? He fingered the green velvet drape. *Non*, it was all Riley's fault. That meddling female had cost him his daughter's love, her respect, her trust. If she hadn't barged in, he'd never have grabbed Amira.

In the moment, Riley's taunts had enraged him beyond his control. Amira had been in the way. He'd had no choice.

But her respect mattered. A lot. He didn't want her to see

him eliminate Riley, but he hoped the blows had been fatal. Then Jacob Coulter would be his only worry.

And Jacob was about to wish he'd never tangled with him.

A smile pulled at his mouth.

Just a few more days now ...

Klagenfurt, Austria

RILEY'S HAND felt so cold in his. Bandages covered the head injuries. In the ICU cubicle, monitoring machines bleeped and chirped beside her like protective birds. The overhead lights blazed on her face, chalky against the pillow, her auburn curls, a splayed halo against the dead-white sheets. If only there were something he could do for her. Jacob hadn't felt this helpless since Noel died in his arms. He shifted on the chair, haunches aching from hours on the hard chair, but the nurses hadn't thrown him out when visiting hours ended.

He stroked her hand, bent to her ear. Her breaths seemed so shallow. "Hey hon, the doctor says you're doing great. Going to be fine." It wasn't a lie. God was her physician. "I'm here for you."

Dear God, give us a breakthrough. She's been through so much.

A nurse stood in the doorway. "I'm sorry, but you'll have to leave now. We'll call you if there's any change."

He squelched the desire to yell, tell the nurse to get out. Instead, he forced a nod. "I'll see you in the morning, hon." He leaned over the bed, kissed Riles' cheek, brushed her icy lips with his. "I love you with all my heart. Never forget that."

He lifted his face a few inches, and her eyelids fluttered.

"Nurse, did you see that?"

"See what?" She moved to the bedside and checked the monitors. "Her vitals are improving."

"Great. But her eyelids moved." He feathered his knuckles along Riles' jaw. "Honey, wake up now. You're safe." His tears dribbled on her cheeks, but he didn't care. "Armand's gone. I'm here."

Her lashes flickered upward, a butterfly shedding its cocoon. She blinked, shifted her gaze toward him. "Hey, handsome." Her voice croaked, but her cockeyed smile zinged through him like a haywire pinball.

"Sorry the Cavalry was late."

"Thought I was reenacting Custer's last stand."

A chuckle twisted his sob. She was back. Humor and all.

He pressed the palm of her hand to his lips, kissed the chill from her fingertips. *Thank You, God.*

22

Where had yesterday flown? The nights in ICU had stolen her sense of time. Good thing Jacob had been there to drive them back to Wien.

Veering Gussi's car into the right lane of the A 22, Jacob leaned across the gear-shaft console, the warmth of his hand seeping through her skin. "Sure you'll be all right?"

"Right as a Texas rainstorm." She hoped. If only the headaches didn't nauseate her. Picturesque villages outskirting Wien whizzed past her window. Today was her first *Probe*, rehearsal, at the Staatsoper. If the vertigo didn't zap her, it was a career dream come true—a leading role at one of the world's most historic and prestigious opera houses.

The furrow between his brows deepened. "You're still so pale."

"You're used to seeing me in makeup." Was it only forty-eight hours ago she'd snuck out of her hotel room and driven to Armand's estate?

"Maybe you should've let them keep you another night or two."

"I'm fine. Besides, you need to be in Wien. Whatever kept Armand in Austria must be so huge it justified the risk." More than anything, she wanted Jacob to uncover Armand's evil ops and take the man down. Anyone who'd kill his own child should be behind bars. Permanently.

"If he held his own daughter in so little regard, what would he do to other peoples' children?"

"Yeah. Check in with me as soon as your rehearsal is over." The worry in his eyes nearly undid her. "Please?"

"I will." She was too tired to argue. Anyway, he didn't need more stress, concerned she'd collapsed.

He took the exit for the *Innere Stadt*, the first district and the historic Ring Circle. Home of the Staatsoper, and more palaces and statues than she could count, the famous Lippizaner horses. One stunning Baroque building after the next. The majestic mosaic roof and steeple of St. Stefan's Cathedral soared above the rooftops. At the next break in the traffic, he turned into the opera house parking garage.

"Gussi said to keep her car as long as we need it. I'll get her some comp tickets to the opera." And a slew of pastries from Heiner's *Konditorei*.

"Sounds good." He pulled into the first available parking slot. "I don't want you taking public transportation until you're well."

There he went again, telling her what to do. A sigh slipped between her lips. "Yes, master." What was the difference between loving care and overprotectiveness and bossiness? The boundaries seemed so thin.

He helped her from the car and gave her the keys. One arm around the small of her back, he walked her to the stage door entrance. "You'll be smashing." His lips lingered on hers.

"Right." If Armand hadn't knocked her voice and breath

control out of whack. The Queen of the Night wasn't onstage much, but her arias were tour-de-force crowd-pleasers. If well executed. A soupçon of unease niggled her stomach. Should she have hired the claque? This was her debut. And the Viennese could be merciless.

Chin high, she smiled, entered the theater, and signed in with the portier.

PRESTIGIOUS EUROPEAN OPERA houses switched singers for leading roles as often as Americans changed their clothes. A pity her contract didn't include a stage rehearsal with her colleagues to practice the blocking and ensemble numbers.

If only the director would walk her through the staging today, point out stage windows and doors. Those could be hard to tell from the backside of a period set. There were hilarious tales of famous singers entering through a window by mistake. No way did she want to become the next statistic.

Riley entered the vast rehearsal room and greeted the Intendant and the conductor. "Lovely to meet you. Delighted to have the chance to work with you, Maestro."

"And I with you. *Küss die Hand, gnädige Frau.*"

Despite the conductor's perfunctory hand kiss, she loved that about Austrians. And in high society, single adult women were referred to as *Frau.*

"Thank you for coming on such quick notice," the conductor said.

"My pleasure. Our vacation was cut short, so I'm glad to accommodate you."

Dear God, please don't let this be another performance from the stratosphere.

Score in hand, the stage director pointed upstage. "You will enter from here."

"*Ach, wunderbar*. On the ground."

"*Nein*, you'll be on a catwalk above the stage."

A wave of dizziness washed through her. Not another staging from outer space. "I see." Perspiration pooled beneath her armpits. "Do I sing the entire aria from the catwalk?" she said through gritted teeth.

"*Ja*. You're an experienced actress. Use whatever gestures you feel are appropriate."

Clutching the railing would be more like it. "That's most kind of you." Chances were, she'd survive these performances if she didn't throw up from the rafters. The way her body was reacting, maybe she hadn't conquered her fear of heights. "And the dialogue lines?"

"You will do your dialogue from the stage."

"Lovely." Compared to the Antwerp staging, this one was positively tame. She wouldn't be jerked around the stage in a faulty hydraulic lift. "Will I be working with my colleagues before opening night?"

"*Nein*, that won't be necessary. You're all seasoned performers in this production."

Stifling a gulp, she nodded. The staging wasn't complicated. She could do this. Make herself sing inches from the roof. She wouldn't faint. Memories of the terrifying performances in Antwerp wouldn't haunt her. "Is this a period staging or avant-garde?"

"*Aber nein*. Traditional. Our audiences prefer it. Tickets sell better."

"*Wunderbar*." A traditional staging was more fun to sing. "And my costume fittings?"

The Intendant consulted his clipboard. "The wardrobe mistress can see you at ten in the morning, eight days from today." He grimaced. "The last Queen of the Night was considerably larger than you."

"Hopefully she wasn't three feet shorter."

He laughed.

Or a foot taller. At five-nine, she often left the seamstresses madly stitching on three-foot borders so she didn't look like Little Bo-Peep. Maybe all they'd have to do was remove a few sections of boning from the bodice, nip in the waist. Uh-huh. Right.

The pianist launched into her first aria. The words and melody poured from her mouth as she focused every inch of the evil Queen's malice upon the intendant and the stage director. Why couldn't she have a regular rehearsal like every other singer? Someday she'd have the clout to insist on it. Finally, her career was ratcheting upward.

As long as she didn't faint on the catwalk.

23

Wien, Day 6

The rehearsal had been ninety minutes of sheer willpower over her body's attempts to collapse. Refusing the dark curtain that threatened her vision. Perspiration drenched her body. She'd hit all the high notes, nailed the lightning-fast runs, one hand clutching the rim of the piano. Hopefully her facial expressions befit the malevolent queen. A queen who ordered her daughter to murder her own father, lied to her future son-in-law, and intended to rule the land.

Why did her roles mirror the events of her life? She tottered out of the opera house and sat on a cement bench, dialed Jacob. Somehow, she had to help him catch Armand.

"How'd it go?" His words tumbled so fast she smiled.

"Just peachy."

"You're calling from the car, right?"

"On my way." She would be. The rumbles in her stomach she'd ignored during the rehearsal returned with a Viennese vengeance. She glanced up the Kärtnerstrasse, now a walking street that tempted pedestrians with the world's most exclusive

129

shops. Her favorite *Konditorei*, bakery, was only a few minutes' walk. If she didn't rush and walked close to the shop doors and windows, she could reach Heiner's. "Talk to you later." She smooched into the phone.

"You'll go straight to the hotel?"

"No worries. Bye." She disconnected before he could say anything. Heiner's was exactly what her body needed. Saliva pooled in her mouth. Should she order Stefanietorte, with its spiderweb icing and vanilla cream oozing between thin layers of ground-hazelnut cake?

She headed for the stoplight behind the opera house, then ambled up the Kärtnerstrasse. A few yards later, she paused, caught her breath outside La Rosa's display window of cashmere and alpaca sweaters. One more door and she'd reach Heiner's. She scanned the pedestrian shoppers. Now that it was autumn, there were fewer tourists, and more locals.

A petite girl decked out like a model in thigh-high boots emerged from the shop across the pavement. A breeze fluttered her long black hair.

Amira. What was she doing here? This was the first place Armand would search for her.

Shopping bags from Gucci and Fendi in hand, Amira's glance swept Riley's side of the street. The girl's lips parted. Blinking rapidly, she turned and strode toward the cathedral and U-Bahn stations.

Would she alert Armand? Cell to her ear, Riley stumbled after her. Jacob picked up on the first ring.

"Home already?"

"Amira's heading toward the U-Bahn station at Stefansplatz. She's been on a very expensive shopping spree."

"Where are you?"

"Trying ... to ... follow ... her." Riley gasped. "But I can't keep up. She's too far ahead. I think she recognized me."

"Leave it to me. I'll alert Interpol to check the security cameras in the subway station. Go. Home. Now."

"Have to eat first. Or I'll pass out."

"Where are you?"

"I'll be at Heiner's on the Kärtnerstrasse. It's closest to me." How could a bump on the head leave her so weak?

Legs jellying, she walked back to Heiner's. Inside the nearly two-hundred-year-old café, the scent of dark chocolate, coffee, and roasted nuts enveloped her. She crept along the glass cases filled with Kremschnitten, Apfel Strudel, Sacher Torte, and a myriad of other delectable desserts. Far more fun to spend a fortune in here than in Gucci or Fendi's. Of course, Amira's purchases would last longer and not end up in massive hips.

"Riley?"

She turned toward the woman seated at a tiny table for two across from the display case. "Countess." Riley shook the woman's hand.

"Please join me." The woman gestured toward the vacant Bentley chair, gold bracelets jangling on her slender wrist. She straightened her pale pink bouclé jacket that must have come from the house of Chanel.

"Whatever happened to you." She touched the butterfly bandage on Riley's forehead.

"Oh, this? I fell and hit my head on a coffee table."

"How dreadful. Perhaps you should be in hospital."

"I'm fine."

"No, you're not. You're white as a ghost."

"Uh-huh." She'd just seen one outside. Someone was housing Amira. Otherwise, she'd need those euros to pay rent and buy food. The girl must have one serious shopping addiction.

A server took Riley's order for an open-faced sandwich, a *Melange*, and a piece of Stefanietorte.

"I just had my first opera rehearsal." Survived was more like it.

"How exciting. But you must take care, my dear. Head injuries can be nasty."

"So I've discovered."

The countess pulled a slender silver-covered notepad and pen from her Gucci bag, jotted something. She tore out the sheet and gave it to Riley. "Dr. Falken's private Klinik is excellent. You'll receive outstanding care."

"*Danke.*"

"In two days, I'm having a cocktail party." She leaned across the table, voice dropped. "Catered by Heiner's. I hate to cook."

"I'm sure you have better things to do with your time."

Head tilted back, the countess's laughter lilted across the table. "*Jawohl.* You can be certain of that."

Riley's order arrived. Her eyes drank in the delicate blue-sprigged dishes, the small water glass topped with a tiny spoon, the foam-topped coffee, all arranged on a small silver tray.

"Eat, eat." The woman brushed her fingers toward the food. "And then you must agree to come to my party."

"That's so kind of you, but—" Riley dabbed the napkin against the foam on her lip.

The countess's perfectly arched brows shot upward. "And who might this handsome man be?"

Gasping, Riley glanced over her shoulder, then sighed. Jacob. Thank God, it wasn't Armand. "This is—"

"Her fiancé."

Right. A fiancé who'd wanted to remain anonymous.

"Countess von Felsenstein. I saved Riley's life in the casino."

"*Vielen Dank* for coming to Riles' rescue. That was fast thinking. And brave."

"I'm a risk-taker. It's the only way to live. Maybe that's why I feel so sympatico with Riley." Almost purring, she extended her hand, curved for him to kiss.

"Charmed." Smiling, he kissed her hand.

At least he didn't give her a Sir Raleigh flourish and bow. Riley ducked her head. Oh, these Viennese. Still using courtly gestures and manners. And she loved it when they kissed hers too. These days, they often ditched the kiss and spoke the words as a greeting.

"And now I insist you come to my party. Both of you."

Riley opened her mouth. "But—"

"We'd love to. Thank you for the invitation." Jacob squeezed Riley's shoulder. A say-nothing squeeze. What had he found out?

24

Wien, Day 6

Hand clasped around Riles' elbow, Jacob slowed his steps to match her pace, a crawl compared to her normal racewalk. Thankfully, she'd chosen a bakery near the opera house and the parking garage. With his free hand, he cradled a package from Heiner's, filled with Riles' favorite treats. Given her passion for dark chocolate, surprisingly few of the slices were chocolate. "I'll fetch the car and pick you up on the corner."

"Thanks, no. The exercise is good for me." She shifted her weight away from him, but her huffing breaths worsened.

Watch it, Coulter. Don't micromanage. If only she'd listened to him and gone straight home. But they'd have lost the lead on Amira. Riles was right. He couldn't have it both ways, chiding her for disobeying him when every time her instincts had been spot on. "If you want a local doctor, Margot can recommend a good specialist."

"The countess gave me the name of a first-rate physician."

"Okay. Will you go then?"

"Yes." Riles' voice rasped into his ear. "Who do you think is housing Amira?"

Tiredness rimmed her eyes. Riles should be home in bed, not playing sleuth. "No idea. You think Armand's in Wien?"

"Could be. From the way her gaze roved, she was surveilling the area before she'd stepped five feet from the store. Her duffle bag in Klagenfurt wouldn't hold much clothing."

He kept his hand on her elbow as they neared the crosswalk. "If she shopped at Gucci and Fendi, the bag may have been full of euros and little else."

A sudden breeze whipped fallen leaves and Riles' curls into a frenzy. "They call this type of wind a Föhn. Did you know in Austria, if you commit a murder during a Föhn, you can't be held guilty."

"An acquittal—you're kidding."

"Nope. Better not try to have Armand arrested during one." Riles glanced at him. "Why did you accept the countess's invitation?"

"Armand moved among the wealthy and elite in London. She fits the ticket. It's too dangerous for him to circulate here right now, but she may have social connections worth investigating. Maybe a little name-dropping wouldn't hurt."

She elbowed his ribs. "So now I'm your entrée into high society."

"Yeah. He chuckled. "You've got great creds."

"I hope she doesn't expect me to sing for my supper."

"Thought divas salivated at the chance to strut their vocal stuff."

She harrumphed. "Not this one. I'd like a relaxing night off. With maybe a little networking thrown in."

"Knew you couldn't resist." He grinned. "Bet you three slices of those tortes, the countess begs you to sing."

"You're on."

"Guess I'd better rent a tux." His cell chirped in his pocket. "Agent Coulter speaking."

She took the package of tortes from him and leaned against the building wall.

"CCTV here. We have sightings of the young woman. Sending you the photos now."

"*Danke*." He clicked on the pictures. Glanced toward the U-Bahn entrance behind them. "Could you also please forward them to the local Interpol office? *Danke*." He thrust the phone in his pocket. "The subway CCTV captured Amira boarding the subway heading toward the Westbahnhof, the train station. But the cameras picked her up again disembarking at the Volkstheater where she hopped on the U2 headed toward Karlsplatz."

"Then she's circling back downtown."

"Looks that way." He checked his watch, squinted toward the parking garage. He ought to walk Riles to the car.

"I can make it back to the hotel without you."

If only he could be in both places. Riles needed him. But he had to get Amira in protective custody. "Are you sure?"

"Yes. Go catch us a fugitive."

***

BREATHLESS, Jacob sat at the fountain's edge outside the Karlskirche, an ornate Baroque, green-domed church. He doubted Amira had gone inside. She might take her Muslim faith seriously. Although he'd never heard reports of Armand darkening the doorway of a mosque.

Given the speed of the U-Bahn, Amira might have surfaced long before he reached here. He phoned Margot, brought her up to date. "Could you run checks on CCTV cameras at the Karlsplatz station and the surrounding area?"

"*Ja*, but Austrian law requires the erasure of the films within seventy-two hours unless they're needed for a court case."

"Then we'd better hustle. I'll check for evidence of her shopping at Fendi and Gucci."

According to Google, both stores were on the Kohlmarkt, near Michaelerplatz and the Kärtnerstrasse. Today he'd get in his exercise.

As Jacob stepped through Gucci's glass doors, the subtle suggestion of old money pervaded the décor. Rich dark wood furniture and paneling, intricate patterns in the glass-tiled floor. Professional smile in place, an elegantly dressed saleswoman approached him. She smoothed her narrow black skirt, tweaked her matching jacket.

Interpol ID held up, he pulled out his pictures of Armand and Amira. "Do you recognize these people?"

"The girl, definitely. She spent several hours trying on outfits today."

"Did she purchase anything?"

"*Ja*." The clerk checked the register drawer for the sales receipts. "She purchased two blouses, a jacket and matching skirt and slacks."

"How did she pay for the items?"

"With cash."

"Do you often have such young customers?"

"*Nein*. But her father, the man in your picture, has accompanied her in the past and told us to sell her whatever she wishes."

"Has he ever charged the purchases?"

The woman bristled. "Is there a problem?"

"We're concerned for her safety. Her life may be in danger."

"Isn't a search warrant required for such information?" She straightened the purses on the backlit shelves.

Sometimes an informed public who knew their rights

wasn't a blessing. Like today. "We may have only hours to find her. Did you know she's thirteen?"

The woman blinked. "*Aber nein.*"

"Afraid so. If she returns, or you see her on the street, will you please call this number immediately?" He handed her his business card.

"Of course."

He turned to leave, then paused. "When was the last time you saw her father?"

The woman frowned. "Not recently ... six weeks ago?"

"Was he here with his daughter?"

"*Nein.* A woman."

"Can you describe her?"

"Stunning. Tall. Wears her clothes beautifully. Blonde. Perhaps forty-five?"

Bingo. Another lead to track down. "Would you recognize her again?"

"Perhaps ..." The woman shrugged. "Then again, maybe not."

Venice, Italy

How DID priests and nuns survive cloistered living? Armand crumpled the velvet drape in his fingers. The space had grown unbearable. He had to get out of here, out of Italy fast. But if Interpol had border police watching for him, they'd have blocked every means of transportation. His one shopping trip in Venice had yielded a straw fedora, several suits and pairs of shoes, a sumptuous meal and a bottle of wine on the Grand Canal. Soon he'd have to access more cash.

He grabbed his cell on the first ring.

"*Liebling*. I thought you'd want to know Interpol was asking about you at Gucci's."

"Gucci's? I've never charged anything there."

"But you took me there, remember? Apparently, the saleswoman recognized me. She called a little while ago, said she told him only that she recognized the pictures they have of you and Amira."

Fist working, he carved another path across the room. The net was closing in on him.

"How do you want me to handle this?"

"You mean, how much to pay her for her silence?"

"Precisely."

"I don't know." He raked a hand through his hair. "Make her your personal dresser, take her to lunch. Invite her to one of your parties. Give her money—" His voice rose.

"I'm sure all the above will work. The woman has a career to nurture."

"Fine." He disconnected, threw the phone on the bed. Poured himself a glass of brandy. Soon he'd be out of liquor too. Head tilted back, he drained the fiery liquid in one gulp, then snatched his phone.

Time to launch an attack. Make Jacob sorry he'd ever come to London. Or Austria.

He placed another call, blew out brandy-scented breaths until the woman answered.

"Get the girl."

25

At the knock on the hotel room door, Riley tightened her dressing gown sash over her lounge pants and top. Eating in the restaurant had been more than she'd wanted to face tonight. Jacob hovered at her side, his face wan. Lines etched the corners of his eyes, his mouth. She opened the door, rubbed the ache in her skull.

A tray balanced on his shoulder, the room-service waiter arranged the plates for two on the desk, handed Jacob the bill. Riley removed the silver domes and inhaled the scent of melting butter and garlic oozing from the steak and frites. Not very Austrian, but they needed some serious protein.

Jacob seated her, snagged a plate, and plopped onto the easy chair, feet perched on the ottoman. He forked a bite of meat with a French fry and groaned. "Great idea, Riles."

"How much longer can we afford this place?" Their rooms cost more than she'd wanted to spend, but worrying Armand's goons would attack her in her apartment was too much stress on Jacob.

He mumbled around another mouthful. "If we catch Amira soon, we'll have leverage against Armand."

Savoring the garlic butter on her bite of perfectly grilled steak, she nodded. If they had room for dessert, they could dig into the Heiner's treats.

Using her last *frite,* she mopped up the garlic butter and popped it in her mouth. Now she could face life. She stacked his bare plate on hers, then snuggled on his lap. "Let's do this again, lover boy."

"How about tomorrow night, doll?" His lips brushed her forehead, her hair, sending shivers down her spine.

"Can't. We have a cocktail party."

He groaned. "Wish we could get out of that."

"Now, now. It's business, remember?" Angling herself on his lap, she tilted her chin and settled her lips on his for a long, slow kiss. Sparks shot through her. His arm tightened around her, and their breaths quickened. Boundaries—

His cell beeped. Sighing, he pulled away and took the call. "Hey Tracy, how's it going?"

"Do you know where Amira is?" Tracy's voice wobbled.

"No. Wish I did." He put the call on speaker. "She's in great danger. Have you heard from her?"

Riley straightened in the chair. *Dear God, please let her be honest with him.*

"Why do you ask?" That spiteful teenager tone again. "You know Papa Ar—her dad said she couldn't contact me."

"But that doesn't mean she obeyed him." Sternness etched his tone.

Silence filled the room.

"Allowances are a privilege." His sigh reached into Riley's soul. "Tracy, I have to know I can trust you."

"You've been spying on me! What are you doing, listening to my phone calls?" Her shriek reverberated through the cell. "I hate you. You never loved me." The call went dead.

The lines on his face deepened. He shoved the phone in his pocket, rubbed the shadows beneath his eyes. "So much for effective parenting."

"You've got to admit, Tracy's pretty smart."

"Yeah. You recommending her for Interpol training?"

"Nope. I'm first in line."

"Not without a doctor's certified bill of health. I had Margot contact a highly recognized neurologist who has his own private clinic. She made you an appointment for the day after tomorrow."

She pulled away from him. There he went, micromanaging her life again. "Cancel it. I told you I was seeing the countess's doctor. I'm quite capable of making my own appoint—"

"I know. But you could barely make it to the car this afternoon. Right now, I can't take more personal stress."

"That was sweet of you." She fiddled with her sash. She hadn't meant to add to his burdens. But she'd see Dr. Falken instead.

26

"I hope we won't have to stay too late." Inside the elaborate foyer of the countess's apartment building, Riley let Jacob hold the elevator door open for her.

She lifted the hem of her formfitting, red silk evening gown and stepped inside. Cocktail parties were so not her thing. But she was here to help Jacob. She adjusted the single strap that crossed one shoulder.

The doors whooshed shut, and he pushed the button for the fifth floor. He tweaked his tux bowtie in the mirrored walls. "Sure we aren't overdressed?"

"No worries. If so, I'll play the diva."

"And I'll be your trusty sidekick." He kissed the tip of her nose. "Better still, your bodyguard."

"Hmm ... I like that idea."

The doors opened, and her heels sank into the plush carpeting. The crystal chandelier gleamed on the hallway furnished with ornate Baroque furniture. Too posh for her tastes. Although she wouldn't mind living in a penthouse. This one occupied the entire floor.

"Ready, milady?" Jacob pushed the bell outside the gilt-edged doors.

The doors swung open, and the countess welcomed them with open arms. "*Liebling*, how good of you to come. I thought you two might beg off." She swept back the folds of her cream satin gown. Pearls glimmered in her French twist and on her wrist.

"We're delighted to be here." Riley clasped her sequined clutch. Definitely not overdressed. "Thank you for inviting us."

"How sweet." The woman planted air kisses near Riley's cheeks, then extended her hand for Jacob to kiss.

Riley bit back a grin as he complied.

"Let me introduce you." She looped beringed fingers through their arms and walked them across the salon. The furniture and paintings were as costly as those in the hall.

If Jacob hadn't attended a European cocktail party, he was in for a surprise. Guests didn't circulate. They sat and conversed with the people beside them. None of the American cigarette in hand, cocktail in the other, roaming the room full of loud laughter and banter. Instead, she and Jacob entered a salon with muted conversations, a drink on the table beside the guest. Hopefully their hostess had chosen pleasant seatmates for them, or the evening might be excruciating. Riley pasted on a smile.

The countess stopped beside a portly, silver-haired man seated with his back to them. The gentleman across from him paused mid-sentence.

"Herr Doktor, may I present soprano Riley Williams and her fiancé—" She tapped her lips. "How silly of me. I don't know your name."

"Jacob Coulter."

The man rose and turned around. Riley choked. The

magistrate she'd met outside Armand's room. Would he tell the countess?

A question in his eyes, Jacob glanced at her.

The judge's brow shot upward. "We've met." He stood, shook her hand, the touch brief.

What? No *Küss die Hand* for her? She forced a smile. "Nice to see you again."

"And I thought I was connecting Riley with someone new." The countess's laughter tinkled like broken glass.

Blue eyes drilling Riley, the judge gestured her to his partner's vacant seat. The defendant's chair. "On the contrary, I look forward to continuing our conversation."

Her cheeks warmed. "How delightful." Another interrogation.

The other gentleman sat on her right. Jacob took the last seat, brow furrowed, body poised to pounce.

With her stay in the ICU, then spotting Amira, she'd forgotten to tell Jacob about her run-in with the judge. She chose a glass of soda water from the white-coated waiter's tray.

"Your fiancé? And how long have you been engaged?" Judge Krank asked.

"Three months." She turned to the man on her right. "We haven't been introduced."

"Heinrich Markowitz."

Great. Was he a prosecuting attorney?

Judge Krank cleared his throat, fixed her with his soul-piercing eyes.

Thighs clenched against the seat, she squeezed her whitened knuckles over her evening bag. Here it comes.

27

———————

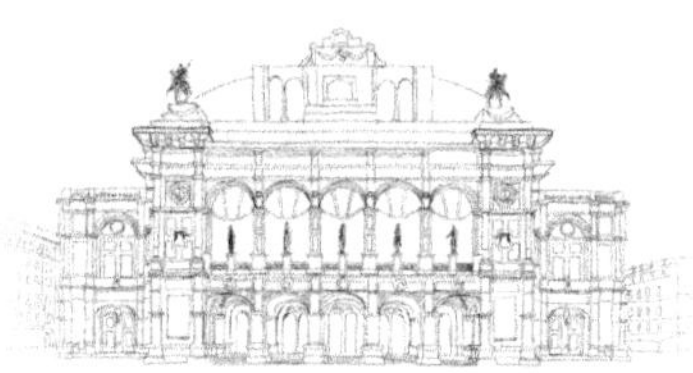

"Are you feeling better?" the judge asked.

"Oh, much, *danke*." If she didn't get out of here fast, her reputation would be mud. What was she thinking? As soon as she left, he'd tell the countess, and ticket sales for the opera performances would plummet.

"The Herr Doktor feels it's—appropriate—for you to be out?"

"What doctor?" Jacob zeroed on the judge.

"The psychiatrist—"

"I've never been treated by one in my life."

Jacob blanched, and Markowitz squirmed on his chair.

No way was she letting him get away with this. Shifting in her chair, she played to her audience of three. "The judge is referring to my abduction in a Klagenfurt hotel by a known terrorist." Giving the magistrate a beatific smile, she touched the bandage on her forehead. "An abduction," she gestured to the judge, "he failed to report to the police."

Crimson swept upward from the judge's bow tie.

146

Eyes bugging, Jacob gripped the armrest.

Markowitz sank in his chair.

"Sadly, my captor escaped, but my fiancé arrived in time to call an ambulance and saved my life." She sipped her soda water. "It's so important to gather all the facts, don't you agree, Judge Krank?"

Face dark as a purple beet, he drained his champagne. "*Natürlich.* You'll excuse me." He lumbered to his feet and headed for the bar in the corner.

The longing in Markowitz's eyes suggested he'd like to flee too.

Maybe it was the head injury. She'd just tanked her career in Vienna. But she was tired of injustice, people jumping to conclusions, and so-called upholders of the law leaving victims to flounder on their own.

THE JUDGE WAS responsible for what happened to Riles? She'd never have gone docilely with Armand. Right now, he'd like to bravo her for humiliating the man. Unlike Germans, Austrians favor the indirect, oblique approach. Not in-your-face facts and statements. Jacob took the judge's seat, warmed her hand in his palm.

A woman lurched away from the bar, clutching a glass of red wine. The chandelier glinted on her long, blonde hair, her sequined jacket. Dressed in a white evening suit, she tottered toward them, her stride taxing the floor-length straight skirt.

A warning niggled his stomach. If only he and Riles could leave, but the guest laid her red-taloned fingers on Markowitz's shoulder.

"*Schatzi,* have you recovered from all the tra-la-la today?" The woman rolled her eyes, slurped her wine. "The press doesn't usually get involved, but you handled it with aplomb."

The press? He'd have Margot check into this. Jacob hoisted his glass in Markowitz's direction. "It's tough being in the public eye."

"*Ach*, you speak German," the woman said.

"*Jawohl.*"

"They both do." Markowitz's warning tone was lost on the guest. She'd had far too much to drink.

"Journalists can be such a nuisance. What were they up to now?" Riles asked.

"Some religious group was protesting the visa/work permit laws. Accusing the government of sh-shanctioning prosh-titution as honest labor." Despite her slurred words, she took another sip of wine.

"Oh?" Jacob asked.

Tittering, the woman plopped into Jacob's vacated chair. "The fact that immigrants can get a permit to work as prostitutes but not as maids. In fact, prostitution is the fastest way to earn a living in Austria. And it's legal." She raised her glass to Markowitz.

Riles jerked, chin thrusting forward. "You mean the government supports prostitution?"

"Well, not really." The woman gave Riles a once-over.

"They facilitate it then." Jacob set his soda water on the side table. Prostitution wasn't only a source of enormous income for the pimps and brothel owners, it was great for money laundering. Was this why Armand hung around Austria?

Red splotches peppered Markowitz's cheeks. Blinking like a semaphore, he glanced toward the countess.

Flashing them a thousand-watt smile, she sauntered over. "My dear Riley, won't you please honor us with an aria or two?" She swept her hand toward the grand piano in the next room, the lid propped open.

"I-I'd love to, but—" Riles paled.

"Unfortunately, she's on a day of vocal rest." They'd joked about this, but she'd always acquiesced in the past.

"Then perhaps a few *Lieder*?" The countess's eyes lit. "My guests would enjoy it so much."

Jacob helped her from the chair. "The fall left her dizzy. How's that headache, hon?"

"Actually," Riley touched her bandage, "It's throbbing."

"Countess, it's been a delightful party. Thank you for inviting us, but I need to get Riles home." Jacob reached for the woman's hand and brushed his lips on her soft skin. No point waiting for the command to do it.

She took Riles' other arm and escorted them to the elevator. "You must come back and take tea with me." She kissed Riles' cheeks. "When you're feeling better."

"*Danke*, that would be lovely."

Once the elevator doors closed, Riles leaned against the wall. "What did you make of all that?"

"I think Interpol may have its first serious lead on Armand's business interests in Wien."

"Disgusting, isn't it—a government sanctioning prostitution with easy work permits. If Europeans weren't so class conscious, I'd have told them I worked as a maid when I first moved to Austria. Not fun, but at least it was honorable. And certainly not degrading to me as a woman." She sighed. "What's the world coming to?"

Venice, Italy

THE PHONE PINGED on Armand's bedside table. How was he supposed to sleep? Grappling for the cell in the dark, he stared at the text message.

Time's up.

What had happened to trigger the warning? For whatever reason, a phone chat had been deemed too dangerous.

In the past month, his life had burgeoned from one nightmare to the next. And now, no calls from Amira. She refused to open his text messages. Each apology had spilled more emotional blood than he'd thought remained in his veins.

Duvet thrown back, he shoved the cell into his pajama pocket and padded across the cold tile floor. With his chief lieutenant in prison, he needed to hire new ones to manage his ops. Trustworthy men. Ruthless men.

He forced three deep breaths of Venice's polluted air into his lungs. He needed a plan. A foolproof plan. And a way to reach Wien without detection.

A laugh worked its way up his throat. Having friends in high places helped. And once Riley and Jacob were dead, his life could resume.

Address pulled up on his cell, he texted one of the few people he could trust.

Do it today.

28

"Tell me about the brothel industry in Austria." Jacob turned his office chair to face Margot.

"Austria has many kinds, not just classic sex clubs or night clubs offering customers alcoholic drinks and sexual services." She ran the coffee machine in the corner. "In those types, sex workers don't pay a fee, but they share their earnings with the clubs."

"Hmm." He jotted a few notes on a legal pad.

"We also have the FKK sauna clubs, big Wellness centers where sex with females is allowed."

Jacob stifled a shudder. What happened to godly standards? Didn't people care anymore?

"To work there, the sex workers pay a daily fee to the FKK owners as do the customers."

"So, the owners rake in euros from everyone."

"*Ja.*" She sipped her coffee. "It keeps the women from sleeping on the streets. They rent the rooms weekly or monthly, and the house owner manages the building. But the girls keep all their earnings."

"Then we have sex studios, small, cheaper brothels. The owners take a cut from the girls' earnings, the clientele is seedier, and working conditions are sometimes awful." She slid a page across his desk. "These are the most well-known brothels in Vienna, registered with the police. Anyone can find the list online."

"Wow. Almost every district in Wien is listed." Many with scads of establishments. He made more notes. Maxim's at Kärtnerstrasser 61 and Babylon Vienna's at Seilerstätte 1, both in the *Innere Stadt*, close to the wealthiest apartment owners and the most elegant hotels.

"Maxim Wien is considered one of the best nightclubs in the city. A reputable classic sex club with parties and very high-class girls. And no entry fee. The club prides itself on providing a fresh lineup, always introducing new—talent."

New girls. That could mean sex trafficking behind the scenes. "Sounds like we ought to check it out."

"Because prostitution is legal in Austria, and brothels generate sizable income, Interpol's hands are tied."

"Unless we uncover sex trafficking."

She cocked an eyebrow at him. "You think the government doesn't know about this?"

The pencil snapped in two. He was a protector. An upholder of the law. How could he do his job with immoral governments watching over his shoulder?

"If young ones aren't a man's fancy, Maxim's also has women with many years of experience." She popped another coffee capsule into the espresso machine. "One even has a choice of rooms, standard, VIP, super VIP. For those in a hurry, their website lists the girls and the days they're available."

"Enough." The roil in Jacob's stomach threatened to erupt. Was Armand involved in this business?

"You really ought to check out Babylon Vienna."

He didn't want to have to check out any of this. How could any self-respecting man take advantage of a woman?

"It's still the biggest and most expensive brothel in the city. It used to be extremely discreet. Not long ago, they did no online marketing. They relied on their reputation and referrals from their elite clients." Margot sipped her fresh cup of coffee, leaned against his desk. "Their stunning interiors, all-inclusive luxurious service, and beautiful women appeal to upper-crust society."

Babylon, the ancient hedonistic kingdom. Glitz and glamour in its day. Masking the evil that permeated its society. Like Wien and a host of other cities today.

"If you want to know more about what they offer—"

He held up a hand. "Spare me the details."

"Brothels are a thriving industry in Austria. These days it's part of the tourist appeal."

If he had to listen to anymore, he'd barf. "Armand may own a hefty portion of this industry under shell companies."

"We've so few resources. Are you sure staking out brothels is the way to find Armand?"

"I don't know, but it's the most logical business venue for a man of his interests."

Venice, Italy

GRINNING, Armand clicked the video icon on his iPad screen. A pity he couldn't have attended the meeting himself. From the filmed angle, the cameraman had chosen a table across from Tracy and his recruiter. A crowded Brussels café. Good choice. Middle-aged women chatting over coffee and cake. Not the place Tracy's bodyguard would expect to find her.

"You said your brother had you under surveillance." The recruiter stirred a packet of sugar in her coffee.

Despite her twenty-five years, the blonde goddess could pass for eighteen. Someone the girls would idolize. So far, she'd reeled in thirty teens, signed contracts and all. Armand settled in his chair. Business was booming, requests for au pairs coming in from Dubai, Qatar, Egypt. None from Paris.

"Don't worry. I ditched the guy when I pretended to try on dresses at the department store. That's why I was late."

"Very resourceful. An outstanding trait for an au pair." The recruiter leaned back in her chair, preening as if she'd discovered the latest Mensa candidate. Overboard IQ and all.

Armand chuckled. If she kept up her current recruitment rate, he'd have to raise her pay. Just what he'd expected from German efficiency.

"You're still interested in the job, aren't you?"

"I don't know ..." Tracy's hands skittered across the table, toyed with the spoon on her saucer. "I'd better think this over. I really need a job, but leaving school ..."

Her Belgian school uniform was no more flattering than the British one. He glanced at her chest bulging from the blouse. Such a waste of talent as an au pair.

"I thought you weren't happy in Belgium." The recruiter flicked her long blonde hair from her beige-suited shoulder. "Brussels isn't the most exciting place to live. Or the easiest to make friends."

"But Paris is so far away."

"Not really. If you take the Eurostar, you can be there in two hours. And there's so much to see and do there. You'd make friends with other au pairs."

"Hmm ... I don't know." Tracy slicked her lips, glanced around the café. "Kind of odd, though. The agency sending me an application. I never receive any mail."

"It's serendipity. Most of the girls in your school don't meet our standards."

Tracy startled. "You sent letters to my classmates?"

"Oops. Shouldn't have let that slip. That's confidential." The recruiter tapped Tracy's hand. "Think of all the money you'd earn. All of it yours, to spend as you like."

The girl's eyes lit. Her fingers fluttered to her throat where he'd fastened many a jeweled necklace around her neck. "I've been bugging my brother to let me get a job. Parttime, of course."

Armand chuckled. No doubt she missed the unlimited shopping sprees he'd provided her. Her lavish, loving Papa Armand. If only she knew he was the one dropping this gem in her lap.

"Would you like to sign the contract?"

"Umm ..." Tracy twisted her knuckles. "What would I be doing, exactly?"

"Taking care of the children."

"That's all?"

"That's what au pairs do." The recruiter softened her words with a winsome smile.

For a second Tracy relaxed in the chair, then leaned forward. "I'm not into cooking, cleaning house, or anything like that."

Armand chortled. Or cleaning up her bedroom in his townhouse. But then, neither was Amira.

"You could try it for a semester. Go back to school next term if you want to. After all, it's only a six-month contract."

"That doesn't sound so bad." Tracy stared toward the wall, chewed her lip. "I have to go. Thank you for the drink." She pushed her coffee aside, pulled her shoulder bag from the back of her chair.

Armand leapt toward the screen. "No!"

"The family really wants you to come. They fell in love with your picture and your essay."

For a second, light flickered in Tracy's eyes, then dimmed. "But I know nothing about taking care of children." She squirmed on the seat, hands tucked beneath her thighs.

"As any mum will tell you, it's on-the-job training. You'll get the knack of it in no time." The recruiter's smile could melt the scales off a snake. "Trust me."

"Really?" The pleading in Tracy's eyes was almost pathetic.

Armand pushed his chair back from the screen. He'd never met a more love-needy teen. She'd eaten up his pats on her head, a stroke of her cheek. Just like the children at the orphanage.

"You haven't told anyone about our meetings, have you?" The recruiter sipped her coffee.

"Of course not. My Bomma thinks I'm having coffee with a girlfriend."

"Good. I like the way you think." The recruiter leaned across the table. "You know, we're very selective in the girls who reach this stage of the interview process."

Tracy sat taller in the chair. "Really? When would I start?"

"Quite soon, if you'd like." The recruiter slipped a small phone from her purse. "We'll call you on this cell. First, we need to finalize arrangements with your host family. In the meantime, keep working on your French skills."

"I will. But you said they wanted the children to learn English." Alarm riddled Tracy's voice.

"Most definitely. But on the street, you must be able to fend for yourself in French."

"Yeah. Uh, what nationality is my host family?"

"We work with many different nationalities."

Good sidestep. Armand fingered his upper lip. Few were French. Many were from the Middle East. The Ukraine. Russia. Even Asia. He gave the clients what they wanted. Not his problem if they hadn't heard of workers' rights, fair pay, and good treatment. Or if Papa expected to sleep with the hired help.

"Yes, but what about my family? You said they liked my essay so you must know something about them."

Careful now. Armand clawed the leather armrest. Reel her in slowly. This was one fish he couldn't let fall off the hook.

"We don't divulge information about your employer until you've signed the contract." She slipped several sheets of paper from her purse. Offered Tracy a fountain pen.

Hand trembling, Tracy slid the pages in front of her. She stared at the pen as if it might bite her.

"It's standard legalese. Just sign here." With an angelic smile, the recruiter tapped a line on the second page.

"I ... I don't know ..." Tracy pushed the contract back to the recruiter. She shrank in her chair, slid her hands into her lap. "I need to go. Bomma expects me home by five."

"*Liebling*, the family is so eager to welcome you into their household." The recruiter laid the pen on the contract and scooted it in front of the girl. "I know you won't regret this. They're so loving and kind."

Tracy's gulp bled into the microphone. Her fingers crawled toward the pen.

Armand's fists throbbed. If only he could be in the room when Jacob found his sister missing. Despite that expensive bodyguard.

29

Wien, Day 9

Seated at his cubicle in the Vienna Interpol office, Jacob's knuckles blanched on his cell. "You're kidding." Until now, the bodyguard's daily check-ins had been reassuring. No sign of anyone else watching his sister or Mrs. DeBeers. But this—

"How could you lose Tracy?"

"I followed her inside a department store. She pulled a few dresses from the racks and took them into the dressing rooms. No way could I go in there. And ..." The bodyguard's hard throat clear sent chills through Jacob. "She disabled her phone so I couldn't trace her whereabouts."

Jacob's toes cramped inside his shoes. What was she up to? Without warning, rain and hail peppered the windows.

"Twenty minutes later when she hadn't come out, I asked a salesclerk to check on her. She said the dresses were on the hook, that she must've slipped out via the staff door at the end of the dressing room hall."

"She deliberately ditched you." Jacob slapped a fist on the

padded cubicle wall. Why? Had she fallen in with the wrong crowd at school, kids doing drugs? "When did this happen?"

"An hour ago. I searched the store, the streets. Sounds to me she was keeping an appointment."

"But with whom?"

"No idea. Normally, she heads out of school, head down, backpack on her shoulders, and scuffs her way back to the apartment. There's been no sign of anyone else watching her. Or Mrs. DeBeers. Every morning she hobbles out with her cane to grocery shop, then heads home."

"Good." The Brussels area was a hotbed of terrorist groups. Groups responsible for bombings at the airport, in Paris, and other cities over the past years. It'd be easy for Armand to hire someone there, especially since the police refused to enter certain neighborhoods without backup vans of armed officers. Even then, sometimes the cavalry failed to show up. "What's next?"

"I take up my post in the café across the street from the apartment. Until my night relief shows up and camps out in his Peugeot in front of their building."

"She could've been sneaking out the back door of the apartment building."

"I don't think so. Mrs. DeBeers says Tracy stays in the apartment once she gets home from school. She calls me every night once Tracy's gone to bed."

"Where are you now?"

"In the café across from the apartment building. So far, no show."

"When Tracy spots you, does she acknowledge you?"

"A few eye rolls now and then." He chuckled into the phone. "Yesterday she asked me outside the school if I wanted to correct her homework for her."

"We should've tagged her with a prisoner's ankle bracelet." Jacob's growl huffed against the microphone. If evidence didn't point to Armand's presence in Austria, he'd book the next flight to Brussels. Give Tracy a tongue-lashing she'd never forget. Didn't she understand the stakes here? Jacob sank into his desk chair. Had Armand managed to get to her?

Dear God, please help me. What should I do?

"I know you're doing the best you can. Keep me posted. And thanks." He disconnected the call.

Margot's heels tapped across the wood floor of his cubicle. "Trouble?"

"Tracy slipped away from her bodyguard." He filled her in.

"I know how torn you must feel, being here, far from her."

He loosened his necktie. The woman had no idea.

"You'll want to see this." Jacob caught a whiff of her perfume as she set a manila folder on his desk. "The latest intel on Austrian casinos with unusual wins and losses."

"Thanks." Jacob flipped through the printouts, the grainy pictures of the major winners and losers. "No sign of Gold Tooth or the sniper, the one Riles calls Flattop."

"Armand probably withdrew him from circulation after the botched attempt on Riley's life."

"Question is—permanently?"

"No unidentified bodies in our morgues fit his description." She leaned a hip on his desk.

"Odd, this guy's showing the same pattern at every casino." Jacob jabbed a finger on a man's photo, gelled dark hair gleaming beneath the casino lights, every stitch of his suit hand-tailored. "And he visits them all. Regular as clockwork."

Jacob studied the copy of the man's passport, required to purchase and cash in chips. "Klaus Amersfoort, if we can believe that. Have your guys run a background check on him."

"Already done. His Amsterdam apartment is registered to a Mohammed Kalil. Six bank accounts registered to Amersfoort in Switzerland, the Netherlands, Belgium, France, Germany, and Austria. All with hefty deposits and shifting of funds."

The tiniest leap zinged through Jacob's chest. Had they found a solid lead to Armand's money laundering in Austrian casinos? "Where's the money coming from?"

"Probably human labor and sex trafficking."

His stomach wrenched. "How's business in Austria?"

"Sadly, sex trafficking is booming. Law enforcement turns a blind eye to all those brothels. After all, Vienna is an international city, home to the UN, OPEC, the International Atomic Energy Agency, diplomats, businessmen looking for a good time. It's lucrative for our economy."

He slapped the folder shut. How could men treat women like this? "Keep digging on Amersfoort. I want to know what he eats for breakfast, where he shops and hangs out, and everyone he contacts."

"On it." Heels clacking, Margot headed toward her office.

If he could mount his own stakeout at the casinos—no, but he couldn't, not until Riles was well. And if Armand nabbed her—*Be wise, Coulter.* The enemy's tactic of divide and conquer had worked well in the church for centuries. Was Tracy's disappearance a feint, or the first step to harm her?

Was Armand dangling a casino bag man in front of them to keep their attention away from where it should be? Jacob slid out the list of dates the guy had visited the gambling houses. Not exactly predictable. No if-it's-Tuesday-it-must-be-Vienna schedule. He ran his finger over the data. Sometimes, after gambling in another town, the bag man had returned to a casino he'd visited two days ago.

With the botched attempt on Riley's life at Casino Velden, Armand surely realized Interpol would be watching the casinos. Maybe this guy didn't work for Armand. "Hey Margot, the way he zigzags back and forth, do you think he's meeting with someone, picking up more funds to launder?"

She stepped from her office, ashen faced. "Could be." She

handed him a printed-out photo. "This just came in from the police."

"Gold Tooth." The man had been shot execution style. His crumpled body lay on a shaded hillside between a copse of trees. "Any idea where they found him?"

"In the Vienna Woods. Above Grinzing."

Grinzing, one of Vienna's historic wealthy suburbs, home to vineyards and new wine that could turn imbibers into dithering idiots. "Then he was still tracking us. But who'd take him out?"

"Maybe Armand eliminates shoddy workmanship." She leaned a hip on his desk. "Do you think he's called off his assassins?"

"If Armand pulled the Czech off the assignment and had this guy killed, no doubt he assigned someone new. Someone we won't see coming."

Someone we won't suspect.

30

"Why are you having me stalked?" Tracy fumed into the phone.

In the background on his cell, a Dutch game show blared on Mrs. DeBeers' television.

Tracy must be in her bedroom. Thank God, she'd finally decided to answer his calls. At his office desk, Jacob shoved aside his cold coffee, the latest police reports on Gold Tooth's death. "Why did you shake him this afternoon?"

"None of your business. I don't like that you don't trust me."

"How can I, when you pull a stunt like this?" Harshness clipped his tone, but he couldn't help it. The bodyguard had reported she'd waltzed into the building shortly before five. Three hours ago.

"I'm thirteen. Almost a grown woman." Raucous laughter burst from the television.

How was he supposed to respond? She might look like an adult, and she'd displayed alarming savvy this afternoon, but her naïveté could get her killed. Blackness cloaked the office windows. "I didn't want to tell you this, but Armand tried to assassinate Riles and me last week."

"How do you know it was Armand?" A tremble crept into her voice.

"He has contracts out on us. I hired a bodyguard to keep you safe."

"Why would Papa Armand come after me?" Her voice shrilled into a wail.

Jacob gritted his teeth. How could she still think of that man as her papa? "Because you know enough about his operations to see him incarcerated for life."

The silence on her end melted into minutes. "When are you going to increase my allowance?" The petulant thirteen-year-old had returned.

"I'll think about it when your behavior is trustworthy."

"I want two hundred euros a month."

"Two hundred—after that shenanigan you pulled today—"

"I was home by five."

"That's not the point."

"Then what is? I want to get a job."

"You're underage. No one will hire you."

She snorted into the phone. "A lot you know."

"What you did today can't go unpunished. You're grounded for the next month."

"A month?" She screamed into his ear.

"You will be escorted to and from school. Daily. No meetings with friends. No movies. No coffee dates." If it weren't potentially dangerous, he'd take away her phone too.

"That's not fair. All I did was shake your tail."

"A very expensive tail whose job it is to keep you alive." Jacob's voice exploded into the cell. Why couldn't she understand he had her best interests at heart? "I love you. I care what happens to you."

"You have a funny way of showing it. Some parent you'll make."

He winced. What if she were right? He was never there for her. Or for Noel's orphaned son.

"I bet I know more about taking care of kids than you do."

"Probably so." What he knew wouldn't fill a text message. He forced a calm into his voice. "Nevertheless, the punishment stands. Your lockdown starts in the morning."

"I hate you." Tracy disconnected the call.

Right now, he'd like to wring her neck for frightening him. What other tricks did she know besides disabling her phone?

Venice, Italy

"THE RABBIT HAS NIBBLED THE CARROT."

"Ah, perfect." Armand saved his computer work, closed the laptop. Now he could activate the next part of his plan. He'd take out everyone Jacob held dear, then go for the man's jugular.

"I miss you. Do you think there's any way we could meet?"

"At the moment, it's too risky."

Her sigh reached through the phone. "I thought you'd say that. Aren't you concerned I'll look elsewhere?"

The phone nearly bent in his grip. They'd been together ten years. She'd refused to marry him, but that didn't mean he was ready to share her. "Would a pay raise change your mind?"

"What did you have in mind?"

"Name your price."

"Let me think about it. In the meantime, I'll watch over your interests here."

"What would I do without you?" He made kissing noises

into the phone. "Thank you, darling. I know I can count on you."

At her sultry laugh, his heartbeat shot into overdrive. "You haven't much choice, *Liebling*." Her phone line went dead.

For ten years she'd been his voice of reason. He poured a glass of water from the bedside carafe and drained it in one long gulp. She was right. The sniper had failed. The poison injection had failed. Tracy was still on the streets, free.

But not for long.

Wien

RILEY WHACKED the carrots into small slices on the cutting board. After years of living in Wien, she'd expected to visit favorite haunts, not be confined to her Vrbo apartment except for a short jaunt to the little Billa grocery store around the corner. An U-Bahn station lay only forty steps from her apartment. An easy subway ride to the opera house. And everywhere else in Wien. She plopped chunks of chicken into the pot, splattering the broth.

After watching the Austrian checkout clerk accuse two Muslim boys of stealing today, shopping elsewhere would be preferable. She tossed the veggies into the simmering broth. No wonder terrorist groups weren't starving for recruits.

With Jacob's office off-limits, she barely saw him. She thumped the dinner plates on the table in the living room.

No way was she staying cooped in here until Armand and his henchmen were caught. What part of let's-cut-our-vacation-short so we can find Armand didn't Jacob get?

His pre-arranged knock pattered on her door, and she let him in. As usual, the hallway was quiet as a tomb. One of the perks of renting a refurbished place in a 175-year-old building. Older neighbors, up-and-coming businessmen and women.

"Hey there." He rubbed the dark circles rimming his eyes. His suit looked as if he'd slept in it. How could she stay irritated with him?

"Hey there, yourself." She shut the door behind him and wrapped her arms around his neck, inhaled his faded aftershave, then settled her lips on his. He snugged her to him, and she sank into his kiss that tasted of coffee and bratwurst.

When he broke off the embrace, she rested her head on his chest. *Oh, God, please grant Jacob a breakthrough in this case. We can't survive like this.* More than anything, she wanted to be with him. Share his life, his heartaches. But if he kept shutting her out ...

"Tell me you were a good girl and didn't wander all over town today."

"Scout's honor." She raised two fingers. "Any news?"

"Yeah."

She served the chicken soup and salad while he filled her in on Gold Tooth and Tracy. After praying over the meal, she handed him the breadbasket. "Did Tracy give a reason for her vanishing act?"

"No. Just a demand for a two-hundred-euro allowance."

Riley choked on the broth. "What's she into with that kind of overhead?"

"Drugs?" His eyes begged her to say no.

But these days, so many families faced this crisis. She reached for his hand. "What are you going to do?"

"I don't know. I need to be there." Anguish ripped his voice. "And here."

"If I weren't in rehearsals, I'd fly to Brussels for you."

"No, you need to rest. Doctor's orders, remember?"

She cleared their plates and served the dessert. "Heiner's Stefanietorte." The thin layers of hazelnut cake and custard filling was one of her favorites. What was not to like from a family-owned *Konditoriei* in business since 1840? "With Gold Tooth out of the picture, I can move about the city."

"Not if Flattop is still on his payroll. Or if Armand hired a replacement." Sharpness edged his tone. "An assassin more efficient than the one I'm certain he had killed."

Every day now Jacob seemed more like Dad. She'd vowed never to marry a man like that. What would he be like, ten years into their marriage? Could she live with this? She massaged her temple. Easy now. Jacob had been under so much pressure. "I'll call the countess, hang around town with her. She made a great bodyguard at the casino."

"Sounds safe enough, despite her taste in party guests." He pushed aside his empty plate. "You know, two hundred euros is such a specific amount."

"If you ask me, it's absurd. I doubt you can come up with a list of tasks that merit even half the money." She put the dishes in the kitchen sink to soak, then walked him to the couch beneath the floor-to-ceiling windows. Everything had been tastefully decorated, classy contemporary furniture, a Persian rug over the antique herringbone flooring. Just the place for a good cuddle. She let him pull her onto his lap and snuggled against his chest.

"With Tracy under surveillance and no activity on her phone, she couldn't have had an appointment with anyone, other than a classmate." He rested his chin against Riley's forehead, his evening stubble tickling her skin. "Tomorrow I'm having security cameras installed in Mrs. DeBeers' apartment. Tracy won't be able to sneak out undetected."

31

Wien, Day 10

The owner of Jacob's apartment had furnished it with Biedermeier antiques. Satin striped upholstery and duvet, a beautiful clothes cupboard made of inlaid wood. Even Julia Child would balk at his tiny kitchenette. But not at the tablecloth on the two-seater table. Or the Persian rugs scattered on the herringbone floor. Personally, he would have gone with contemporary, but he might as well enjoy his piece of Austrian culture. Definitely wouldn't find it in Texas.

Laptop set aside on the table, he glanced at his watch. Tracy's bodyguard still hadn't checked in. If von Bingen hadn't kept him on a two-hour Zoom call, demanding fresh strategy to uncover Armand's ops and location before the night's end, he could've followed up earlier. He listened to his voicemail, then dialed the man's number. No answer. Fingers flying over the keyboard, he texted him.

Where are you, man? How's Tracy?

For the umpteenth time that day, Jacob's phone rang. Who

169

was it now, von Bingen? Margot's latest list of casino wins and losses? Riles wanting him to come for supper? Right now, he needed to hatch a new plan for his boss. Contact the security detail.

"Jacob, Jacob," Bomma's voice shrilled into his ear.

His blood ran cold. "What's happened, Mrs. DeBeers?"

"Tracy's missing."

"How do you know?" The question came out hoarse.

"She didn't come home at five, and it's after seven now." Sobs peppered her words.

Dear God, no, no, no. And he was eleven hundred kilometers from home. "I haven't been able to reach her bodyguard."

"He's not at the café. I went over there as soon as she hadn't come home by five thirty. I've called and called her cell but there's no answer. What should I do?"

"Nothing. Stay in, stay safe. I'll call the police."

"This is all my fault."

"No. You mustn't blame yourself." It was his fault. He should've been there for Tracy.

One thing was certain, his sister didn't leave of her own accord. But she'd warned him. If he hadn't refused to increase her allowance, she wouldn't have run away. Unless she had a place to go. She was too much a creature of comforts. Armand had seen to that.

If her abductor planned to take Mrs. DeBeers next …

"Mrs. DeBeers, I want you to go to a hotel right now. Phone me when you get there, let me know where you stay."

"No, I won't do that. If Tracy comes home, I must be here."

"But you may be in danger." He filled her in on how Armand worked, pitting one person against the other. "I need to alert the police now. Talk to you shortly." He disconnected, then filed a report with the police sergeant.

"Do you know how many runaway cases I'm looking at on my desk right this minute?"

"More than you ever thought you'd see. But a known terrorist orchestrated this kidnapping. He has a contract out on Tracy, my fiancée, and me." The decibels in his voice soared close to a shout. By now Armand might have Riles too. "And the elderly woman who was looking after my sister in our absence may be next on the list."

The sergeant huffed into the phone. "These days, kids are always running away from home. I'll see what we can do. I have your contact information. We'll be in touch."

How could the man be so blasé? "Thank you." Jacob dialed Interpol. "I need a check on the whereabouts of a private bodyguard I hired to protect my kid sister." He left his contact information, called Riles. When she answered on the first ring, he choked back tears. "Hon, are you okay?"

"Yes. Why do you ask?"

"Tracy's missing. I think Armand's behind this. You may be next."

"Are you sure about Tracy?"

"I don't have any proof, but her bodyguard is MIA too."

"What do you want me to do?" Her voice was as taut as a guitar string.

"Stay in your apartment. Keep the doors bolted. I'll be there as soon as I can. Don't answer the door unless you recognize my signal."

"One of our old hymns?"

"You got it." Right now, he ought to hum a few of them for himself.

"Honey, sure you don't want me to come be with you?"

"No. Best stay where you are. I've got to think this through, plot a strategy."

"I'm pretty good at plotting."

The soothing lilt in her voice almost sold him. "Yes, but I don't want you out on the streets. Tracy didn't make it home from school."

"What about Mrs. DeBeers?"

"She's fine." Sweat dribbled down his armpits. "This was an abduction waiting to happen." He knew it. Why hadn't he been able to prevent it? He was supposed to be a protector, wasn't he? An Interpol agent. A future husband. Big brother to a kid sister who didn't know right from wrong most of the time. "I-I've got to go. Love you." He smooched into the phone.

Jacob paced the Persian rugs. Raked his hand through his hair. *Dear God, help. Only You can fix this situation. I come to You for wisdom.* He couldn't afford any wrong moves here. *Give us swift breakthroughs.*

"Please, God, I'm asking You for miracles." Choking back tears, he fisted his hand to his lips. *Be with Tracy right now.* She must be terrified. How had Armand managed to lure her?

No matter what it took, he'd find the creep and bring him to justice. *Really? How realistic is that?* He shoved away the thought.

His phone rang again. An unknown caller ID. "Jacob Coulter here."

"Sergeant Villiers, Interpol police." The man cleared his throat. "I found your bodyguard."

Tentacles of dread wrapped around Jacob's chest. "How is he?"

"Dead. Someone left a perfectly placed stiletto drilled between his ribs. Bloody hilt and all. Must've punctured his heart."

One more death he was responsible for. Jacob sank onto the kitchen chair. Did the man have a family, a wife, and kids? "Where did you find him?"

"Near a dumpster behind the café where he staked out the apartment building."

Why hadn't he insisted Mrs. DeBeers leave? "Please go to apartment twenty-five across the street." Jacob gave the address. "Insist and accompany Mrs. DeBeers to a hotel." Tracy wouldn't be coming back tonight. Maybe never. He'd have to tell their parents. Sooner or later. They had a right to know. The more people praying for her, the better. "Text me with Mrs. DeBeers' hotel address please. Make sure you're not followed."

"Will do. I'm so sorry." The officer disconnected the call.

Jacob called von Bingen and filled her in.

"I'm sure you want to hop on the next flight to Brussels. Don't. If you do, you're falling into Armand's trap. He's trying to lure you away from Austria, from his operations."

"I agree." At least their Zoom chat hadn't been a total waste of time. Jacob dialed Brussels Interpol, brought the officer up to date. "I'm sending you a picture of Tracy. Expand the search through all Brussels' neighborhoods. No doubt Armand has numerous terrorist contacts in the area. See if anyone saw her. If she made it to school this morning."

"On it."

"Thanks." He pocketed his cell, gave in to the sobs he'd barely suppressed. "Oh, God, forgive me. I'm such a failure. I failed to protect those you placed in my hands. Forgive me." But even forgiveness wouldn't bring back Tracy. With everything in him, he wanted to book the next flight to Brussels, but he couldn't leave Riles unprotected. And if Wien was Armand's base of operations, this was the place to be.

The text ping sounded on his phone. Riles.

You have a job to do.

Maybe this is what that scripture meant, laying your family on the altar, choosing whatever God has asked you to do over your family's welfare. Riles was right. He couldn't guarantee Tracy would survive, but clearly, Armand wanted him out of Austria. No way was he falling into that trap. He grabbed his overcoat, left her a voicemail. "I'll be at your place in about half an hour. I don't want you staying alone."

The studio apartment Margot had found him offered an

elevator. When it chose to work. Tonight, he double-timed the stairs to the ground floor. He raced to his car, popped a blue police light on top of his vehicle, and headed for Riles' apartment. Why hadn't they rented in the same building? He slapped the steering wheel. Because she insisted having her own place in the district she preferred.

Getting a grip on himself, he texted Margot the news.

> Tracy was too money hungry to leave
> home without a job in place.

> No doubt, courtesy of Armand.

> She'd hinted she could earn at least 200
> euros a month. Any ideas what type job
> she found?

Three dots bounced on his screen. Margot's response came through.

> An au pair position? Some agencies are
> quite unscrupulous.

His chest ignited. Some of those girls ended up sex-trafficked.

Lord, please don't let that happen to Tracy.

32

Venice, Italy, Day 10

Package delivered.

Chuckling, Armand allowed himself another glass of champagne while the room service waiter set up his dinner on the table. The text was almost too good to be true.

What wouldn't he give to see Jacob's reaction. The agent thought he was invincible. Well, he'd show him. He was on a super roll. Why stop now?

Bill signed for, linen napkin whipped over his lap, Armand tucked into his meal. The bechamel sauce on his pasta oozed across his tongue. Exquisite. If he stayed in Venice much longer, he might have to set up some operations here. After all, the city wasn't that far from Vienna. Maybe he should rent a yacht, sail around Italy, and enter Austria from another border.

He texted a return message.

Call me when you can.

His phone rang almost immediately. "Tell me all about it."

175

"*Liebling.*" Her laughed tinkled into the phone. "I wish you could have been here to see this one."

"Hmm. I'm sure it was sweet."

"Oh, very."

"Did she sign willingly?"

"Yes. She called me on the special phone, and said she was ready to sign. I arranged a pickup date and place. Somewhere I was sure she'd never been. But not so seedy she'd be suspicious."

"Was she?"

"Oh, no. She arrived, backpack in hand. As soon as she signed the contract, she asked if we could buy some extra clothing. To avoid arousing suspicion, she'd left home without a suitcase. I told her she wouldn't need clothes where she was going."

"How did she take that?"

Another laugh in his ear. "I wish you could've seen the alarm on her face. She backed away, head whipping left and right, looking for somewhere to run. My two cohorts crept up behind her. Before she could scream, one of them shoved the chloroformed cloth over her nose and mouth, then dropped a burlap bag over her head. She was off in La-La Land in no time. You can see for yourself how she takes it when she wakes up."

He grunted. Not likely. Jacob probably had alerts out for his face on every CCTV camera in the city. "How did she get rid of her bodyguard?"

"Easy. I told her to leave school by the janitor's room. That gate isn't locked during school hours."

"Well done. You thought of everything. Did you get the pictures?"

"Of course. You'll love them. They should be coming through any second."

At the ping on his phone, he clicked on the first photo. Above Tracy's panic-stricken face, the Stella Artois sign glowed red. The architecture was unmistakably Belgian, the narrow building, the gabled bricks. "How ever did you manage that?"

"Photoshop, *Liebling*."

He held the picture closer. It had fooled him, but would Jacob spot anything wrong? Nabbing her in a Brussels neighborhood where no one would care what happened to her had been one of his more brilliant ideas. Not even the police entered the area. If only he could be a fly on the wall, watch Jacob suffer when he saw Tracy's abduction.

"I recorded our meeting at the café."

Static crackled in his ear.

"There." He recognized Tracy's voice. A thump on the table. "Serves him right."

At her grumpy tone, he chuckled. "I'm indebted to you for a job well done."

"Anytime. When will I see you?" Her voice was melted butter to his ear.

He toyed with his fork. Did he dare risk letting her come to him? Her presence would relieve the boredom.

"Or do you have other business deals for me to close for you right now?" Once again, she'd tactfully bailed him out.

"Soon, but it might be best not to come right now. I'll be in touch."

"As you wish."

"A courier will deliver your reward."

"I'd much rather have you."

If she purred into the phone one more time, he'd tell her to hop on the next plane. Instead, he said, "In due time."

She blew a kiss into the phone before he disconnected.

Now on to his next victim.

Wien

WHAT KIND of big brother was he, leaving Tracy alone with an eighty-five-year-old surrogate grandmother? Jacob sank on the easy chair in Riles' apartment, the stiff cushion unforgiving beneath his thighs. Steam escaped the soup pot on the stove, slapped the lid. The scent of chicken and garlic nauseated him. Right now, he didn't care if he ever ate again.

Each tick on the mantle clock jangled his nerves like a firing squad cocking their rifles. He'd known Armand was dangerous, that he'd lash out where it hurt most. *Oh, Tracy, forgive me.* He cradled his head in his palms.

"Honey." Riles settled on the armrest, her Chanel No. 5 enveloping him. Her fingertips squeezed his shoulder, barely penetrating his knotted muscles. "I know how you feel—"

He yanked free from her touch. "Do you?"

A gulp escaped her throat. She slid her hand onto her lap. "It ... may not be the same, but I blamed myself for Lacy's death. I carried that pain for years."

But her twin sister's death from leukemia wasn't the same thing. Medicine had done all it could to save her life. What had he done to safeguard his kid sister? A security detail, but ...

"My parents left Tracy in my charge." Vinegar curdled his voice, but he was beyond caring.

"No ..." Her gentle tone dinged off his invisible armor. "To protect her, they chose to put her in boarding school and left you to fill the holes in her heart." Her fingers fluttered to a wayward curl at her temple. "That may sound harsh, but you're assuming a guilt load God didn't intend you to carry."

"You don't understand. Being separated from their children is agony for missionaries." But had it been for his parents? He could tick off both thumbs, the times he recalled any tenderness from his mother. Forget about Father.

Nestled against his side, Riles pressed her cheek against his, his muscles rigid as steel. "Perhaps your parents blocked off their feelings, thinking it would shield you from their anguish."

"Yeah. Uh-huh." But he wasn't counting on it.

"Nevertheless, we must forgive others." The wetness from her tears dribbled onto his face. "And if we don't forgive ourselves, guilt, shame, and condemnation will destroy us from the inside out."

"But if only I'd been there—" The crack in his voice ripped his throat.

"Armand would've gotten to Tracy another day."

"Maybe."

Riles' warm sigh brushed his cheek. "I'll bet the hardest parenting lesson is letting go of your children."

"We aren't dealing with her first bike ride without training wheels." At the snarl in his voice, he cringed.

"Tracy's a teenager. She wants to try her own wings. Mistakes and all."

"Yeah, I get that." But he'd promised himself to keep her safe. How could she trust men again? "I'm a law enforcement officer. I'm supposed to *protect* citizens."

"Okay, Superman, apart from God, you can do nothing. Let's ask Him to reveal His strategy to rescue her."

A smile quirked a corner of his lips. Take-charge Riles. He needed her almost as much as he needed God. Sighing, he bowed his head. "Okay." But forgive himself? No ... never.

33

Wien, Day 11

"Riles, I'm thinking of leaving Interpol." Jacob sagged against her refrigerator door. His day had been fruitless. No new clues on Tracy's whereabouts, or the goons running Armand's casino ops.

"What?" She wiped her hands on the dish towel. "Why?"

"I'm tired of putting my loved ones in danger."

"You can't be serious." She thumped two dinner plates on the kitchen table. "You're a superb agent. Look at all you've accomplished the past three months."

"Right. You've nearly been killed—how many times now?" He swallowed over the boulder jamming his throat. "You don't really think Armand intends to let Tracy live, do you?"

With a sigh, Riles turned to the counter, knife whacking through the carrots, onion, potatoes, a ninja chef on steroids.

Obviously, she didn't think so, either. "You deserve to build a career without one eye over your shoulder to spot the latest murderer on your tail."

"Okay." She laid down the knife. Turned to him, her face placid.

How much had it cost her to paste on that expression?

"If you're determined to leave Interpol, what do you intend to do with your life?"

He shrugged. "Go back to the police force."

"Where? In America?"

Hand raked through his hair, he shrugged again. "I guess so. Can't think of anything else I can do over here."

"Honey." She wrapped her arms around his chest and kissed his cheek. "Whatever you decide to do is fine with me. But this is exactly what Armand wants you to do. He's trying to intimidate you, destroy you emotionally." She led him to the couch in the living room. "He's hit you where it hurts most."

Not quite. He hadn't taken Riles. *Thank God.*

"Let's pray about this and come up with a solution. Do you think Armand is in Vienna?"

"I don't know." Jacob sat, kneaded his knuckles. "He could be anywhere. With today's technology, you don't have to be in a country to control it. He lost his top lieutenant but he's not hurting for people willing to work for him. Willing to assassinate for him. Willing to kidnap—" His voice broke.

She scooted closer, her palm warm on his, and brought his hand to her lips. "Lord. we need your help. We need a miracle, and we need it swiftly. Please protect Mrs. DeBeers and those searching for Tracy. Comfort her, wherever she is. May she know Your tangible presence, Lord. If she's never asked You to be her Lord and Savior, I pray she'll do that right now."

Fresh moisture pooled in Jacob's eyes. Riles was right. The last thing he wanted was Tracy to die and not spend eternity in heaven. He had to leave her in God's hands, no matter what happened to her. *God promises to work things together for our good,* the voice niggled his mind. *Do you really believe that?* Yes. God's word is truth. "I'd like to sleep on your couch tonight.

Make sure you don't have any visitors." He'd probably lie awake wherever he spent the night.

"Of course." As she slid her arm around his chest, his phone rang.

"Mrs. DeBeers, how are you?" He activated the speaker.

"Fine." Her voice wobbled. "I'm at the hotel."

"Yes, Interpol notified me." He braced himself before asking. "Have you heard from Tracy?"

"No, I'm afraid not."

"Could you walk me through the last forty-eight hours with her? Did she do or say anything out of the norm?" He laced his fingers in Riley's. Snuggling close, she nestled against his chest.

"Well ... when we watched TV together on the couch, I'd catch her staring at me, tears in her eyes. I didn't know what to make of it. I thought maybe she thought I was such an old woman I wasn't gonna live much longer. Instead ..." Sobs bled into the phone.

"I understand." He compressed his lips against his own flood of tears.

Finally, she sniffed a few times. "This morning—no last night when I went in to say goodnight to her, she shoved some clothes inside her cupboard. She closed the door and tried to block it. I guess so I couldn't see what she'd been doing. Then she ran to me, clung so tightly I could barely breathe."

Oh, Tracy, Tracy. What were you about to do? Was Armand behind her disappearance, or were the police right? She was a runaway who'd found a way to earn money on her own. But where, and how?

"I should have known something was wrong. I should have recognized the signs. I'm so sorry, Jacob. Please forgive me. I failed you."

"No, no. It's I who failed you, Mrs. DeBeers." He'd failed everyone. Everyone he loved and cared about. Riles squeezed his hand. Swallowing hard, he forced himself to continue.

"When she left for school this morning, did everything seem normal?"

"Yes. Well, no. I didn't think about it at the time, but her backpack was bulging."

"Did she take her textbooks?"

"I always check her room after she leaves. To make sure she made her bed. She'd taken all her schoolbooks and notebooks."

If Mrs. DeBeers were still at home, she'd probably find some clothes missing. His sister had planned this. She must have been in cahoots with someone. Someone who lured her out of her safety net. Convinced her she'd have all the money she wanted. For whatever reason.

If only he'd upped her allowance. No. That would never have worked. This was about something deeper than increasing her cash flow.

"I want you to stay at the hotel until I tell you it's safe to go home. Rack up that room service charge or eat in the restaurant, but do not leave the building. You hear me?"

"Yes, Jacob. I don't want to cause you anymore worry. Take care, my boy. You're in my thoughts and prayers. Give Riley a kiss for me."

"Will do." He hung up, pulled Riles so close their heartbeats synchronized into one galloping roar.

RILEY SLID from Jacob's embrace. What had happened to the man she'd fallen in love with? Bouts of depression were so unlike him. Was it a massive guilt trip because he couldn't protect them?

"I'm starved. Let's go out to dinner." A good meal usually pulled him out of the doldrums. She hopped off the couch, grabbed her coat from the wall hook. Plopped on her hat, wrapped the cashmere scarf around her throat. Some people thought singers' neck-scarf fetish was an affectation. But the fabric helped protect the throat from the damp Viennese weather and impossible-to-cure catarrh. That blight had hindered many a singer's career. She waited by the door while he shuffled over to her.

"I thought we were eating here."

"Nope. I'll make the stew when I get home. We can have it tomorrow. A bit of fresh air will do us good." And time away from this oppressive atmosphere. She grabbed her purse, linked arms with him, and headed them toward the elevator. "We can plot a way to flush out Armand."

"How do you propose we do that?"

"Make things so hot for him that he comes to Wien to check it out. Two can play his game, you know."

For the first time since he'd arrived, a light shone in his eyes. "I'm open to suggestions."

"We've prayed about this. We must believe God has a solution. Armand is going to lose this battle. Permanently." She didn't know how, but it had to end that way. Somehow.

His phone rang. BRUSSELS INTERPOL. He put the call on speaker. "Any news?"

"No, but we may have figured out where Tracy was kidnapped. Our satellite imagery matches the building in the photos that were sent to you. It's in Molenbeek."

"Great. Terrorist territory. No surprise there."

"We've canvassed the café. No one saw her. She was never inside the building, if we can believe the owners," the agent said.

"Either they're lying, or ... could the picture be photoshopped? Thanks." He pocketed his phone. "We're still flying blind. With no idea if they've hurt her." His voice choked off. "Or if she's still alive."

34

At their restaurant table, the scent of Wiener Schnitzel fried in olive oil and butter and garlic almost nauseated Jacob. He ought to eat but his appetite had fled with Tracy's disappearance. He stabbed a bite of parslied potato, choked it down.

"Let's review what we know about Armand's ops in Austria."

He speared another bite of potato, pushed the rest of them around his plate. "Not much."

"You have proof he's using casinos for money laundering."

"Check."

She stabbed a bite of Wiener Schnitzel. "We know government-backed prostitution is right up his alley."

"Check." He sawed off a bite of Wiener Schnitzel. Forced himself to chew it.

"We uncover who finances these brothels, check into their history."

Napkin to his mouth, he dabbed his lips. "Margot and I are

185

working on that. But none of this leads us to Tracy." He pushed his plate aside.

"Jacob ..." Riles stroked the back of his hand. "You can't bring her back."

Her words sucker-punched his gut. But she was right. As usual.

"That's up to other agents. Instead, we try to capture Armand, her kidnapper."

"Okay." He sipped his water. "Let's focus on what we can do right now, stuck in Vienna."

"We have to rip this man's operations apart scene by scene."

"Spoken like a true opera singer." He snatched a Semmel from the breadbasket and took a bite. "I've had Margot checking bank accounts for exorbitant cash deposits."

"What if he's not using banks this time? What if he's flying low level, funneling it through purchases of goods instead?"

"That's harder to trace."

"Exactly." Riley set her knife and fork on her plate. "Regarding prostitution, I had the impression all the countess's guests wear horse blinders."

Jacob signaled for the bill. "We don't know that for a fact."

"Okay. Where does the judge stand on the issue since he was so quick to condemn me? Apart from you, Austria's legal beagle may have been the only honest man at the party. Scary thought, huh?"

35

Day 12

Seated on the doctor's examining table, Riley crossed her ankles, pulled the paper sheath closer around her body. He'd run so many tests she felt like an over-jabbed pin cushion.

The door opened. Stepping inside, Dr. Falken thrust his hands into his white lab coat pockets. "I can find nothing wrong with you."

"*Gut.* When will the headaches go away? Singing makes me dizzy." She might not have to ride a motorcycle in this production, but she'd be performing from a catwalk six miles above the stage. Maybe he'd give her something for her fear of heights. She shuddered. Just what she wanted, more meds.

"I need to make certain I have the strength to do my role. This debut is quite important." Like make or break her career.

"I understand your concern, Fräulein Williams. I can give you something for the headaches and the vertigo." He rolled over a stool, pulled out his prescription pad. "The good news is, there is no brain bleed, and you have no blood clots. Your

187

arteries are clear, so you should be fine in time. Get plenty of rest and try to stay stress free."

Stress free, with Tracy kidnapped? Peachy, just peachy. "Thank you, Doctor." She took the prescriptions, shook his hand.

He left the room, and she drew on her pantsuit and low-heeled shoes. As she passed his office, Dr. Falken held a microphone to his mouth. "The male patient, a citizen of the UK, shows signs of syphilitic infection which he claims he caught in the brothel Excalibur."

Excalibur? She stopped outside his door. She'd seen the place in the first district. Super ritzy. It looked more like an exclusive hotel than a den of iniquity.

"I have recommended the following treatment."

A nurse glanced at her from the desk down the hall.

Fussing with her shoulder bag, she ambled toward the Kassa.

While the receptionist processed her insurance card, Riley signed the paperwork. Card in hand, she walked through the waiting room.

Seated in the corner, a man held his forehead in his hands. The buttons threatened to burst from his too-tight suit jacket. The woman next to him massaged his shoulders, her voice barely above a whisper.

Riley startled. British accents. Where had she seen these people? She opened her purse, took her time slipping her insurance card inside her wallet. Think, think. They weren't in Velden. Or at the countess's party.

"Don't worry puppy cakes." The woman patted his hand. "They can treat that disease these days."

"Yes, but I'm already seeing a neurologist for it."

"You just need to stay clean for a while. Stay away from the girlies."

Eyes closed, Riley searched her memory bank. A gasp

caught in her throat. London, at Armand's gala. They'd sat on the first row. Shivers zinged across her shoulder blades. She'd never forget the man's lecherous gaze as she sang that night.

Outside the clinic, she headed up the street. Orange and gold leaves fluttered at her feet. Riley wrapped her scarf close around her neck, pulled up the collar on her trench coat, and dialed Jacob. "We have a lead."

"Aren't you supposed to be at the doctor's office?"

"I am. I mean I was. He gave me a shiny gold star." She told him what she'd overheard him dictate and about the couple in the waiting room.

"Are you sure?"

"Absolutely. Wouldn't forget that guy." She entered the park and sat on a bench. "The doctor even named the brothel. Excalibur."

"If the man told him the truth."

"True. But it's worth checking out, don't you think?" Leaves fluttered from the branches and settled at her feet.

"We know Armand hires others to do his dirty work, keeps his own hands clean. Makes sure he's out of the country or out of the way when his biggest ops go down."

"Okay. Maybe this slimebag is doing his dirty work for him now."

"You think he's hired a new lieutenant?"

"That overweight lech? No. But we know he's hired several somewhat incompetent assassins. Thankfully, for our sakes." A woman walked toward the bench, her hand around a toddler's wrist. "Jacob, do you really think Tracy would go off with that man?"

"No. No, I don't. I think she went off with a woman."

"A female she trusted." The toddler stopped to pick up a fallen leaf, and the woman's smile radiated utter adoration. "Someone who made her feel good about herself, gave her the affirmation she so desperately needs."

"Yeah, and all I do is tell her no allowance and straighten up and fly right."

"That's your job, Jacob." Riles turned aside on the bench, lowered her voice. "You're a surrogate parent, trying to recalibrate her moral compass."

"Yeah. Right. And doing a brilliant job with that." His sigh settled in her heart. "So, we look for some woman in Brussels who acted as Armand's go-between."

"Yes. In the CCTV photos of Amira, a woman accompanied her. I'll bet Armand has them chaperone his daughter and report what she says and does." A pigeon waddled toward Riley and waited at her feet expectantly. "Why not approach Tracy the same way?" She rummaged in her purse for a packet of crackers.

"Finding needles in haystacks would be simpler than locating Amira's female bodyguards. Or Tracy's."

"I suspect Amira would turn to a man as easily as she'd run to a woman. If she felt the man wouldn't betray her to her father." Riley tossed the bird a few cracker crumbs.

"I agree. If only we could bring her in, check her phone, trace her calls, see if Armand tried to reach her."

Riley scattered the rest of the cracker bits on the sidewalk. "From those shopping bags, Amira didn't seem too worried about lack of money."

"You think she has access to Armand's bank accounts?"

"I don't know. She could be staying with a woman she trusts, someone who can loosen his purse strings." Riley stashed her trash in her purse and rose from the bench.

"I think you're right, Riles. Send me your consulting fee for Interpol."

She laughed. "Von Bingen would love that. Seriously, we've seen how susceptible he is to female charms. I think he assigns men to do the dirty work, buys their loyalty, but doesn't trust them with the checkbook."

36

Voices thrummed throughout the Interpol office, cell phones shrilled, nervous agents tapped computer keyboards. A headache hammered Jacob's eye sockets. He pushed aside his fourth cup of coffee, stomach revolting at the smell of more caffeine. The black hand on the wall clock dropped with the finality of a guillotine.

Every minute without a lead on Tracy's whereabouts hurtled them closer to losing her. Or finding her lifeless body. Armand would never let Tracy live. Her knowledge of his operations had become a deadly liability.

No, don't go there. Focus on something uplifting. A Bible verse that offered comfort, hope. A decree of victory he could cling to. God's word was filled with those.

"This just came in from von Bingen." For once, Margot's perfume had faded, and the faint scent of sweat clung to her black suit.

Jacob stared at the All-Points-Bulletin she'd laid on his desk. "A five-thousand-euro reward for any information leading to Tracy's whereabouts." Good. No mention of terrorists or Tracy's ability to lead to their arrest. *God, bring us someone who'll speak the truth.* "Who put up the money?"

A flush colored Margot's cheeks. "Is there anything I can do for you?"

"Thanks for asking." He swiped a hand over his stubbled jaw. "Sometimes people become arrogant, too confident. That was Armand's mistake in London. He overplayed his hand, hadn't counted on Riles' savvy and my—my—"

"Bulldog tenacity," she said. "All we need is our fangs into one solid clue."

Maybe there was a compassionate bone in her body. Maybe he'd misread her. One thing was clear, he hadn't laid Tracy on God's altar. Abraham had to do it with his son, Isaac. Tears clogged Jacob's throat. He hadn't let God be solely responsible for her and the outcome of her abduction. He squeezed the corners of his eyes.

God, help me truly trust You to take care of her.

"You're thinking if you went to Brussels, you'd be the one to find her. But our agents there are excellent."

Not trusting his voice, he nodded. Every fiber in his body urged him to take the next flight out of Austria. He clicked the mouse to a web search.

Margot's intake of air was sharp. "Armand wants you to do exactly that. Then he'll move in for the kill here in Wien."

Move in for the kill—was Riles next on his list? His scalp tingled at the thought. The screws in his muscles ratcheted a notch. Oh, God, what should he do?

That verse in Psalm 92, God gives us the ability to stay calm in the time of adversity until the wicked have been caught.

Right now, he needed an overdose of Godly calm. He might not be able to rescue Tracy, but he'd bring down Armand. Somehow.

"Let's set a few traps for Amira and the woman who'd shopped with Armand."

ONE MORE HOUR in her apartment, and she'd have gone bonkers. No matter how desperate Jacob felt, he wouldn't break Interpol rules and invite her to his office. Even if she could help him find Tracy.

Riley stepped off the U-Bahn in the first district, strolled along the Graben, another elegant walking street that intersected the Kärtnerstrasse and turned onto Kohlmarkt. Home to Russian oligarchs and a dizzying array of designers' stores. Bulgari, Burberry, Dior, Fendi, Gucci, and others. The amount of wealth lurking in the first district was staggering. No wonder Amira felt at home here.

The scent of designers' perfumes wafted onto the street. Almost every Baroque-era building had been renovated inside, sleek, modern with brightly lit interiors. She gawked at the exquisite outfits and accessories hanging in the windows. Even a button was out of her price range.

Expensively dressed customers roamed inside, but the shops weren't mobbed with customers like Stieffel's Department Store. She passed Fendi's, then paused outside Gucci's. A well-dressed salesclerk stood near as a woman thumbed through a rack of blouses. The client turned sideways.

No. Could that really be Margot? Since when could Interpol agents afford designer originals?

She pulled out three items, handed the garments to the salesclerk, then glanced toward Riley. Margot's face hardened.

Yikes. No place to hide. An open walking street. Flat glass-paned storefronts. Not even a potted plant she could duck behind.

Head high, Margot followed the sales assistant to the fitting rooms, her high-heeled steps as confident as a five-star general. There could be a back exit, a dingy alley. Should she tail her?

Was Margot an agent on the take? A mole inside Interpol could explain why Armand was always six miles ahead of them. And the woman's antagonism toward Jacob, wanting him ousted. Riley strolled to the outdoor café across from Gucci and sat at an outdoor table. She dialed Jacob's cell.

"Riley," a voice called out from the street.

Rats. Just what she needed. An interloper on her surveillance. She disconnected her call. "Countess, how lovely to see you."

"And you too." The woman sat beside her, smoothed the navy cashmere slacks she'd paired with a cream turtleneck and subtle Burberry plaid shawl.

Someday Riley would earn enough to afford nice clothing. Not from Fendi or Chanel or any place special, just quality made. Right now, she had to invest in stunning evening gowns, *de rigeur* for a singer. Thankfully, the IRS considered them her professional uniform.

"How are you feeling?"

"Much better, thank you." Not exactly true, but she wasn't a sympathy seeker. The countess might have a loose tongue and loose lips still sank ships. A few rumors of ill health, suggesting her performances wouldn't be up to par, could sink Riley's reputation at the Staatsoper.

"Won't you come for tea?"

"That's so kind of you." What was taking Margot so long? If she had vanished via a back alley, Jacob would see to it she was caught.

The woman's gaze narrowed on Riley. "Tell me how you really feel."

"Fine. Absolutely fine, no more headaches." Well, maybe a few. Margot came out of the dressing room, snagged several hangers of slacks, a few jackets, an evening gown. "Rehearsals are going well. How are you?"

She patted Riley's hand. "You must come to tea. How about tomorrow at four?"

"*Danke.* I look forward to it." Tea with the countess. She'd need a hostess gift.

"*Gut. Auf Wiedersehen.*" Leaving a cloud of perfume in her wake, the woman strolled toward the Kärntnerstrasse.

How much longer was Margot planning to shop? Riley ordered coffee and a *Wurst mit Senf*, a sausage with mustard. Savoring each bite, she sipped her coffee. If she sat here much longer, the waiter might accuse her of loitering.

Storm clouds brewed overhead, scenting diesel fumes and dust with the promise of rain. Being caught in a chilly drizzle wasn't good for her throat. *Hurry up, Margot.* Hadn't Jacob noticed her absence from the office?

The first big drops slithered through Riley's curls, moistening her turtleneck. Jacket collar flipped up, she scrunched her neck into her damp wool scarf and scurried inside the café, watched Gucci's from the window. In this downpour Margot wouldn't stroll down the street.

She could call Jacob again, but his plate was overloaded, searching for Tracy, Armand, and Amira. Nope she'd make this her mission.

When the shower let up, Margot stepped out of the store. Riley blocked her path, shivering. "Find something you liked?" She nodded toward the bulging green sacks in Margot's hands.

The agent's chin shot upward. "*Ja,* I did."

"Hmm ... must be nice shopping at Gucci's."

"It is. Maybe someday you can do it too." Margot's icy smile needled beneath Riley's skin.

Not likely. "Does Jacob know where you are?"

"*Ja.* Thank you for not blowing my cover."

"Your cover?"

"*Ja*, he wanted an undercover agent here in case Amira or the woman Armand was seen shopping with came in."

"Brilliant." But who was paying the tab?

A sliver of a smile flitted across Margot's face. "I don't need my job at Interpol. My inheritance and trust money provide quite nicely for me."

"Oh." Why didn't the pavement open and swallow her? Once again, she'd misjudged someone. Armand had bamboozled her in London. Now she'd allowed jealousy's tentacles to poison her opinion of Margot. "Did you see anyone we're looking for?"

"*Nein*. But according to our records, this is the time of day they were sighted."

"Uh-huh." Spotting Amira, no problem. But unless the salesclerk pointed out Armand's mistress, how would Margot recognize her? Maybe she was relying on women's intuition.

"Happy hunting, enjoy your new clothes."

"I shall." Margot's superior smile was back in place.

Riley smoothed her jacket lapels. Compared to the countess and Margot's designer outfits, her pantsuit wasn't even shabby chic. Maybe that's how Tracy felt, losing access to the finest couturiers in the world. Doing without or living with less was a tough lesson to learn. Always better to be satisfied and grateful for what you have.

Sidestepping puddles, Riley strolled the glistening pavers. Fingers of sunshine pierced the ominous clouds, God's hand separating the darkness. Right now, they needed a ray of hope. Fast. Her days in Vienna were numbered.

She strolled toward Tuchlauben, the medieval street named for cloth cutters, with the oldest secular frescoes in Wien, now home to Chanel, Louis Vuitton, and Jimmy Choo shoes.

A few doors down, the British woman from Dr. Falken's waiting room entered the Chanel store.

No way was she missing this op. Phone out, Riley snapped

the woman's photo as she meandered around the display table, picked up a quilted leather bag. Pasting on a curtain-call smile, Riley strode inside and sidled next to her. "Hello. How delightful to see you again."

The woman turned, her face stiff as baroque stonework. "You too."

"Do you shop here often?"

"When I'm in Vienna." The Brit examined another purse on the table. "And what are you doing here?"

Ignoring the veiled insult, Riley opened a clutch, nearly choked at the price tag. "I'm making my debut at the Wiener Staatsoper."

"Hmm. Another round of antics as the Queen of the Night I suppose?"

"The Queen of the Night, yes. Antics no." At least she hoped not. Her London and Antwerp fiascos were enough for a lifetime. "Where are you staying in Vienna?" A rude question but Jacob needed every lead she could get.

The woman drew herself taller, her chin barely reaching Riley's chest. "We always stay at the Hotel Sacher."

"A lovely place. I enjoy it so much." Not that she'd spent the night there, but she'd dined there. Once.

"If you'll excuse me ..." The woman snatched the bag in Riley's hand and walked to the Kassa.

Now what? Flee in humiliation or stay?

A saleswoman gave Riley's pantsuit a onceover. "May I help you?"

"*Ja* ..." Riley scanned the shop. What color didn't they have on the floor? "I was looking for a pale lavender pantsuit."

The woman's brow rose. "I believe not, but I shall check."

"*Danke.*" *Dear God, don't let them have a slew of lavender suits in the storeroom.*

The Londoner chose a second bag. The salesclerk rang up

the sale and the woman brushed past Riley and sauntered out the door.

She could hardly follow her outside, but she needed to know where the woman went.

The saleswoman returned to the floor. "I'm afraid lavender is not one of Chanel's colors this season."

What a relief. "That's too bad. Perhaps I'll check back later."

"Please do."

Letting the Londoner disappear in the milling crowds, Riley tailed her. The Sacher Hotel wasn't far.

Instead, the woman turned up a side street and headed toward Excalibur, the brothel.

37

"What's up hon?" Jacob sounded as if he were munching carrots.

"You need to check out the brothels. I just followed the British woman I saw at the doctor's office to Excalibur. Sending pic now." She forwarded the grainy photo. "I spotted her in Chanel's. The handbags she bought could finance a world cruise. I bet she's a money launderer for Armand."

"Riles, you need to quit playing Paul Drake."

Perry Mason, huh? At least he hadn't called her Miss Marple. "But you're stuck at the office, and I'm on the street." She bit back her words that Interpol needed more field agents. And a few more females on the force.

"Did she go inside?"

"Yes."

"Don't tell me you followed her into that place."

"You kidding? No way." A fresh burst of rain pelted the pavement, and she slipped under the hotel portico. "But I saw her approach the madam, and they chatted for a few minutes."

Sounds of tapping on a keyboard trickled through her phone. "Where are you now?" he asked.

"I'm outside the hotel where she's staying."

"Which one?"

"The Bristol. She told me they were staying at the Sacher—"

"Riles. Do. Not. Approach. A suspect. Got that?"

"Sure, sure, but I spoke with her at Chanel's." Declining the doorman's offer to hail her a taxi, Riley moved away from him. "She remembered me from London. I could hardly play dumb."

Jacob groaned into her ear.

"Anyway, I followed her inside the hotel. Discreetly of course. She used a key card to access the elevator."

"Thanks, Mata Hari. I'll put someone on it. You've been a big help. Now get out of there and go somewhere safe."

"And where might that be?" Honestly, special agents could be so exasperating. If Interpol had a little help, she and Jacob could get on with their lives. "Are there any updates on Tracy?"

His sigh squeezed every inch of her heart. "No."

"Okay. Talk to you soon." If only one of her leads could help uncover Armand.

***

JACOB WALKED over to Margot's office cubicle, almost as devoid of personality as his. She swiveled her chair from the computer desk to face him.

Did the woman own anything other than power suits and heels? He brought her up to date on Riles' sleuthing. "She photographed the suspect for us."

"Has she billed us for her services?"

"Not that I know of." They ought to pay her, but he wasn't

fueling any latent dreams of an Interpol career. "How can we get an undercover agent into the brothel?"

She cocked an eyebrow. "What did you have in mind, male or female?"

"Neither." No way was he volunteering, nor would he contribute to his colleagues' moral delinquency. "How about access to CCTV cameras in the area?" If the government hadn't been convinced not to install them there.

"I'll check on that." She inserted the woman's photo into the facial recognition program, pulled up her passport picture on the computer. "Elizabeth Bower. Born in Manchester, England. Age fifty."

"Why did she visit the brothel?" He brewed himself another coffee at the corner table. "She didn't avail herself of its services."

"Pardon my saying so, but Riley isn't the most discreet tail. She saw them at the Klinik and followed her today. Perhaps the woman was warning them Interpol's tailing them."

"Or she's a money launderer." The first sip of coffee scalded his tongue. "Or a courier for Armand, stopped by to discuss a cash delivery or pick up."

"Riley might have missed an exchange of funds."

"Could be." Whatever the purpose, it bore checking out. "If the woman's a courier, she may be assigned to collect from other brothels he owns. Possibly in other cities." The London Met and Interpol had investigated everyone on Armand's gala guest list. Had these two slipped through the police net? If so, not happening again. Not on his watch.

THE DAMP BREEZE flowing through the subway tunnel whisked Riley's curls from her shoulders. She wrapped her silk scarf around her throat, scanned the people waiting for trains. Jacob would expect her to stay alert.

But she needed to drill her wicked runs and high notes, reset her psyche into the malevolent Queen of the Night's persona. She scurried inside the Staatsoper and signed in with the blue-smocked portier, followed his directions to her rehearsal room.

"*Küss die Hand, gnädige Frau.*" Tufts of white hair surrounded a shiny bald spot on his head as the pianist brushed his lips on her extended hand.

Most of the time, the kiss was faked. Not today. Maybe because she was singing a leading role.

"*Bitte.*" Shoulders wrapped in a wool sweater that had seen better years, he gestured her to the bend of the piano in the center of the room.

Would she be able to croak out her runs, the high notes? "Might I have ten minutes to warm up my voice?"

"Of course." He bowed and shuffled out to the hall.

The knots in her throat refused to budge, stiffening every run and roulade. Great. All she needed was to make a bad impression. People talked. He'd report on their rehearsal. *Oh, God, help. I need this job.* She did a few more deep breathing exercises, and the door opened.

Ready or not here we come. She flashed him a smile and moved to the piano.

"While you were warming up, this came for you." He handed her a vellum envelope fit for royalty.

"*Danke.*" Probably from the countess. Riley slit the flap with her fingernail, pulled out the engraved card.

WE'RE WATCHING YOU WHEREVER YOU GO.
YOU WON'T GET AWAY THIS TIME.

Breath lodged in her throat. We? Now it was multiple

watchers, multiple assassins? Fingers shaking, she shoved the card in the envelope. Now her prints were all over it. She had to get this to Jacob ASAP.

"A well-wisher?" Smiling, the coach sat on the piano bench and opened *The Magic Flute* score.

"Something like that. Who gave you the card?"

"A runner for the portier delivered the envelope while I was waiting in the hall. I told him I'd make sure you received it."

"How kind." She'd been followed to the opera house. And someone knew she'd set up the impromptu rehearsal, only early this morning. She shoved the card in her purse. Fresh knots gripped her throat. Was her apartment bugged?

The pianist leapt into the introduction of the Queen's Vengeance aria.

How was she supposed to sing over this stress, the trauma? Gaze riveted on the corner of the wall, she opened her mouth, willed the notes and text to come forth. She could do this. She *had* to do this.

"Brava." The pianist nodded and turned to her next entry, cueing her dialogue in his Viennese accent.

The rehearsal passed in a blur. She thanked him for his time, fled to the restroom, locked herself in a stall and phoned Jacob.

Ten rings. No answer. Not even his voicemail kicked in.

Where was he when she needed him?

She hadn't a clue how to reach the Interpol office. A quick web search yielded nothing other than the office was called a National Central Bureau, no address or phone number, and that Interpol had been birthed in Vienna in 1923, the brainchild of an Austrian policeman. Great. What should she do now? She left the ladies' room and headed for the portier's desk.

"Pardon me." She flashed the card she'd received. "I'm Riley Williams. Could you describe the person who left this for me?"

The man pushed the sign-in book toward her, handed her the pen. "A messenger boy, a delivery service."

"Oh." Not what she wanted to hear. She signed herself out. "Then there's no record of the company or the delivery man."

"Correct."

"*Danke.*" Why couldn't something go right for a change? Armand seemed to hold the entire deck of cards, while she and Jacob weren't sure what game they were playing.

38

Outside the opera house, she glanced left, right, for anyone who might've written the card. Men and women stared back at her. How could she have forgotten Austrians love to stare? Avoiding their gaze was a giveaway you were a foreigner.

She hailed a taxi. An extravagance, but given the warning note, streetcars and subways made her even more vulnerable. With her debut in a matter of days, she'd returned Gussi's car to her. Along with a huge box of treats from Heiner's and two comp tickets for *The Magic Flute*.

Vienna's stunning palaces and ornate statues passed in a blur. Half an hour later, she paid the driver. Maybe she shouldn't have been so predictable. Rehearsal. Home. She glanced around the half empty street, then let herself into the apartment building. Thankfully, Austrians kept the doors locked 24/7. No key, no entry.

Best forgo the elevator. What if someone was waiting for her inside? She trudged up the three flights of stairs.

Jacob had fussed when he found out she'd rented in the tenth district, but it was such a charming apartment. After all, the rent came out of her singer's salary. These days, disgruntled jihadists probably lived in every district in Vienna. Not just Favoriten.

Inside her spacious foyer, she stepped out of her heels and dropped her purse on the kitchen chair. She grabbed a roll, cut off a chunk of cheese and laid the knife on the kitchenette counter. Munching her snack, she stared at the mug in the sink.

Odd.

Not a dish had been out before she left for the rehearsal.

Had Jacob been here? With trembling fingers, she tried his number again. This time his voicemail kicked in. "Hey, were you in my apartment today? Call me." She told him about the warning note, tried to stifle the wobble in her voice. "Please come over."

Just what he needed. A clingy woman in his life. Snarfing another bite of her cheese roll, she entered the living room. The three pillows on the couch had been rearranged. The hairs on her nape shot on alert. Jacob wasn't into decorating.

If someone was hiding in the clo—the toilet closet—next to the front door, she wouldn't make it out into the hall. She backed out of the room, the antique floorboards creaking with every step. Glanced toward the bathroom off the kitchen. Was someone in the apartment?

Waiting for her.

Waiting to kill her.

Sweat slicked the soles of her feet.

Everything inside her screamed to pack an overnight bag, check into a hotel. She tiptoed into the bedroom. The cheese roll tumbled to the floor.

Someone had artfully draped her sheer white nightgown on the bed, the spaghetti straps properly spaced on her pillow.

Hand clasped over her mouth, she choked back moans. Who did this? How had he gotten in here?

Heart pulsing her throat, she crept to the foot of the bed. A note lay on the lace bodice of her nighty. The block letters spun before her eyes.

WEAR THIS TONIGHT. YOU LOOK LOVELY IN IT.

How COULD he have been so stupid? Of course, Armand would come after Riles. One way or another. Jacob raced up the stairs to her apartment. As soon as he'd listened to her voice message he'd left the office, his car swallowed in rush-hour traffic.

If she didn't have these performances coming up, he'd book her on a flight to Texas. Send her home where she could patch up things with her parents. And get her out of Armand's clutches.

Panting, he took the last two steps and pounded on her door.

It whipped open and she fell into his arms and buried her head against his suit jacket. "Jacob, oh, Jacob."

"*Shh*, it's okay." He stroked her curls, inhaled her rosemary-scented shampoo. "Everything's fine. I'm here now."

"Where have you been? I couldn't reach you. Yon never gave me your Interpol info."

The accusation in her voice stung. But it wasn't like her to become hysterical over a note.

"Someone's been in my apartment." Through her sobs, she told him about the mug, the pillows, the nightgown.

Red-hot rage throbbed every vein in his skull. How had the man gotten in? What was this—a campaign to terrorize Riles, work her up into such an emotional state she couldn't think straight, made dumb decisions? Then ruin her performances. And pick her off at will.

"Stay here while I search the apartment." He eased her inside the foyer and examined the door, the lock. No sign of a forced entry. Did the intruder have his own set of keys? He checked inside the clo, walked through the kitchen to the bathroom, scanned the living room. Then stepped into her bedroom.

He had no idea what Riles slept in, but the sheer negligee laid out on the bed was appropriate for her wedding night. And for no man's eyes except his. Fist balled like brass knuckles, he drove it into his palm. If the pervert were here, he'd kill him. How dare he handle her nightgown. Or envision his fiancée wearing it.

Focus, man. You're Interpol.

Phone whipped out, he photographed the note, her negligee, the embarrassing intimacy of the layout. He thumbed through her wardrobe. Nothing but neatly hung outfits, pairs of shoes in a straight line, and two suitcases above the cupboard.

Surveillance kit unzipped, he combed every inch of the room for hidden cameras and microphones. Wall joints, windows, framed pictures, the mirror, every piece of furniture. He skimmed the device above the bedroom doorframe. *Beep, beep, beep.*

Using his pocketknife, he pried out a miniature mic/camera, fingers itching to pulverize it on his palm. The sicko had observed her every toss and turn in bed.

The floorboards creaked behind him. He thrust the devices and folded knife into his pocket. "Hey, hon."

Arms hugged across her chest, Riles crept into the room. "I was saving the gown for our honeymoon. But now I feel so violated—" She curled against his chest, and he hugged her to him.

Some protector he'd turned out to be. The jerk had invaded

her privacy. Made lewd insinuations. How dare he attack his bride-to-be. Tightening his grip around her back, Jacob struggled for a calming breath.

He hated to ask, but he needed a probable timeframe for his Interpol report. "Have you worn the gown since you moved in?"

"I tried it on my first night here." Pink flushed her cheeks. "And twirled in front of the dresser mirror." Her voice shrank to a whisper. "Thinking about wearing it for you."

White-hot coals in his chest ignited into flames. Then the camera had already been in place and activated. And whoever left the note, knew where she would be staying in Wien.

39

Wien, Day 14

"Wonder where Amira is?" Seated at his office desk, Jacob texted his CCTV contact and requested a follow-up search for Armand's daughter. He turned to Margot waiting by his cubicle. "You think she's returned to her father?"

"It's possible."

"She could've ridden across the border with someone." He plucked her picture from his desk, stared into her sullen eyes. How badly did she want to elude her father?

"Does she have the savvy or financial means to live on her own?" Margot asked.

"Or is she more interested in inheriting his empire?"

His cell rang. The caller ID read Interpol Brussels. "Yes?"

"Thought you'd like to know your sister's phone pinged."

Invisible bands squeezed his lungs. "You mean you heard from her?"

"No, the caller ID read Amira Découvrir."

"Can you send me the number?" Jacob covered the phone, whispered to Margot. "Get a trace on this. It's Amira."

"On it." Margot dashed for her cubicle.

The text message appeared on his screen. "What time did the call come through?"

"Five minutes ago."

"Thanks. Keep me posted." Jacob disconnected, then dialed the number Amira had used. With each ring his heart sank. *Come on girl, pick up the call.* He pulled the cell from his ear and a faint voice came through the speaker.

"Who is this?" The words spat into his ear.

"Special Agent Jacob Coulter. You just called my sister."

"So?" Vitriol dripped from Amira's voice.

"She disappeared days ago. We believe she was kidnapped."

A sharp intake of air reached his ear.

"Any idea where she might be?'

"How should I know?"

"Your father tried to kill her last month." Jacob struggled to keep his voice even.

"He let us know he's responsible for her disappearance."

The silence on the other end stretched until he wanted to reach through the phone and shake her by the shoulders. How could she be so insensitive, was she as blackhearted as her father?

"Tracy trusted you. You were her best friend. Are you going to let something happen to her?" His voice broke. Did the girl have a compassion molecule in her DNA? "Amira, I beg you, please help us find Tracy. For once in your life do something noble." Did she even know the meaning of the word?

A sigh heaved into the phone. "My father has many business interests. He thinks I don't know about them, but I do. Well, some of them. One of his schemes is luring girls into au pair jobs."

A sick feeling wormed through Jacob. "Where are they located?"

"They could be anywhere in the world. At this point, Tracy may not even be in Europe."

His blood iced. Not in Europe? Then she could be working for some Middle Eastern potentate, or any other culture where women weren't valued. "Can you get me information on how to find her?" Eyes riveted on the clock, he counted the seconds. How much longer to trace the call, her location? "Please, Amira. Please help me. For Tracy's sake."

Another seconds-long silence. Why wouldn't the girl come clean?

"I don't know. If I still lived with him ... He's so secretive." For the first time, her voice quivered.

Poor kid. Still dealing with the trauma of her father's death threats. "Do you have access to his records right now? Maybe a password for his computer files?"

"That's it. No more questions." The call disconnected.

Jacob thumped his forehead in his hands. He'd been so close. If only he hadn't pushed her so hard.

"I'm sorry." Margot approached his desk, laid a hand on his shoulder. "Is there anything I can do?"

He shrugged. "Amira seemed shocked at Tracy's disappearance, so my sister hadn't told her about planning to work as an au pair. But why didn't Amira give me the information we need to try to find Tracy?"

"She's afraid." Margot dropped her hand from his shoulder. "She doesn't want to turn herself in."

If she didn't, how would they find Tracy? Or Armand? "Amira's a critical key to this puzzle. If she won't help us—" No, focus on the positive. "Now we know about one of her father's operations. An international operation."

"And she's too scared of her father to risk going to any of his hideouts to try to help us."

Could he blame her? "She might fancy herself a woman of

the world, but she's still only thirteen. I doubt Armand would spare his own daughter's life if it would cost him his own."

"I'll run a check on au pair agencies in Europe. See if we come up with anyone dodgy." She headed for her cubicle.

"Thanks." He called his communications contact. "Don't suppose you were able to trace that call ..."

"Not precisely. Our satellite link narrowed the region to Europe."

Great, just great. That much he'd been sure of. "Thanks."

SEQUESTERED behind a screen in the costume shop, the seamstress parted the back of the Queen of the Night's star-studded skirt. Riley stepped into the black brocade dress, and the woman pulled the boned bodice over Riley's torso. Six inches of airspace gapped beyond her shoulders and the sleeves. "There's room for two linebackers in here."

"No problem." The costumer pinned sections of the boning together, but the bodice and sleeves still swam on Riley.

"Is there another gown we could use?"

"*Nein*. This is the one the director has chosen. All our Queens of the Night wear it."

"But this one will fall off if I move. Can you take it in enough to make it fit?"

Teeth clamped around a row of metal pins, the woman shrugged.

Great. Why couldn't she sing a debut without some sort of bizarre hitch?

"*Bitte*." She motioned Riley to turn around.

As she pirouetted, straight pins scraped her waist. Some singers welcomed the boning for breath support. Personally, she found it restricted her lung expansion. This time she'd need every inch of rib girth she could muster, or the dress would sluice down her hips faster than a luge team at the Olympics.

"Sit, please." The woman gestured to the chair.

Riley plopped onto the seat and the dress gapped open like an unclasped accordion.

The woman *tsked*.

"Have you removed every possible section of boning?"

"I'm afraid so." She reached for the Queen's headdress, positioned it on Riley's curls, and pinned the cap along her scalp.

Breath whooshed from her mouth. She'd worn worse contraptions. Maybe they could attach a few peacock feathers in case the dress fell off. Then she'd fake a Gypsy Rose Lee fan dance from the catwalk. She brushed a curl from her eye. The worst part of stepping in already launched productions was the lack of stage rehearsals and properly fitted costumes.

Every Queen of the Night she'd sung seemed destined to appear onstage as close to heaven as possible. She shuddered. Maybe she should find a new role as her signature piece.

She stood and surveyed herself in the full-length mirror. No way was this costume going to fit. Even her mother's clothes had looked better on her when she'd played dress-up as a child.

The woman pulled the sleeves toward Riley's shoulders.

What should she do? Throw a diva tantrum? "I'm sorry, but I can't go onstage like this. How can I sing, worrying the gown will fall to my feet?"

"*Ja, ja*, it works." The woman zipped the dress, but the boning came nowhere near Riley's back.

Right. Even if they wrapped a rope around her ribs and stuffed the bust line with a dozen pair of socks, it was hopeless. She flicked a hand across her brow. Why couldn't she have worry-free performances where she could focus on her character and singing her arias flawlessly? Instead, she'd be anxious about an impromptu strip tease.

"This gown will have to be replaced. I need a reasonably fitted costume. This is totally unacceptable."

The seamstress's eyebrow shot toward her hairline.

Okay, so she was a newbie, but she deserved a fair shake at success, didn't she? She forced a smile. "I'll stop by tomorrow to see how much progress you've made. In the meantime, please try to find me a suitable alternative costume." Riley stepped out of the gown, handed it to the woman, and pulled on her pantsuit.

"*Auf Wiedersehen.*" Riley closed the dressing room door behind her and headed for the rehearsal room. This was one drama she'd have to handle on her own. Jacob had too much on his hands. Moisture welled in her eyes. Maybe someday she'd laugh at the trials and tribulations of being an opera singer.

Once again, fate seemed determined to sabotage her career.

40

Day 14

Would the headaches ever cease? Fingers massaging her throbbing temple, Riley rang the countess's doorbell again. The antique paintings on the green-silk wallpaper swam before her eyes. No footsteps pattered inside the apartment. Bouquet in one hand, she lifted her coat sleeve and checked her watch. Four fifteen. Had she misunderstood the invitation?

A wave of dizziness hit her, and she leaned against the antique table until it passed. Traffic in Vienna could be unpredictable. Maybe the countess was out shopping. Checkout lines could be so slow.

Pen in hand, she flipped over her business card. She wasn't up to this today anyway.

Sorry I missed you. Thank you for the invitation.

Riley Williams

She wedged the notecard between the door and the jamb.

The door squeaked open. Surely the countess wouldn't leave her door unlocked. Riley's pulse shot into overdrive. Had something happened to her? After all, the countess had saved her life at the casino. One of Armand's assassins might have found her, harmed her too. "Hello?"

Heart in her throat, Riley stepped inside. What if he were still in the apartment?

A tea service was laid on the coffee table between a couch and two pale-blue silk easy chairs. Lace sheers and pale-blue silk drapes framed the floor-to-ceiling windows. A blue Persian rug covered much of the herringbone wood floor. The mixed décor of antiques and comfy contemporary screamed expensive. Even the scent of the countess's perfume hung in the air. Riley headed for the note card propped against the tea tray.

Dear Riley,

I'm running late. My maid has left, but please help yourself to tea and cake. I'll be here as soon as I can.

Flowers laid on the table, she tapped the side of the pot. Hot. Eating without her host felt so rude, but the countess might be less embarrassed if she drank some tea. She poured herself a cup and sipped the steaming liquid. Its licorice sweetness rolled over her tongue, slid down her throat. Black dots peppered her vision. Missing lunch had been a mistake. But she was meeting Jacob for dinner.

Protein. She needed protein. Maybe a cucumber sandwich? The strength bled from her ankles. Every inch of her leg muscles oozed into rubber. Must—lie—down. She shoved the cup and saucer on the table beside her, staggered toward the open bedroom doors. How could she feel ill from a cup of tea? Or was it the walk to the apartment, or the pesky headache again?

Sweet tea. She never sweetened her tea. Or her coffee. A maid wouldn't have known. But the front door had been unlocked. Someone had been in here. Messed with the pot of tea.

Tremors fluttered through her heart. Her pulse skyrocketed. An allergic reaction to an artificial sweetener? She stumbled toward the king-sized bed. A little nap ... Surely her hostess would understand.

Riley wobbled across the flokati rug, fingered the pale pink silk spaghetti-strapped sheath laid out on the duvet. Next to it, a fire-engine-red dress. A red silk band joined the see-through mesh bodice to another mesh section from the navel to the thighs. Slinky. Nothing left to the imagination. Hardly seemed like the countess's taste.

Shudders jolted through her shoulders. A fresh wave of nausea pitched in her stomach. The man who'd been in her own apartment had been here too. Flattop? The countess was in danger. He'd probably seen them talking at the café near Gucci's.

She shouldn't be in here. Cramps gripped her stomach. Overhead, the chandelier swayed like a pendulum. Edgar Allen Poe.

Must go.

Now.

Purse—must find, call Jacob. The walls zoomed toward her. Furniture whirled about her in circles. But the open door, the—

Sparklers danced before her eyes. Her knees whacked the floor.

Blackness slid through her head, her eyes ...

———

WHERE WAS RILES? She'd promised to meet him here thirty minutes ago. Jacob roamed the foyer of the Sacher Hotel Rote

Restaurant. Tonight, the red brocade wallpaper, crimson carpet and drapes were suffocating. The eyes in the oil portraits on the walls tracked his every step. He tried her phone again. It went to voicemail. Again.

If only he'd insisted on meeting her at the countess's apartment. It wasn't far from here.

The maître 'd approached him a second time. "Shall I continue to hold your dinner reservation?" He gave a discreet nod toward the diners waiting to be seated, some of whom had arrived without a reservation.

Jacob tugged at his tie. It wasn't like Riles to not alert him she was delayed. Ever since his business trip to Vienna three months ago, he'd promised himself he'd bring her here for a romantic dinner.

No way had she stood him up. A sinking feeling twisted his gut. Armand's assassins must have found her. "No, thank you, cancel the reservation. I apologize for the lateness of this."

"Understood sir." The maître 'd turned to the first couple in line and ushered them into the dining room.

Jacob texted Margot with the details of Riles' disappearance.

> I'm headed to the countess's apartment.
> Please check CCTV video to trace Riley's
> steps. Thanks.

Legs barely functioning, he forced his steps faster along the few blocks between the restaurant and the woman's apartment building.

The elevator worked with agonizing slowness. *Come on, come on.* He bolted from the cage, rang the woman's doorbell, knocked on the door. Jiggled the lock.

No answer. From the street, none of her windows seemed lit. Had they both been nabbed?

Margot texted him back.

Have alerted CCTV. Will keep you
informed.

He texted back his thanks. Emotions a whirling dervish, he put a trace on Riles' phone.

If only she'd worn the hair clasp he'd designed for her months ago. With its miniature microphone and GPS tracking, he'd have a fix on her location. Had she even brought it with her? From now on he'd insist she never leave home without it. Not while he worked for Interpol.

First Tracy, now Riles. Everyone dear to him. *Dear God, please don't let me lose them.* He shoved a lid on the panic churning his stomach. He had to get a grip, stay strong. He'd need all his wits and God's intervention to find Riles, bring her home.

If she were still alive.

41

Day 15

Head throbbing worse than ever, Riley struggled awake. Opened one eye. Where was she? The odor of dank walls, mold, and mildew hit her nostrils. Nearby, the sound of water lapped the walls. Whimpers crept up her throat. Was she in a ship's hold? Arms numb, shackles held her wrists above her head, the back of her hands brushing cold, slimy bricks.

Her gaze dropped and she gasped. Someone had stripped her clothing down to her underwear. Her heart nearly burst from her chest. Had he—they—she couldn't bring herself to finish the thought. Tears trickled down her cheeks.

The odor of poop, pee, and puke wafted from a wooden bucket in the corner of her cell. Her gag reflex worked overtime.

How long had she been here? The last thing she remembered was arriving at the countess's apartment. Then feeling woozy. Drinking a few sips of tea, eating a cucumber sandwich to be polite since she was meeting Jacob for dinner. Then nothing. Had that been all there was to remember?

Jacob must be panicking. He'd lost Tracy and now her. If only she could get word to him. She struggled against her chains, but the metal bit into her wrist bone.

Dim light filtered through a metal grated window. A motorboat *put-putted* past, and water sloshed the windowpane. Growls knotted their way through her stomach. How long had she been here? Days? No, not days or she'd be weaker, even more dehydrated. Her tongue clung to the dry skin on her lips.

Armand. What did he intend to do with her, or to her? No, no. Focus. She had to get out of here. She needed to be prepared. A giant cockroach skittled over her bare thigh. She clamped a shriek between her teeth.

In the distance, footsteps trudged on what sounded like stone pavers. A metal door screeched open, and thuds came from a room nearby. A girl screamed. "Please, please, no. Don't hit me anymore."

Chin sunk to her chest, Riley's tears dribbled onto her thighs. *Dear God, no.* The victim sounded so young.

The cries died to moans. Was the girl dying? The metal door slammed, a lock clicked. Footsteps stopped outside her cell.

Her breath clutched in her throat. *Oh, Lord, help me be brave.*

A key ground in the lock, and the door swung open. Bare bulbs in the hall nearly blinded her. The light glinted on the man's blood-covered hands.

Staring him down, she forced herself not to squirm. Show. No. Fear. Isn't that what they said?

"*Gut.*" His lips spread in an evil grin, his breaths heavy. "You're awake."

Please God, no. Don't let him touch me.

A tic pulsed the corner of her eye, an erratic SOS. Jacob would never find her.

The man backed into the hallway, locked her door.

Breath whooshed from her mouth. Spared. For the moment.

Somehow, she had to convince him to unlock her shackles. If she grew any weaker, she wouldn't have the strength to fight him off.

Surely he'd be back with food and water. Unless he intended to feed her himself, he'd have to unchain her, wouldn't he?

Weeping filtered through the walls. Girls, some childlike, others the voices of young women. Had they all been abducted too? Was this a holding tank? If so, she'd stumbled onto another layer of Armand's evil operations. He could be supplying the brothels with girls and raking in the cash for himself.

Moist stones beneath her legs pimpled her skin. Didn't sex traffickers usually beat their victims into submission, then rape them? Shudders shook her spine until her teeth rattled. Was that to be her fate?

Dear God, help us!

Outside her door, a cart rattled on the stone floor. The door screeched open. The jailer stepped close enough to smell his sour breath. She cowered against the wall. Leering at her, he ran a grubby finger down her temple, her jaw, then stroked her lips.

Oh, God, oh, God, help, she screamed inside. Eyes squeezed shut, she waited for what was to come.

Instead, he unlocked one of her wrist shackles. The muscles quivered as she lowered her arm to her lap. He set a metal bowl of watery, brown liquid and a spoon on her lap. "Eat up, girly. You need to put a little meat on those bones. Get you ready for what's coming."

Her stomach revolted and she vomited on his shoes.

Swinging one arm back, he whacked the side of her face.

Stinging nettles spiked through her skin. The metallic taste of blood pooled inside her mouth.

"Don't ever do that again."

"It-it was an accident. I didn't mean to. I'm sorry." Already she'd lost her moxie. She was kowtowing to her captor. How could that have happened so fast?

He walked to the doorway, his hulking body blocking half the light.

Hand trembling, she spilled half the liquid on her bare stomach as she brought the spoon to her mouth. "Oh, delicious. *Danke*." She forced herself to swallow the vile-tasting broth. It reeked of organ meats, the heart, kidneys, and other offal she didn't care to know.

The door locked behind him, and the cart clanked down the hall. One by one, other doors unlocked. With each slap and scream bleeding through the wall, she flinched. She mumbled her thanks to God for the meal, that she was still alive. If only she sensed His presence with her in the room.

I will never leave you nor forsake you.

Peace flooded her spirit. She could count on the Lord. He was all she had.

She finished the disgusting gruel and set the bowl beside her leg. One thing was certain: she had little time to escape. Armand clearly had plans for her and if she were going to flee, it had to happen now.

When the cart drew near her cell, she readied herself.

The door swung open, and her jailer entered.

"Please. I-I need to use the latrine."

"It's not time."

"Tell that to my bladder. I don't know how long I've been here, but I've got to go. Please." Lips quivering into a smile, she willed her eyes to radiate innocence and trust.

"Women." Grumbling, he lumbered over to her. Entwined her curls in his fingers.

Don't flinch, don't flinch. But her leg muscles itched to bolt.

The shackles dropped, clanked against the wall.

Steady now, she could do this. "*Danke.*" She forced another smile, and he leaned close, lips parted to kiss her. Fighting the urge to gag, she gripped the dangling shackle, clubbed the back of his head.

Groaning, he fell to his knees. She clobbered him again and again until he collapsed on the stone floor.

Free, she was free. She staggered to her feet, grabbed his keys. If only she could release the other girls, but they might be too weak to walk out of the dungeon. She could help them better if she escaped and brought help.

No matter she was half naked, the Viennese wouldn't care. She had to get out of there now. Clutching the slimy brick wall, she stumbled into the hallway. Climbed the stairs out of the dungeon.

A boat putt putted nearby. Was she on an island? Maybe she wasn't even in Austria. Panic sieved through her.

She made it to the top of the stone stairwell, rattled the steel doorknob in front of her. Locked. Hands palsying, she inserted the first key on his ring. No go. She tried another one. Then another. Did he have two key rings?

Groans and thudding steps schlepped into the hall.

Heart clambering up her throat, she glanced over her shoulder. Staggering like Quasimodo, her jailor lurched up the stairs. She inserted the final key. The lock turned. *Thank You, Jesus.* She pulled back the heavy door. Darted through an office with multiple file cabinets, two metal desks, and chairs. Surely she was almost there, almost free.

Her jailer stumbled through the cellar door. He wrenched open a desk drawer, snatched a pistol and aimed it at her. "Halt."

Adrenaline surged through her veins. *Oh, God, please help.* If she didn't risk it now, she'd never get out of here alive. She lunged for the final door, flung it open.

And fell into Armand's arms.

42

Day 15

The mid-morning sunlight streaming through the windows nearly blinded him. Seated at his Interpol cubicle, Jacob tried Riles' phone again. No answer, no voicemail. Where was she? She'd promised to tell him where she was going. And she'd never stood him up on a date.

Face ashen, Margot crossed to his desk, a photograph in her hand. "This just came through our general channels. Our team's trying to trace the web path." She swallowed hard. "And possible locations."

Jacob riveted on the photo. Rage throbbed his veins until spots swam before his eyes. Riles. Shackled to a stone wall, head drooped on her chest, flesh bare except for her underwear. A dismal shaft of light filtered into wherever she was being held. "Armand did this."

Calm down. *Be logical, and you can outwit this fiend.* In the picture, Riles was still alive. But for how long? What did Armand intend to do to her? Forcing a deep breath, Jacob pulled out a magnifying glass and studied the photo.

Something glinted on the stone wall around her. Moisture, perhaps?

A sick feeling wormed through him.

With so many centuries-old buildings in Wien and Austria, thousands had basements, cellars. Or ancient dungeons. He peered closer, angled the glass over the photo. Something was growing from the stones. Moss. The last ounce of strength drained from his muscles.

She could be anywhere.

And she was being held underground.

He choked back a sob. *Dear God, don't let Riles and Tracy be taken from me. But we don't always get what we want,* an inner voice taunted. *Maybe this is a test to see how well you deal with an agonizing loss.* No! He slammed his fist on the photo. "My God will provide." And the first thing he was asking of Him, was to spare Tracy and Riles' lives.

Margot cleared her throat. "Interpol police are asking to search every basement in the first district. That's where Riley was last seen."

"Yes, the countess had invited her for tea."

"We've checked CCTV cameras. Riley entered the countess's apartment building."

<hr>

"Going somewhere?" Armand blocked the doorway, dug his fingers into Riley's arm until she winced. Cool air rushed over her skin, pimpled her exposed flesh. Eyes glittering, he swept his gaze over her body. "My, my, in such a state of undress too."

Squirming against his grip, she covered her chest with her free hand. "You." She spat the word with every bit of venom she'd saved up since he tried to kill her in Klagenfurt.

"Don't tell me you're surprised."

"Hardly."

He spoke over her shoulder. "Go check on the others."

"*Jawohl.*" Her jailer slammed the door where she'd fled the dungeon.

Armand threw her inside the office.

Stumbling backward, she slammed her hip against the metal desk. A fiery ache burned inside her leg. What did he intend to do with her? Or to her? She hefted her chin. "No wonder Amira left you."

Arm swung wide, he slapped her face.

Clutching her stinging cheek, ears ringing, she roved her tongue around her teeth. Still attached. "Not even your own flesh and blood wants any part of you."

"You—" He went for her other cheek, and she dodged the blow. One knee up, she rammed his groin. Yowling, he doubled over, and she dashed for the door. *God, help.* She flung the door open and darted into a room done in dark paneling, velvet-covered couches, and book-lined walls. Where was she? She'd expected to step outside a warehouse of some sort. She stumbled toward the wood-paneled door across the room.

Locked.

No, no. It couldn't be.

Groaning, Armand lumbered through the doorway.

Legs jellying, she staggered toward the velvet-draped window. Searched for a way to open it. Pounded on the glass. "*Hilfe, hilfe!*"

"Nice try." He stripped off his belt, whipped her arms behind her, and lashed her wrists with the leather. "One I promise you'll regret."

Sobs wracked her chest. She'd come so close to escaping. He'd make certain she couldn't try again. *Oh, Jacob, please, please find me. And Tracy, wherever she is.*

Breaths ragged, Armand dialed his cell. "Come get her. Put her in the special cell."

Special cell? Nausea ripped through her gut. A sudden urge to pee hit her.

SEATED AT HIS OFFICE DESK, Jacob did a data search for the countess's phone number.

She answered on the first ring. "Allo?" Her silky voice oozed over him like whipped cream.

He told her about Riles' disappearance.

The woman gasped. "*Aber nein.* Who would do such a thing?"

Jaw clenched, he ignored the question. "Could you tell me about your afternoon together?"

"We shared tea and sandwiches. Riley told me how excited she was about her debut at the Staatsoper. She seemed much stronger than the last time I saw her." Her sigh reached into the phone. "I wish I could be of more help."

"She didn't seem upset about anything?"

"*Nein*, she was quite upbeat. Radiant."

Maybe someone had nabbed Riles en route to the Sacher Hotel. "How long did she stay?"

"*Ach*, about ... an hour, I think ..."

Only sixty minutes for tea? Wasn't that kind of short? Most women he knew could gab for days. But then, Riles didn't know the countess well. "Did she mention where she was headed afterward?"

"I haven't the foggiest idea."

Dear God, no. Not another dead end.

43

Day 16

Scritch, *scritch*. Ignoring the ache in her shackled arm, Riley dug her diamond engagement ring into the wall. Only a few more letters to carve. Were they even legible?

RILEY WILLIAMS WAS HERE.

Should she add the date? What was today? Living in darkness had distorted her sense of time. Had she been here two days, three?

Steps thumped on the stairs to her dungeon cell. She relaxed her arm, muscles quivering from the effort to write the words. Would anyone ever find her message?

The iron door screeched open, the hall's bare bulbs flooding the room. A rank odor spewed into her cell as her jailer stalked across the room, eyes brimming with lust.

Cowered against the slimy wall, she drew her feet to her chest, wrists shaking against the shackles. What was he going to do to her? Had Armand decided to have her tortured?

The man crouched in front of her, his breath sour from too many beers. "Time to get you ready."

Ready for what? The word screamed in her mind. Her heart pounded so hard she gasped for air.

Face shoved in hers, she jerked her head aside. He forced the key into her shackles and the chains clattered against the wall. He yanked her to her feet, his grip on her arm searing her flesh. "Let's go."

Ankles numb, legs mush from sitting so long on the floor, she stumbled beside him into the hall, stubbed her toes on the stairs. Damp slime coated her bare feet. Where was he taking her?

Oh, God, help. No matter what happens fill me with Your peace. Your word says You'll never leave me, never forsake me. Never leave me, never leave me. Never—

At the top of the stairs, he opened an iron door to her right and shoved her in front of him. She huddled a few feet inside the doorway. A bathtub smudged with grime, an equally dirty sink, an overflowing toilet. Bile spurted into her throat. What now? A wadded bath towel lay on a stool beside the tub. Icy cold from the tiles seeped through her feet. She shivered, hands across her chest. Squeezed her thighs against the urge to pee.

"Get cleaned up."

"In this pigsty?"

"This is your lucky day." Running his gaze over her, he slicked his lips.

The quaking in her shoulders rattled down her spine, but she held her ground. Not even a tiny window with a metal grate. No point screaming for help.

"I'll be back." He slammed the door behind him. A key grated in the lock.

The last ounces of strength that had held her upright oozed from her body. She sank to her knees. *Help me, God. I can't do this.* The odor from her unwashed body assailed her.

Sink or bathtub, which would be worse? But every inch of her longed to be clean. She shuffled over to the sink, splashed her face with cold water, then forced herself to use the toilet. Good. They'd provided toilet paper. For once.

She turned on the bathtub tap full force, but the water's roar didn't budge the black grease on the sides. Or dim the awful what-ifs whirling in her head. Stepping into the tub, her foot skidded on its slick floor. She squatted and splashed her body from head to toe, letting the hot water rinse off the filth.

What evil did he have in mind?

Would she ever feel clean again?

Tears streamed down her cheeks. Now she'd never have a chance to work things out with Jacob. Why had she been so adamant he change? Couldn't they have resolved their differences with God's help? But now—

Oh, God, walk through this with me. Hand palsying, she reached for the towel, shut her eyes to its dinge. How many women had used it before her? She patted her body dry, then wrapped her torso in the grimy terry cloth.

Seated on the stool, she pressed her thighs tight.

And waited.

44

Wien, Day 16

J acob scrolled through the list of police-registered brothels on his office computer. Where should he look next? His cell rang. Father. Bracing himself, he answered the call.

"Any word on Tracy?"

"No, Father. We're doing everything we can to find—"

"And you call yourself a policeman."

"I'm not a policeman. I'm a special agent analyst."

"Find. My. Daughter." Father's voice thundered in Jacob's ear.

If his parents had never sent her to boarding school, they probably wouldn't be in this mess. "We're doing everything possible."

"It's not enough."

"I'll be in touch. Have to get back to work." Jacob cut off the call before he said something he might regret. He drew three deep breaths, but Father's voice still echoed in his ear.

Focus. Focus.

The last place he wanted to find Riley was in a brothel. But if she were still alive, he wanted to marry her, no matter what she'd been through. If she'd still have him. Somehow he'd find a way to change, to be the kind of man she needed.

Where do we go with this, Lord? He muttered the prayer under his breath, but it played nonstop in his heart. If he couldn't save Tracy and Riles, maybe he could rescue some of the women being used by Armand. He had no proof, no leads that Armand was involved in Austria's brothel industry. Nothing but a niggling in his gut. An instinct that wouldn't let go.

Soft footsteps approached his cubicle. He swiveled his chair away from his desk. Margot waited, twisted a button on her jacket. "Can I help?"

"It's possible Armand owns a hefty portion of this industry in the city under shell company names, and we wouldn't know it."

"*Ja*. But is this where we should spend our time searching for Riley?"

"Since Riles spotted that couple from Armand's gala in London last month and followed his wife to a local brothel, I think yes."

"Then this man could be an investor in more ways than one."

"You could say that."

Margot paced his tiny cubicle. "We have so little to go on. And we lack the manpower to stake out every brothel in Wien."

"It's the most logical business venue for a man of Armand's interests. Why settle for laundromats and car washes?"

He pulled the CCTV photos of Tracy in Brussels, Riles entering the countess's apartment building. "How could they have disappeared out of sight of these cameras?" It made no sense. Unless they didn't leave these locations on foot or in a recognizable state.

"If they were shunted out of the building inside a giant

laundry cart and tossed into the back of a truck, no one would know." Margot's voice died to a whisper.

"Yeah." The Armands of this world left nothing to chance. "This wasn't some haphazard plot hatched at the last minute. Découvrir would've plotted their abductions beyond the nth detail."

Margot sighed. "At least there've been no signs of their bodies."

"True." But did that mean they were still alive? Or was it wishful thinking on his part? He raked a hand through his hair. *Where are you Tracy? Where are you Riles? Speak to me.*

What wouldn't he give for one of those dreams and visions the prophet Joel spoke about. Too bad Interpol dealt in hard facts and evidence, not dreams and visions from God.

Von Bingen wouldn't fund requests for additional personnel without evidence to support the expenditure. Jacob called his contact at the CCTV monitoring desk. "Any updates on photos of the countess?"

"*Ja,* she was seen leaving the building an hour before Miss Williams arrived."

"An hour *before*?" His phone dinged and the photo appeared. Wearing oversized sunglasses, the woman emerged from the building in a designer-looking suit, a Louis Vuitton overnight bag in one hand and a Chanel purse. As usual, she'd dressed like a high-class fashionista. "And no pictures of her returning an hour later?"

"None."

"Any other photos of her coming and going in the past day or two?"

Soft clicks sounded over the phone. "*Nein.* No sign of her return to the apartment."

Was the countess involved in Riles' disappearance? Had the woman played them for fools all along?

"However, our guys found one thing that might interest you."

"What's that?"

"Out of curiosity I skimmed our data recovery bank of CCTV tapes back a month ago. There were shots of her leaving Gucci's with several shopping bags and a good-looking man at her side."

Jacob's heart ratcheted. This could be the clue they've been praying for. "Could you shoot me a copy of that please?"

"*Jawohl.*" Buttons clicked in the background. "Just sent it your way."

"*Danke.*" Jacob clicked on the file. A grainy image of the countess and Armand. *Thank you, God.* The connection they'd been searching for had been there all the time. So where were they now? "The guy's a terrorist financier. Got any more photos of him?"

Jacob drummed his fingers on the desk. The officer's breaths blew into the phone, keyboard clicks punctuating the silence.

"You'll love these photos. En route now."

"*Danke.*" Jacob opened the new file. Clear shots of Armand entering the countess's apartment building, taken three days ago. "Can you find anything with him prior to this date?"

"I can check for you. Our data recovery system is top-notch, but it will take some time."

"*Danke.* Appreciate your help." Jacob printed the pictures and slapped them on Margot's desk. "Our first solid leads."

"Armand's been in Wien right under our noses."

"Looks like it."

"You think he was staying with the countess?" Flames shot through Jacob's chest. If Armand was in her bedroom when they'd attended her party, he'd must've chortled with glee.

THE DOOR BOLTED BEHIND RILEY. She huddled in the corner near the entrance. At least this room had a window with velvet drapes, a settee that had seen better decades, eons ago. She whispered a prayer of thanks. No shackles on the walls and a decent place to sit.

The room seemed reasonably clean too. Beneath a well-lit mirror, a dressing table and chair with an array of expensive top-line cosmetics, trays of false eyelashes and fake nails. She darted to the window, pounded on it until her hands ached. No sash, no bars over the frame. Just a solid pane of glass thick enough to be bulletproof.

Trapped.

She was trapped, trapped, trapped.

Wobbling away from the window, she sank onto the couch. The brocade fabric itched her bare skin. She stared at the two rolling racks laden with glitzy cocktail dresses, a row of stiletto heels beneath, and gulped. Either she was leaving this place, or someone planned to ravage her here.

Tucked high on the corner wall, a red light on a camera blinked. She crossed her hands over her chest. Who was filming her? Already, she felt violated.

Sighing, she forced herself to the larger rack, thumbed through the cocktail dresses. Chills rocked her. It was almost as if someone had riffled through her clothes closet, made a note of her size. Every garment would fit her perfectly.

The other rack held even shorter dresses and a smattering of tiny sizes. Did they line up outfits for the next victim to save time?

At this point, she had no illusions about her fate. But what about this next girl? Obviously someone small. Nausea pitted her stomach. A child? If only she had paper and a pen. Then she'd leave a note of encouragement for her. She darted to the dressing table, scrabbled through the eyeliner pens, and scrawled a message beneath the mirror.

JESUS SAYS, I WILL NEVER LEAVE YOU, NOR FORSAKE YOU. NO MATTER HOW BAD THIS SEEMS.

But no way was she going down without a fight. She searched through the makeup for anything she could use as a weapon. An eyelash curler, eyebrow pencils, makeup brushes, an array of curling irons. With her naturally wavy hair, she didn't need this. But a good, swift jab in the groin of the next man who entered ...

For the first time since she'd awakened in the dungeon, her heart soared. Maybe, just maybe, she could escape.

If she could stay out of the camera's sight when the door opened.

She checked the labels on all the dresses on the rack. Gucci. Alexander McQueen. Prada. Chanel, Fendi, Dolce et Gabbana. Who'd done the shopping? Most likely, a woman. A woman with exquisite taste. A woman who knew what appealed to high-society men.

The rack held an array of crimson, royal blue, turquoise, emerald-green. Not a white dress among them. But her own closet held evening gowns in each of those shades. Her skin prickled. Someone had searched her apartment in Brussels.

With ice-cold hands, she slipped into the emerald-green silk sheath, straightened the rectangular straps on her shoulders, and zipped the form-fitting dress. Would she ever be able to wear this color again, or would she always associate it with tonight?

At the dressing table, she applied makeup base, dabbed cream rouge on her deathly pale cheeks. Added a slick of pink lipstick and eye shadow. Fingers shaking, she glued on a pair of false eyelashes. She slipped on the silk stilettos that matched the dress. The buyer had thought of everything. Every pair of shoes fit her feet. There was even a bottle of her signature scent, Chanel No. 5, on the table.

No. She fought the urge to brush the bottle to the floor. That scent she reserved for Jacob and no other man. Instead, she snatched the largest curling iron, crept along the wall to the door and waited.

Footsteps approached.

Heart pummeling her chest, Riley flattened her body against the narrow corner near the doorknob. Sweat slicked her grip on the curling iron. One good putt shot below his belt, and she'd slip out of the room.

A key grated in the lock and the door swung open.

Riley lunged for the doorway. Make it count, make it count.

She aimed, and the young girl screamed, hands flailing to her head.

Dear God—Tracy.

45

Day 16

The jailer shoved Tracy inside the dressing room and locked the door. Curling iron at her side, Riley ran her fingers over Tracy's bare arms. "Did they hurt you, are you okay?"

"I'm fine. But the other girls—" Tracy fell into Riley's embrace, words tumbling from the girl's mouth. "I didn't know what was going to happen to me. All I remember is signing the contract."

"What contract?"

"The au pair contract in Brussels. The lady was so nice. I-I thought I'd earn lots of money, and Jacob—when he wouldn't raise my allowance, I wanted to hurt him."

Hurt him? She'd devastated him.

"As soon as I signed the paper, I felt funny."

"Did you have anything to drink or eat?" Riley led her to the couch.

Tracy's brow knit. "Yeah, I think I had hot chocolate. We were in a café. That's the last thing I remember."

Drugging victims seemed to be the norm with these people. She didn't recall having tea with the countess. Just pouring a cup for herself and eating a cucumber sandwich.

"Until I woke up in the dungeon here." Tracy twisted her fingers in her lap. "It was awful being all alone. Sometimes I tried to talk to the girls in the next cell. Between their beatings. But he never laid a hand on me."

Another miracle. *Thank You, God.* The first was finding Tracy alive. Now, more than ever, she had to get them out of here.

Riley pointed to the clothing rack with the smaller sizes. "You need to get dressed."

"Dressed for what?"

"We may be forced to do some things we don't want to."

Tracy blanched. "You mean to stay alive?"

"Yes." Riley rolled the rack close to the settee. Not that it would shield Tracy from the evil-eyed camera on the wall.

"Okay ..." Tracy rose from the couch in slow motion, slid the dresses across the rack, one by one. She pulled a shell-pink slip dress from the hanger. "How about this one?" Her voice shrank to a six-year-old's tone.

A log blocked Riley's throat. "It's lovely." She choked out the words.

Tracy dropped the skimpy silk over her shoulders, and Riley gestured her to the makeup table.

"Wow. These are really cool brands." She scrounged through the rouge and eye shadow pots, applied a sheer base, and blended eye shadow on her lids as if she'd been wearing makeup for ages. Maybe Armand had let them when she and Amira visited him from boarding school.

All too soon Riley had glued the strip of false eyelashes along Tracy's lids. The girl studied her reflection in the mirror, smoothed a strand of her new updo in place. Did the child understand what was about to happen, that she'd never be the same?

The door swung open, and the jailor entered, dangled two pair of metal handcuffs at them. "Ready for your big night out?"

HANDS CUFFED BEHIND HER, Riley stumbled out the back door. The brisk night air bit her naked arms. She glanced up at the three-storied stone building. Given their dungeon cells, she'd half expected a moat and a drawbridge. But she'd heard motorboats. Was the Danube beyond those trees?

Pine trees blocked her view more than a few yards. The scent of freshly overturned earth clung to the air. Beneath the spreading branches of a linden tree, two open graves lay beside a body-sized mound. She stifled a shiver. Were those holes for her and Tracy?

Would their identities ever be known? As if in answer, clouds shrouded the sliver of moon.

"Where are they taking us?" Tracy teetered on her four-inch stilettos, a gawky chicken on stilts. In her pink silk slip dress, she could almost pass for a kid playing dress-up. If her chest weren't so developed.

Tears stung Riley's eyes. "I don't know."

Would her scratched messages on the walls ever reach a law enforcement officer?

Tires crunched on the gravel road. A gaily painted bus entered the property and stopped beside the back porch. The doors whooshed open, and nine girls dressed like Riley and Tracy lumbered down the steps. The half-light caught their wan faces, the glazed eyes of the walking dead.

Ice sieved through her body, jellied Riley's legs. In a few hours, this would be her. Tracy.

"Oh, God, help!" Tracy dug her fingers into Riley's biceps.

Teeth gritted against the sting in her muscles, she patted Tracy's wrist. What could she say to comfort her, to reassure her?

"Get a move on." The jailer pushed them past the bus. Shoved them toward a liveried chauffeur waiting by the open side door of a sleek, black minivan. A Mercedes. Wherever they were going, they were traveling in style. Designer dresses and shoes.

Had Armand summoned them? Chills spiked her flesh.

As they tottered toward the waiting driver, he pulled two black blindfolds from his pocket, eye masks with elastic around the back. So typical, hiring someone built like a GQ stud. Handsome. Deadly.

She caught a whiff of the chauffeur's expensive aftershave as her jailer shoved her inside the van, then Tracy.

"Careful," said the driver. "Don't damage the goods. He wants them untouched."

"*Ja, ja.*" Muttering curses under his breath, her captor removed the metal handcuffs, lashed Tracy's wrist to Riley's, then bound their ankles with leather straps. He tied Tracy's right wrist to the passenger strap dangling from the roof. She squirmed on the seat, whimpering.

"Shut up." He raised a hand to strike her.

She huddled against Riley. "I-I'll be good." The pathetic pleading in her tone tore Riley's heart.

"She's just a child," Riley spat the words at him.

"All the better." He flopped Riley's left arm along the seat back and lashed her wrist to the seatbelt hook on the wall. She grimaced, shifted to ease the burning in her muscles. If only he'd left an arm free. Now there'd be no escape.

"Give me those." The jailer snatched the blindfolds from the driver, snapped them in place over Tracy's eyes, then Riley's.

False eyelashes twitching beneath her blindfold, her world went dark. Her heart plummeted. Now they'd never be able to identify the route or the location of the house.

Armand had thought of everything.

Day 16

The graveled road beneath the Mercedes shifted, and the minivan rumbled over cobblestones. Armand's attention to detail was frightening. Screams from the beaten girls would've alerted neighbors. So he'd used an isolated body farm. A snazzy chartered bus to deliver his latest sex trafficking victims to a brothel and back.

The plastic seat glued to Riley's bare back. What thoughts were running through Tracy's mind right now? How could she prepare the girl for what awaited them? Should she pray they survived the experience or not?

Diesel fumes crept inside the vehicle. The driver downshifted, slung the van into a hard right turn. She lurched against Tracy. "Sorry."

"What's another bruise? You should've seen those other girls. They said I was the youngest. What's going to happen to us?" Sobs shattered her voice. "What are they going to do to us?"

Nausea soured Riley's gut. "We're going to have to be brave

and trust God to see us through this—" She clamped her mouth around the word. Ordeal. "No matter what happens, He can make all things new."

"How?" Tracy wailed.

Riley wished she knew. "He has ways of healing His children. And others who want it."

If only she could have alerted Jacob and told him what Armand was up to. And let Jacob know she and Tracy were still alive.

For the moment.

No doubt Armand never intended to let her live, but maybe he'd spare Tracy's life, and give Jacob time to find his sister.

Would he listen to reason if she pleaded with him to spare the child? Convince him how much the poor girl admired him. Shoulders drooping, Riley sagged over her lap. Who was she kidding? Armand was an evil man. He deserved to be caught. He deserved to die and every one of his evil operations uncovered and smashed.

The minivan careened to the left, and Tracy slammed into her. The smell of vomit tainted the girl's breath. Beneath her blindfold, tears stung Riley's eyes.

How many other young girls and women had been kidnapped and forced into a life from the pit of hell? Especially with tacit government approval. All in the name of tourism and the eternal euro. When would the world wake up? Degradation of women and girls, boys and young men thrived not only in Europe but throughout the world.

God do something. Rise from Your throne. You're a God of justice, a God of righteousness.

It might be too late for her and Tracy, but maybe her prayers would save other young women and children from a fate that seemed worse than death.

It was almost nine at night when Jacob edged his car down the metal gangway to the underground garage. As soon as he cleared the grate, metal doors rumbled closed behind him. The brothel owner had thought of everything, a hidden car park to protect his clientele.

If he had to set foot in any more of these places, he'd never feel clean again. But they had to destroy Armand's business.

Best he could tell, no CCTV cameras. From the front, the building's façade had been restored to its eighteenth-century elegance. No amusement park pink, purple, or green lighting to lure in customers like some of the brothels he'd checked out.

He killed the engine, stepped from the car. Diesel fumes and stale cigar smoke sapped the air quality. Maybe this time, some brave soul would admit to having been sex-trafficked, tell him they were bussed to work from secluded houses under pimps' vigilant eyes. So far, poking holes in the women's stories had been impossible. But their palpable fear, the shifting in the seat, and nervous hands told a different story. One he couldn't prove.

A black Mercedes with deeply tinted windows slid in front of him. A beefy gentleman emerged from the back seat, hand-tailored suit reeking of mega-euros. Shoulders thrown into a power stance, he mashed a lit cigarette on the cement floor and strode toward the brothel's underground entrance.

Jacob rammed his fists in his pockets. How could men use women like this? Who was this guy—an ambassador, the CEO of a major firm, a government minister?

This was the type of place he'd expect Armand to own. High society clientele. Given Découvrir's love of expensive antiques, the furnishings and decor were probably pure Armand. And every woman inside an exquisite beauty.

Was he finally on to something? Had he found Armand's lair?

His cell phone chirped. At the caller ID, his heart skipped a beat. "Amira?"

"I'm at my father's—never mind where I am." Voice strident, she gave him the password to Armand's computer.

He entered the code in his phone. "Are you safe?"

"For the moment. I found the file that lists Tracy. She's at a place called Waldheim Villa. I've never heard of it. That's all I can tell you. Don't call me again."

Before he could ask a question, she disconnected.

Now what? He couldn't be in two places at once. Where was this house, what city, what country. He texted the info to Margot, gave her Armand 's computer password. Now all they had to do was find his home, the incriminating evidence, and Tracy.

Another ring on his cell. Margot.

"Do you think she was telling the truth about not knowing where this house is?" From the background noise, Margot must be on the road.

"Who knows? Amira won't take my call. She sounded tense. Probably had to sneak in without him catching her."

"The name doesn't sound Belgian—not Flemish, and definitely not French."

"I agree. Sounds German to me." The doorman in black tails ushered a flush-faced man from the brothel into the garage, a navy cashmere coat over his arm.

"What are the chances he had Tracy brought to Vienna?"

Jacob's blood ran cold. "Sounds like something Armand would do." Waldheim Villa. Meant forest home. "It could be in the Vienna Woods." Was that where they'd find Tracy's body? Even the thought paralyzed his muscles. No, he had to stay positive.

"I'm searching online for that name in Austria."

"Great. I'm heading into Excalibur now." Even the

establishment's name carried symbolism: divine kingship and power. Right up Armand's alley.

He locked the car, walked toward the black metal doors that framed tastefully etched glass. Swans. How classy.

"Hold on. I've got something." Rapid-fire tapping sounded from her keyboard.

The doorman swung back the door for him. *"Guten Abend."*

"Meet me at Ochsnergasse, number eight. The house is called Waldheim Villa."

His pounding heart snatched his breath. "Any idea who owns it or rents it?"

"Khalid Al-Mustafa."

"Send in an Interpol police team too."

"Done." She clicked off the call.

"Danke." Jacob held up a hand to the doorman, then darted for his car.

Dear God, please let Tracy be okay.

Day 16

The van picked up speed. If they didn't escape soon, it would be too late.

Scooted down in her seat, Riley brushed her face against Tracy's hair, teeth searching for the elastic band on the girl's blindfold. Tracy startled, then dropped her head forward. Riley nibbled her way upward until she had the band between her jaws. Her heart hiccupped. *Dear God, please let this work.* She nudged the elastic over Tracy's scalp, pulling the band until it cleared the girl's forehead, then her nose.

The blindfold popped off, clutched between Riley's teeth. Success. *Thank You, God.*

Chin to her chest, she let Tracy nibble the elastic at Riley's temple, then along the bridge of her nose. The blindfold inched up over her forehead. Riley blinked as lights and buildings came into view. She nodded her thanks to Tracy. Tears had bled Tracy's mascara and eyeliner onto her cheeks like a wannabe Alice Cooper.

Tracy grasped their lashed wrists in her teeth, grazing Riley's skin.

How long before they reached their destination? And if they didn't manage to totally free themselves, they'd probably be punished. Keeping her head down, Riley levered the sharp stiletto between her ankle and the leather tie, scraping her skin raw.

Armand didn't want damaged goods. Too bad, so sad.

If she could free them, she and Tracy could be out of here before the van parked.

Digging feverishly, she thrust and twisted the stiletto into the knot until it slacked. If only her hands were free. She'd have them out of the van before the driver could summon help.

The vehicle stopped for a red light. The driver tapped his palm on the steering wheel, keeping time with the rock band's pulsating beat on the radio. The light turned green, and the driver crept past illuminated storefronts, dimly visible through the tinted windows. How much farther now?

Tracy double-timed her gnawing. The leather slackened around Riley's wrist. She inched it apart from Tracy's, and the girl wormed her hand free from the strap.

Thank You, God.

For the first time since they'd been reunited, Tracy's eyes shone with hope.

How much longer before they reached their destination? Riley eased her right foot free from its tether, groped the stiletto over Tracy's feet, searched for an opening along the leather tie. Tracy wiggled her ankles, and Riley thrust her heel into the space, toggled the knot until Tracy lifted her feet from the snare. The girl scooted toward the door, worked her hand free from the thong.

Riley scrambled for the leather around her left wrist. It wouldn't budge. She jiggled her hand, picked at the knot again. Come on, Come on. Had he used a different type of knot?

Sweat beaded her forehead. Her fingernails broke as she picked at the leather. The closure tightened like a noose.

Dear God, no. She was trapped.

She hadn't pictured having to stay behind. Tears clogged her throat. With everything in her, she wanted out of here. Wanted to flee so far away Armand would never find her. The strength drained from her arm, and she sagged against the seat.

At least Tracy was free.

But how long before the driver noticed their missing blindfolds? The best she could do was skewer his eye with her stiletto. She'd have one chance to maim him. One chance to buy Tracy's freedom.

If the van didn't swerve off the road and into a storefront.

Ashen-faced, Tracy stared toward Riley's tethered arm. The girl's jaw slacked.

She motioned Tracy to keep her head down. The longer they went without their captor spotting their missing masks, the better their chances.

Curls falling around her face, Riley prayed under her breath. She elbowed Tracy, lifted her right leg toward the driver, gave a couple practice thrusts, then jerked her head toward the van door beside Tracy.

Wide-eyed, Tracy nodded, head bobbing like a Kewpie doll. A tremulous smile fluttered across her lips. Gulping, she nodded toward Riley's still-lashed arm.

God, please let this work.

Drawing a deep breath, Riley angled her body, leaned against Tracy. She dredged up the last of her strength, rammed her shoe toward the driver's eye.

Howling like a banshee, he clutched his cheek. The car shimmied left then right, tires screeching on the pavement.

Horns honked, vehicles struggled to get out of the way.

Riley shoved the stiletto again. This time it connected with soft tissue.

The driver screamed, one hand to his eye. He braked, dug his fingers into her ankle, ripped off her shoe with his free hand.

Captured leg flailing the air, Riley yelled, "Go, go now. Run!"

Tracy tried the door handle, but the door wouldn't slide back. "I can't get out." Frantic, she toggled the lock. Sobs wracked her voice. "It won't unlock." She pounded on the glass. "Help, help." But her screams bounced back into the van.

Passersby ignored them.

Their chauffeur yanked on the emergency brake and the vehicle jolted to a stop. He stumbled from his seat, whipped back their door, growling like a wounded grizzly. Blood gushed from his eye. Had she blinded him for life?

Blocking Riley, Tracy angled sideways, legs drawn, stilettos aimed like daggers. Riley tried to push her out of the way, but the child drove her heels at his groin, pummeled his body.

He yelped, brushed aside her legs, hefted her up, and threw her on the row of seats behind them. She landed with a thud, whimpering and moaning.

Daer God, please spare her. Don't let anything happen to Tracy.

Murder in his good eye, he lunged for Riley. He jammed his sticky palms around her throat, squeezed the base of her larynx.

Fingers scrabbling at his hand, she struggled for air.

Dear God.

One sip, one sip. Spots and sparklers swam before her eyes. Tears sluiced down her cheeks. They'd never get out of this alive.

48

───────

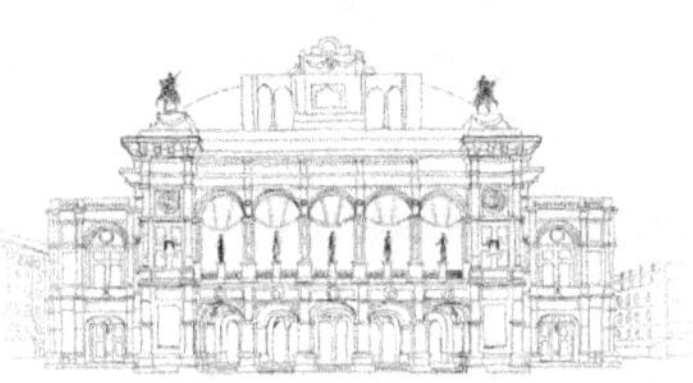

Car slowed to a crawl, Jacob scanned the pine trees for Ochsnergasse Eight, then turned into the driveway. Gravel pinged the windshield as he whipped along the uneven road, braked beside the police van. Its flashing blue lights flicked over a large mound beneath a linden tree and two open graves. Sweat slicked his palms. Had they found a body farm?

He did a quick surveil of the property. Like many older homes, the garage, a four-car structure, was detached from the house. How many people lived here?

Police protective gear over her suit, Margot stood outside her car.

He jogged to her side, motioned over the policemen waiting by their van. "Do we have a search warrant?"

"Sadly no. There wasn't enough time."

"Figures." The stone structure was thick enough to resist cannon fire. Three stories. No hint of lights between the drawn drapes. They'd be at the mercy of whoever answered the door.

His leg muscles itched to dash for the front porch. Maybe they were too late. Had Khalid cleared out and taken Tracy?

He signaled the policemen to surround the house, and a shadow darted across the backyard.

"Get him," Jacob yelled. He sprinted toward the fleeing man, but a policeman tackled him, drove him to the grass. Jacob hauled the suspect to his feet. "Where do you think you're going?"

Breathing heavily, the man slicked his lips, gaze skittering between the house and the garage. "I didn't do anything."

"Right. Just out for a midnight stroll. Why were you running?"

He jerked his shoulder upward. "I don't know. Needed a drink." Stale beer spilled from his breath.

"Why don't we go inside and have a chat?" Jacob pointed toward the back door on the patio.

Whites of his eyes wide, the man stiffened. Another slick of the lips.

"Okay." Jacob nodded to the policemen. Grasping the man's arms, they led him toward the house. Thankfully the guy was too stupid to insist on his rights, ask if they had a warrant.

Jacob tried the handle. Locked.

"Why don't you let us in so we can chat in comfort?" Ignoring the thrumming in his chest, Jacob forced a soothing tone. The man reeked of body odor, unwashed clothes, and hadn't shaved in days. "You're not the owner of this house."

"How would you know?"

"Because we know who owns it. I think you're a thief and you were fleeing. We caught you in the middle of a robbery."

Rubbing his nose, the man snickered. "I'm no robber."

"I'll bet you have a rap sheet fifty kilometers long." Jacob stuck out his hand. "Let me see your ID."

The man blanched. "Haven't got it on me."

"Where is it?"

"No idea." The man's gaze sidled from the house toward the ground.

"Let's go inside and find it." Jacob gestured to the door. "If you don't quit wasting my time, we'll add obstructing justice to the charges against you." The man was stalling. "Search him," he said to the policeman.

"*Jawohl.*" The officer patted down the man's grimy jeans, pulled out a large metal ring of jumbled skeleton keys. The other pocket yielded only a cell phone.

"Call your boss," Jacob said.

The suspect's shoulders twitched. "I-I can't do that." His Adam's apple flipped a double gulp.

"Sure you can. Prove to us you weren't breaking in."

"H-he'll kill me."

"No doubt." If the owner was Armand. Jacob snatched the ring, tried the keys until one clicked back the lock. He stepped inside an office furnished with two desks and chairs and filing cabinets. Without a search warrant, they couldn't paw through documents. The next door took him into a lavishly furnished living room.

Using the heavy metal keyring, he unlocked an iron door. The metal screeched open into a bathroom. Must and mildew hung in the air. Layers of filth coated the tub, toilet, and sink. Who used this place? He knelt beside the sink. Tears blurring his vision, he stroked the rough lettering in the plaster.

ARMAND OWNS THIS PLACE. HE KEEPS SEX-TRAFFICKED GIRLS IN THE DUNGEON. I WAS ONE OF THEM. R.W.

He gripped the sink so hard it shuddered against the wall. *Oh, Riles, Tracy, forgive me, forgive me.* This time he was too late. Amira had been certain Tracy had been brought here.

Heels clattered on the steps and Margot entered the room.

"I found where Riley was kept. She left a message on the wall. '*Riley Williams was here.*'"

"Yeah," he said, barely able to speak. He pointed to her words beneath the sink.

Margot crouched toward the sink wall. A groan escaped her mouth. "There are eight locked cells in the basement, but no sign of Riley or Tracy. We found four girls each, shackled in six of the rooms. They've been badly beaten, and I think ... likely sexually abused. The tracks on their arms indicate they've probably been given drugs, possibly hooked on them now."

His gut knotted. Bile rose in his throat, and he retched into the stained toilet. And Riles, Tracy? What had Armand done to them? He'd kill Découvrir with his bare hands.

"Where do we go from here?" Margot asked.

Swiping a hand across his mouth, Jacob hauled himself to his feet. "I suspect Armand has Riley and Tracy."

Margot paled. "Where do you think he took them?"

"I don't know. His house? Since you feel these girls have been or will be sex trafficked, Armand's goon was probably assigned to rough them up to make them compliant. Once their bruises heal, they probably go into some sort of brothel in Vienna."

"These girls are only fifteen or sixteen years old." Margot choked out the words. "We have no leads on Armand's house here."

Why couldn't something go right for a change?

"Do you think Armand sent Riley and Tracy to a brothel?"

"It's possible." Everything in him screamed, *No, God. Don't let it be true.* He rinsed his mouth under the sink faucet, wiped his hands on his slacks.

"Where do we start to look for them?"

"Their pictures haven't been posted on websites as currently available or 'new talent' so let's head to the brothel I was about to check out tonight. Excalibur. They don't advertise their women online."

"Request police backup." He snapped a photo of Riles' scrawled message beneath the sink. "But with no search warrant—"

"Getting one now." She dictated a text into her phone. "I'll follow you. Even with sirens and blue lights, we're facing a half-hour drive."

Jacob's chest threatened to explode. Thirty minutes could be too late.

If that creep had harmed Riles or Tracy—

49

Day 16

Every muscle in Riley's arm he'd lashed to the seatbelt ring throbbed. Before the chauffeur had snapped their blindfolds in place, he'd left Tracy on the second row of seats, feet bound to the armrest, wrist tied over her head.

The van braked. Something whirred, then thuds, scrapes, a loud clang. The SUV tilted forward, rattled over metal plates. Riley's knees slammed the front row. Perspiration trickled beneath her armpits. *Please not another dungeon.*

The ride smoothed, and the engine died. Footsteps thumped around the van, and their door clattered open. Diesel fumes and cold, damp air rushed inside.

The urge to pee hit her. The place smelled like a car park. Her teeth chattered.

I will never leave you, nor forsake you.

But we need You right now. Where is Your peace, that peace that surpasses all understanding?

The chauffeur whipped off her blindfold, then Tracy's.

Working swiftly, he untied their wrists and feet. "Welcome to your new home, girls."

Luxury vehicles with astronomical sticker prices filled the parking slots. Inside a chandelier-lit hall, a doorman in black tails swung open glass doors etched with swans. Was this Armand's apartment building? Nausea rippled through her gut.

Their chauffeur grunted, hauled Tracy from the van. He jerked Riley to the edge of the row.

Stilettos wobbling on the step, she eased onto the cement floor beside Tracy. The girl's updo and dress were so disheveled, she looked as if they'd fished her from a dumpster. Her own wasn't much better. Red welts and crusting scabs tattooed Riley's ankles. So much for undamaged goods. But they were still alive.

For the moment.

The driver strongarmed them inside the building, shoved them inside a ladies' room. "Fix yourselves up."

"How?" Riley thrust her chin at him. "We haven't any makeup or a change of clothes."

"That's not my problem."

"Armand might make it your problem." She'd sass him so long as she had the strength.

Shooting her a menacing glare, he slammed the door. The lock clicked behind him.

"Where are we?" Tracy sank onto a Louis Quatorze armchair.

"I don't know." The room was done in Armand blue. No doubt the furnishings were antiques, only the best for him. Riley walked through the restroom. Four toilet stalls. This wasn't Armand's home. A brothel?

Fingers numb, she restyled Tracy's French twist and pinned it in place. The uncooperative strands she tweaked along Tracy's cheeks. Riley's fingers itched to destroy the hairdo. Some men preferred the waif look.

The bolt shot back. "Here. Make these work." The driver tossed two silk dresses on the ottoman, one virginal white, the other layered with pink feathers. Too bad they weren't angels' wings. They could fly away from their fate.

Riley lifted the skimpy dresses. "I can't squeeze into this." She handed Tracy the white slip dress and changed into the feathered creation. As they stood before the gilded bathroom mirror, hands clasped like sisters, the glass reflected their deathly pallor.

"I never imagined it would happen ... like this." Tracy's tone shriveled to a child's voice.

"And God never intended it to be this way." Until now all she'd done was pray for the women who worked in the industry. Cried out in her heart for God to shut down the brothels, the pimps, and bring restoration to these traumatized women. Now she was minutes from a fate like theirs.

Oh, God, please forgive me. She was a Christian. Maybe she should have been speaking out, risking her career and her reputation on behalf of these women and girls. Had her prayers affected any change?

Tracy sank onto the ottoman, heels skewed like a little girl.

Brushing the curls off her neck, Riley stalked the room, a caged lioness. When the moment came, should she submit, or fight with all her might? Scratch out the man's eyes, kick him in the groin. What did she have to lose?

Banked coals seethed within her. How many women had the man from London infected? More than anything, she wanted his disease to run its course, the antibiotics would fail, he'd get his just deserts.

In the stillness of her heart a voice said, "*Vengeance is mine says the Lord.*"

She would have to forgive these men, whoever touched her or Tracy. She'd told Jacob he needed to learn to forgive himself.

Would he ever recover when he found out what happened to them?

Beside her, Tracy sniffled, twisted her fingers in her lap.

No point telling her they'd be fine, just fine. Or raise false hopes Jacob would rescue them. A pit hollowed Riley's stomach. If he found them, it would be after they had been forever changed.

The lock snapped back, and the doorman motioned them into the hall. "Come with me." He gestured them into a plush salon done in gold, beige, and browns. The hues of wild animals.

Tracy's icy fingers pincered Riley's arm as they staggered in their heels toward their fate.

More Baroque furniture and expensive *objets d'art*. The slubbed-silk wallpaper closed in on her, a suffocating beige shroud.

A tiny piece of her had believed she and Jacob were invincible. That right would triumph over injustice and evil. She hadn't pictured herself a sacrifice on an evil altar. Unable to free herself. Unable to fight back.

"What do you think they'll do to us?" Voice quivering like a frightened rabbit, Tracy scooted against Riley on the leopard-skin sofa, shoved the fallen spaghetti straps onto her rail-thin shoulders.

"I-I don't know." Legs trembling her feathered dress, Riley clasped Tracy's clammy palm in hers. How many men would they be forced to service?

Would they even survive the night? Tracy was little more than a child.

From the foyer, a male voice cut through the string quartet wafting from hidden speakers. Beside her, Tracy stiffened.

Shoes clicked across the tile floor.

Came closer.

His larger-than-life presence filled the doorway and bile shot into Riley's throat.

"Papa Armand. You came for me." Weeping, Tracy darted to him, buried her face against his chest. "Those horrible men—" Her shoulders shuddered as he stroked her hair, his smile anything but avuncular. "Oh, thank you, thank you."

"There, there, my child."

Ice froze Riley's veins. This must've been his plan all along. That's why Tracy and she hadn't been beaten or molested. He was saving them for himself. What better way to destroy Jacob than to rape those he loved most?

"Come along, little one. I'll make everything right for you again."

"Oh, thank you, thank you, Papa." Tracy glanced toward Riley, fresh mascara bleeding below her eyes.

"No!" Riley's scream shrilled through the room. "You can't have her. Don't trust him, Tracy."

All pretense of innocence had faded from Armand's face. Lust radiated from his gaze.

Eyes wide, Tracy stumbled backward, knuckles mashed against her lips. The color drained from her face. Her hand fell to her side. "No ... No."

With everything in her, Riley lunged for Armand's eyes. He jerked his head and her nails clawed his cheek. "Take me instead. Leave her alone."

Peeling her hands off the bleeding scratches, he cocked an eyebrow. "How noble."

Tracy cowered on the sofa.

Without warning, he yanked Riley to his chest. His cologne filled her nostrils. "Very well. As you wish."

She didn't wish. But she had no choice. She must save Tracy ... Ankles wobbling, Riley stumbled beside him up the carpeted staircase, his vise-like grip a tourniquet around her arm.

If she lived through this night, would Jacob still want to

marry her? Could he erase the images of what another man had done to his wife?

How would she deal with the aftermath? *Please, God, get me through this.*

Our Father, who art in heaven. Hallowed ... hallowed ... be Thy name.

What came next?

On the first-floor landing, Armand paused outside the three closed doors. With lightning swiftness, he released her arm, jammed his fingers around her throat, opened the middle door. Incense seeped from the suite furnished with priceless antiques and impeccable taste. Giving her a savage shove, she toppled into the room.

The satin-sheeted bed loomed in front of her.

50

Oh, God, help. Riley scrambled to her feet, dug her nails into the door jamb. She'd claw out his eyes. Make him regret he'd ever touched her.

"Police! Stop where you are," someone shouted downstairs.

She glanced toward the balcony railing overlooking the foyer. Her heart pummeled her sternum. Uniformed officers had swarmed inside the foyer, rifles drawn. The waiting girls screamed and scattered. Tracy darted toward one of the policemen.

"Jacob, up here. Help!"

"Shut up, you vixen." Hand muffling her screams, Armand slammed and locked the door. Threw her on the bed. "I get you first."

No! She was so close to being freed.

The doorknob jiggled. Thuds battered the wood. But the door held. Armand's eyes were murderous. Coat off, belt off, he strode toward the bed.

Oh, Jacob, Jacob. Feet poised to kick, she huddled against

the headboard. It had worked in the car, maybe she could fight off Armand.

"Officer, shoot off the lock," Jacob yelled.

Ka-zing, ka-zing. The door flew open. Jacob lunged for Armand, flattened him on the bed, wrapped his hands around the man's throat.

Gasping and gurgling, Armand tried to peel off Jacob's fingers.

"I'll take it from here, sir," the policeman said.

"*Danke.*" Chest heaving, Jacob released his hold on Armand.

The policeman cuffed him, read him his rights, took him downstairs.

Ashen-faced, Jacob sat beside Riley on the bed and cradled her in his arms. "Are you all right?"

Choking back tears, she nodded. "We're fine. He didn't—he didn't touch us. Our jailer said Armand was saving us for—But the girls at the house ..."

"We found them. They're in hospital, being checked out."

"They'll need more than that. They were beaten, sexually abused. Over and over." She buried her face against his neck and sobbed.

He stroked her hair until her tears became hoarse gulps. "God gave you back. Tracy too."

"Is she all right?"

"Yeah. For once she ran right into the arms of the police." He handed her a tissue.

Riley blew her nose, dabbed her eyes. "Smart girl."

"Like someone else I know." He planted a kiss on her forehead.

"She takes after her brother." Riley looked into his eyes, hollow with exhaustion.

Would he still want to marry her?

JACOB CRADLED her face in his hands. "I love you Riles. With all my heart." He helped her off the mattress. "Come on. Let's get out of this place." Cupping her elbow, he walked her to the landing.

Downstairs the foyer hummed with voices. Flashing blue lights flicked across curious faces outside the doors. Inside, policemen rounded up the women and girls waiting to be interviewed by female officers.

At the base of the stairs, Margot stood beside Tracy, the girl's shoulders quaking beneath a pink blanket. Mascara blackened her cheeks. One false eyelash hung at a crazy angle.

Thank You, God, she's alive.

A vise squeezed the last of his air. She hadn't been sexually abused. Moments ago, he'd come close to killing Armand. Seeing Tracy, he almost wished he had.

Matching his stride to Riles' faltering steps, he walked her downstairs.

"Oh, Jacob, I'm so sorry." Tracy fisted the blanket against her throat. "I never should've run away."

"I forgive you. The important thing is, you're safe." Keeping an arm around Riles, he stroked Tracy's matted hair. In a matter of hours, Armand would be behind bars.

His cell buzzed. "Yes?"

"*Bundespolizei* here. We raided the countess's apartment and found a teenager hiding in the closet. According to her identity card, she's Amira Découvrir."

"That's good news. What about the countess?"

"No sign of her."

Jacob turned away from Tracy and Riles, voice lowered. "We'll need Amira's testimony against her father. She's slippery. Don't let her get away." At least the girl was alive and unharmed. He mouthed the news to Margot.

The agent crossed over to him. "She'll be placed in child protective custody. We have alerts out for the countess at every border crossing."

"I doubt she's the only woman connected to Armand we want to reel in."

"Amira can help with that," Margot said.

"If she will." Jacob turned back to Tracy, wrapped an arm around her, clasped Riles' hand.

Tracy clung to him so tightly, he could barely breathe. "You saved me, you saved me."

Nope. He took no credit for the rescue. He'd asked God for a miracle, and a miracle he'd received. *Thank You Lord.* Jacob pulled Riles to him.

51

Day 18

The computer screen blurred before his eyes. He pushed back from his Interpol desk, rubbed his eyelids. Where had the time gone? Tracy had pleaded to return to Brussels and Mrs. DeBeers, but he'd insisted she stay with Riles until she could accompany his sister home. He couldn't blame Tracy for wanting to leave Austria as soon as possible.

He'd called his parents as soon as Armand was in police custody and put Tracy on the phone. They'd refused to speak with him. But Mother's voice and weeping had filtered through the phone, asking Tracy over and over if she was all right.

And now, Riles' debut was tomorrow night.

Thankfully, Amira had chirped louder than a mechanical canary on a music box, spilled what she knew about her father's ops. Given them the address where she'd accessed his computer. A rented house in Döbling on a hilly street overlooking the famous Vienna Woods.

He toyed with his computer mouse. What if she'd withheld a few places to resume the business later for herself? The girl was one shrewd cookie. Give her a few years, and no doubt she could play hardball with Armand's top goons.

He reread Liesl's printout from her interview sessions with Amira. He'd requested the policewoman come from Velden since she'd seem not much older than the teenager. Pull a page from Armand's MO. Go for the relatable type.

And since Amira had told Interpol where to find Tracy, she was entitled to the €5,000 reward. Just what she needed—start-up funds for her own enterprise.

"Good news. Our Geneva office located the countess, took her into custody early this morning." Margot handed him a printout of the police interview. "She's plea-bargaining in exchange for answers to our loose ends. Although she denied knowledge of the British couple being couriers, she's given us the name of the man who snuck into Riley's apartment and wrote the threatening notes. And confirmed the identities of the men who launder Armand's income in Austrian casinos and his au pair recruiter. We already knew about Marta Werner, Amira's tutor."

"With the countess onboard, Armand didn't need lieutenants. Just hire a few assassins." Jacob arched his back, stretching the knots in his muscles.

"She also ran his recruiting ops for sex-trafficked girls. She chose them."

"How could evil appear so innocent, innocuous? She saved Riles' life in the casino, then set up her abduction and—" Shuddering, he reactivated his screen, scrolled through the list of florists near the Opera House.

Margot leaned over his shoulder. "What are you doing?"

"Looking for a reputable florist to deliver some baskets of flowers to Riles after her opening night. Any recommendations?"

"Flowers. You did hire the claque, didn't you?"

"What claque?"

"The scores of people in the nosebleed section." Margot leaned a hip on his desk, folded her arms. "Singers pay them to applaud and bravo their performance."

"You're kidding."

"No. I'm not. The famous tenor, Enrico Caruso, refused to hire the claque in Naples. After his aria, they booed and hissed. If you love her, you'll hire them. That is if it's not too late."

His computer screen went black. Should he listen to her ominous warnings?

"Surely Riley knows how the system works, having lived in Wien before."

His forced chuckle hollowed, thinner than canned laughter on a sitcom. No way would Riles have paid a claque. She was determined to make her career on her own.

"Trust me. You won't be laughing if you ignore them."

"I'm sure she didn't do it."

Snatching a business card from the holder on his desk, Margot scrawled something on the back, set the card in front of him. A phone number. "The kindest thing you can do for her is to call them and pay them now. If you have any money left, then think about flowers."

He drummed his fingers on the desk. "How much do they charge?"

"How many bravos do you want?"

"You pay by the bravo?"

"Not exactly."

He eyed the card. Would Riles be furious with him if he did this for her?

Leaning over his computer, Margot shut down the florists' website. "Trust me. Go with the claque. Perhaps you've never attended a performance of classical music in Vienna."

"No, can't say I have."

"The Viennese are known for sitting on their hands. Meaning a polite titter of applause. At best."

"I see." He reopened his computer search engine.

"If you really love Riley, you'll do this for her. She hasn't a chance without them. All singers use them."

What should he do? He didn't want her to think he didn't believe she could wow the audience all on her own.

"The Viennese can be quite cruel to singers. And the claquers take it personally when they've been rebuffed. If you ignore my advice, expect a lot of booing."

52

———

Day 19

Operagoers crowded the Staatsoper aisles. From his mid-first-row seat, Jacob tried not to gape at the bejeweled guests, the opulence of the house. No wonder these debuts meant so much to Riles. Another red velvet and gilt horseshoe affair, three tiers of seats and loges that were dazzling from the audience.

And probably intimidating from the stage. He bowed his head. *God, please let her debut be free from danger and death-defying experiences.*

He winked at Tracy seated on his left. She'd seemed excited about the age-appropriate silk suit Riles had bought her. "Looking great, kiddo. Turquoise is your color."

"Thanks." Tracy's shy smile morphed into something he never thought he'd see. A full-blown grin and a twinkle of—could it be—hero worship in her eyes?

Stifling a grin, he settled in the plush upholstery. And this was one debut the countess would have to miss. Jails probably didn't live-cast the performance. Margot shifted in the seat next to him, the stage lights twinkling on her jet-encrusted evening suit. If he was going to attend Riles' premieres, from now on he'd have to pack a tux.

Margot fidgeted with her program, her evening bag. After all the tensions between them on this case, maybe inviting her to share Riles' premiere had been a mistake. But Gussi had wanted to sit with her boyfriend. That was the least they could do for her, after loaning her car for so long.

"So." Margot crossed her legs, knuckles whitened over her clasped fist. "Did you decide to leave Interpol?"

Was she still vying for his job? He eyed her so long a tic pulsed near the corner of her lashes. "No. Riles threatened to leave me if I did."

"Really?"

"Not exactly. She parted the clouds for me so I could see straight." As soon as he'd gotten Tracy and Riles settled in her apartment, after Armand's arrest.

"You Americans are so strange."

"Yep. Guess we are." But Riles had kept him from making a decision he'd regret the rest of his life.

How could he walk out of a call to pursue justice? When he and Noel had played cops and robbers at boarding school, they'd been passionate about righting wrongs they'd barely understood as kids. Wrongs that had cost Noel's life. Jacob swallowed the lump in his throat. And almost Riles' and Tracy's.

"You are good at your job, you know." A flush swept Margot's cheeks.

He shrugged. "I try, but it's awfully hard sometimes."

"I'm sorry I undermined you. I doubted you had what it takes to be an exceptional leader." Blinking hard, she dipped her head. "But truthfully, I don't think I could've done what you did—staying on task—having lost everyone you love." She twisted her fingers in her lap. "I-I've learned a lot from you. And I hope you'll give me another chance."

Another chance. Isn't that what he owed his parents? This woman had nearly cost him his job, his exemplary service record. Von Bingen was expecting his writeup on Margot's behavior. But hadn't he pleaded with Riles for a chance to prove he wasn't like her father?

"We all make mistakes." He held out his hand. "What do you say, partner?"

Mouth agape, she stared toward his palm, then her gaze slid to his. "*Danke. Vielen Dank.*"

"*Bitte.*" He'd never understand why the German language used the same word for please and you're welcome. But then, there were things Margot didn't understand about his culture. Or him. "And I want to thank you for putting up that five-thousand-euro reward on Tracy's behalf."

Scarlet bled across Margot's cheeks. She fiddled with the jeweled button on her jacket. "How'd you find out?"

"We Interpol agents have our ways." He'd had to dig and cajole to discover Tracy's benefactor.

"I never expected Amira would win the prize."

"Yeah, there've been a lot of surprises on this case."

Clearing her throat, Margot leafed through the program. "So did you hire the claque?"

"No."

Margot blanched. "*Aber nein.* You're teasing, *ja*?"

"No, I'm not."

"Did you break up with Riley?"

"Of course not."

"Instead, you spent a fortune on baskets of roses, I presume." Margot stared at him, jaw agape. "And threw your fiancée to the ravenous Viennese wolves."

"This is Riles' career. She doesn't need me buying off people to pump up her fame. I promise, once you hear her sing, you'll be captivated. And so will the audience."

Margot cocked an eyebrow, then turned back to her program.

Dear God, please let her be wrong. But he had to trust Riles' decision to sing without the claque's support. Maybe the bravos from others would drown out any booing.

Flipping through her program, Tracy leaned closer. "Cool story, huh?"

"Yeah. Right up Riles' alley."

"You don't mean she's really like an evil queen, do you?"

"Of course not. But she's fierce about going after what she believes in and what she wants. And I love her for it." With every fiber of his being, he hoped she'd be a tremendous success tonight. That the evening would bring everything she ever dreamed of for her career.

The house lights dimmed, and the hum of chatter died. The conductor threaded between the instrumentalists to the podium in the orchestra pit and acknowledged the warm applause. The curtain rose and the now familiar overture of *The Magic Flute* swelled over him.

This was Riles' big night.

53

Day 19

Lifting the voluminous skirt of her star-studded costume above her ankles, Riley climbed the steps to the catwalk. Planted her feet on the see-through metal framework. If the grate were a few inches higher, she could swing from the rafters.

A wave of vertigo fluttered through her skull. *Don't look down, don't look down.* Heart in her throat, she crept across the catwalk to wait for her cue.

At least she could descend a spiral staircase for her second aria when she gave her daughter Pamina the dagger to kill her father. All she had to do was keep the athletic socks from rolling out of the bodice and bouncing across the stage.

Another wave of dizziness overtook her. She clutched the railing, waited a few seconds for the worst of it to pass, then took her position center stage. Chest high, she drew three deep breaths. With the cavernous bodice, breathing deeply wasn't a problem. Keeping the dress up was.

The orchestra launched into the prelude to her aria. The

spotlight in front of her flicked on, blinding her. Runs, roulades, and high notes flew from her mouth, her gestures strong.

She might be playing an evil queen, but in her heart, she stood for justice. She loosed all the vengeance of her aria not toward Pamina's father but on Armand Découvrir. Her high *Fs* popped out, perfectly in tune.

As she finished, the house erupted in tumultuous applause. Thankfully, Viennese singers no longer broke character and walked to the edge of the stage to bow after their arias. Then she'd have to climb those wretched stairs again. She held her position, head high, chin in the air. Take that, Armand.

A roar of bravos came from the loges, the house floor, the *Stehplatz*, standing room area, where the claque held court. *Thank You, God*. She'd won them, she'd won them all.

When the curtain fell at the end of the performance, she took her place on stage with her colleagues. One by one they stepped forward and acknowledged the roaring applause. As she walked forward, the four young pages, boy sopranos from the cast, darted off stage. They returned, each carrying a massive basket of pink roses, her favorite color.

Keeping her chest upright, she moved one leg back in a deep curtsey. Oh, Jacob. If he kept this up, he'd be penniless. She slipped a rose from the basket, tilted the flower toward him. Eyes besotted, he gave her a goofy grin. She kissed the blossom and held it against the athletic socks holding up her costume's bust. Probably room for a dozen roses in there.

Twenty-five solo curtain calls later, she wiped the perspiration from her brow and gave each of the four pages a pink rose. She offered one of the baskets to her stage daughter, Pamina. Always a good idea to oil colleague relationships. Three more performances. She'd done it this time, she'd really done it. *Thank You, God*. For once, she'd sung without a mishap onstage. And unbeholden to the Viennese claque.

As the chatting singers and supernumeraries walked into the wings, a stagehand raised his hands, blocking Jacob as he climbed the steps to the stage. Tracy's arm gripped in one hand, he flashed his Interpol ID. The stagehand moved aside, and Riley opened her arms to receive them. Family. Her family had come to support her. God had been so good to them. They'd have to work through the trauma of their ordeal, the nightmares and flashbacks, but He'd spared their lives, their future.

"Hon, you were fantastic." Jacob swept her into his arms, crushing the athletic socks to her chest.

"Thanks." She drank in the citrusy scent of his aftershave, the deep blue of his eyes.

"Oh. My." Tracy threw her arms around Riley. "You were totally awesome. Wow, you do evil well."

"Thanks, I think."

Jacob rolled his eyes.

Maybe she wasn't such a great actress. Aiming the queen's venom at actual bad guys was a boon.

"So, what's next, you two?" Tracy narrowed her eyes at them.

"You know ..." Riley lifted her left hand, flexed her ring finger beneath the spotlight, letting every facet of the diamond shimmer. Thankfully, her scrawled messages hadn't ruined the stone. "I've been thinking ... We should talk about setting a wedding date ..."

The catch in Jacob's breath strained his buttoned jacket.

Tracy broke into a grin. "That's so cool." She motioned them together, stepped away from them.

Blinking at the moisture pooling in his eyes, Jacob locked his arms around her waist. "Are you sure?" he said, his voice thick.

Life together would never be easy. Perfect husbands and

wives didn't exist, but a right mate was a gift from God. "I'm sure."

His eyes searched hers so long, her pulse hammered her throat. Was he changing his mind? "You're on, doll." He swooped her into his arms and the wadded athletic socks tumbled from her bodice and skittered across the floor. "What's that?"

"Had to have some way to keep the dress on. The seamstress wanted to use super glue, but I refused."

"Oh, Riles." He sighed, then brushed her lips with his, and she melted into the warmth of his arms.

God had blessed her richly. She'd never believed she'd marry, and here she was, committing her life to this Handsome Hunk. "After all, we make such a great team."

"Hey ...." He slid his hands down her arms, a wicked gleam piercing his gaze. "Does this mean you're retiring from assisting Interpol?"

She jerked back. "Are you kidding?" She swept an arm in the air. "I can see it now. During my next concert, I run into a nest of terrorists and their hidden cache of weapons." She fingered his lapel. "Who knows, maybe we'll take down a couple jihadists on our honeymoon."

Groaning, he shook his head. "Oh, honey. I don't tell you how to sing your roles."

"Right. You just rescue me from near death during my performances." She brushed a bit of dust from his jacket. "Think about it. I'll be sleeping with their top special agent. Who knows what you say in your sleep."

Chuckling, he pulled her into the stage wing and kissed the tip of her nose. "I wouldn't have it any other way, Frau Coulter."

"Not so fast, lover boy." She pressed a hand to his chest, his heartbeat erratic beneath her palm. "I've an operatic reputation to maintain. Onstage, I'm Frau Williams. But at home ..." She snagged the velvet wing curtain around them and settled in his arms for a little more PDA. "I'll be the delightfully happy Frau Coulter. Or Mevrouw Coulter if we're living in Belgium."

His arms tightened around her waist. "Sounds wonderful to me."

As his lips searched hers, she deepened the kiss, tasted the hint of coffee and chocolate.

God was so good. Once again, He'd spared their lives, given them another chance. And she intended to use it well.

BOOK CLUB DISCUSSION QUESTIONS

1. In the story, Jacob struggles with juggling job and parental responsibilities, desperately needing to be in two places at once when both are in crisis. Have you ever faced this? How did you choose to handle the situations? How did you find a balance?

2. He must also deal with a sense of responsibility that creates guilt, recrimination, and condemnation. His colleague accuses him of making poor choices and setting wrong boundaries. Have you ever had to deal with this? If so, how did you choose to resolve it?

3. Riley worries Jacob's protective nature, and what she perceives as bossiness, will eventually change him into her father's controlling personality. They are both strong-willed people. She wants him to change before she sets a wedding date. Have you had to deal with relationships like this? How did you resolve the issues?

4. Jacob's kid sister has led a secret life that introduced her to vast wealth and unlimited funds available to her. As a parent or guardian, how have you dealt

with poor moral choices your child may have made? How did you walk them through restoration?

5. Both Jacob and Riley face the need to forgive people who've harmed them and played them for fools. Forgiveness isn't always easy. Ugly memories rear their heads. Have you had to deal with this? How do you handle it?

ACKNOWLEDGMENTS

As always, I am indebted to many people who provided input and critique to make this a better story. With deep gratitude to Susan B. Pearcy, for sacrificing untold hours helping me brainstorm events and coming up with the book title; Bedford Pearcy and Robert C. Goodwin for assistance on the sailing/sniper scene; Heidi Van der Wal for naming the scene of the crime and the company of her precious dogs for two months; the brainstorming class members at Blue Ridge Christian Writers Conference headed by author Lynette Eason, and classmate authors Ane Mulligan, Angel Moore, Kristen Hogrefe, and Press Barnhill; members of the Word-Weavers Page 40 critique group: Carri Colvin, Lynda Courtright, and Norma Gail, thank you for all your input. Thanks are also due to authors Carrie Stuart Parks and Lisa Phillips for their valuable opening chapter critiques at ACFW, and Lynette Eason at the Florida Writer's Conference and her weekend writing retreat.

For me, nothing in writing happens without prayer. A lot of prayer. I am forever indebted and grateful to those who have invested time and energy in praying this book to completion: Peggy A. Bell, who has bathed every writing project I set my hands to for almost thirty years; Susan B. Pearcy, Susan Feiza, Pastors Crystal and Jesse Rangel, and author Delores Topliff.

And as always, kudos to Linda Fulkerson for her brilliant cover design, and heartfelt thanks to editor Elena Hill for her spot-on suggestions to improve the story.

ABOUT THE AUTHOR

Sara L. Jameson won Scrivenings Press's grand prize publishing contract in January 2021. They released her debut romantic suspense novel, *Cruise to Death*, June 2021. *Death in High Places*, (Book 2 in the *Troubled Waters* series), released February 28, 2023, to be followed by *Vengeance in Vienna* (release date: July 16, 2024).

Sara is the pseudonym of a multi-published former university professor who writes non-fiction under her real name. She also writes WWII historical novels. When not writing, she enjoys reading, swimming, cooking, and dog-sitting.

snippets of the terrorists' plans. Plans that seem to involve the same river boat cruise Riley is on.

When Interpol learns of Riley's encounter with terrorists at the café, Jacob's supervisor insists he work with her to identify the terrorists and retrieve Agent X. But their relationship is fraught with distrust because of Riley's suspicious past and a romantic attraction neither of them wants.

Get your copy here:

https://scrivenings.link/cruisetodeath

Death in High Places

Troubled Waters—Book Two

An Interpol agent with a deadline he can't miss.

Urgent intel warns of terrorist cells planning coordinated attacks throughout Europe. Special Agent Jacob Coulter of Brussels Interpol is assigned to find the terrorist financiers supporting these groups and shut down their funding operations.